The Rose Thief

Claire Buss

www.cbvisions.weebly.com

Cover artwork by Ian Bristow

Other works by Claire Buss:

The Gaia Collection
The Gaia Effect
The Gaia Project

The Roshaven Books
The Rose Thief
The Interspecies Poker Tournament – The Roshaven Case Files No. 27
Ye Olde Magick Shoppe

Poetry
Little Book of Verse, Volume 1
Spring Fling, Little Book of Verse, Volume 2
Summer Dreaming, Little Book of Verse, Volume 3
Spooky Little Book of Verse, Volume 4

Short Story Collections
Tales from Suburbia
Tales from the Seaside
The Blue Serpent & other tales

Anthologies
Underground Scratchings, Tales from the Underground anthology
Patient Data, The Quantum Soul anthology
A Badger Christmas Carol, The Sparkly Badgers' Christmas Anthology

The late, great, Sir Terry Pratchett said:

"The thing with having an open mind, of course, is that people will insist on coming along and trying to put things in it."

I'm exceptionally glad he tried and of course, succeeded.

See the glittering black sand and the horizon that stretches for ever?

That is the middle of nowhere. Where normally nothing much happens and usually no one knows about it. It is also where The Great Sadness was created, where love came to die. All because of a stolen rose, an Emperor's infinite wisdom, magic and family. Come closer and I'll tell you the story. Share your snacks.

Chapter 1

He, or very possibly she, was known as The Rose Thief. It was a nickname that stuck despite the best efforts of the thief-catchers to stem public approval for a thief who only stole roses. No one had yet admitted to knowing who, or indeed what, the thief was. He could indeed be a woman, or a troll, or even a malevolent spirit. What was of great significance and importance was that only the Emperor's – *may he live for ever and ever* – rose garden was being violated.

The thief was stealing exclusively from the Emperor – *may he live for ever and ever* – and no one but the Emperor – *may he, oh you get the idea* – had access to the rose gardens. Not even any of his thousand and one wives. It made solving the theft extremely difficult.

It also made the Emperor look rather foolish and was the reason why Chief Thief-Catcher, Ned Spinks, was strung up by his ankles, in the third best reception room of the Emperor's Palace.

Ned was waiting to see what would happen next, and to amuse himself in the meantime, was tracing rude shapes in his imagination with the dark stains on the floor beneath him.

'Do you know why you are here?'

The high-pitched, nasal voice came from the direction of Ned's right knee. It was the High Right, the Honourable Lord Chamberlain. Ned tried to swing around a little so he could at least speak to the ankles of the High Right, but he had no turning circle. The blood pooling in his head was beginning to make it hard to think coherently. He decided against his usual witty repartee.

'It's my turn?' Well, maybe just a little. To lighten the mood.

The High Right ignored Ned's response. 'The Emperor – *may he live for ever and ever* – wants this so-called *Thief of Roses* caught. Now.'

'I'll see what I can do, Sir.'

The High Right did not respond and remained behind Ned, making him uneasy.

Due to the voluminous nature of his shirt, a large portion of Ned's back was on display and he didn't think it was necessarily his best side. Feeling rather vulnerable, he was now thoroughly convinced that love handles were not meant to sag upside down. Gravity was not doing him any favours.

He lurched unexpectedly as he was cut down and crashed to the floor in an inelegant heap of slightly overweight thief-catcher. Shaking the stars from his head, Ned winced as the blood rushed back down his body and made his ears ring. At least he still had his ears. The last time the Emperor took a dislike to the Chief Thief-Catcher, the High Left Inquisitor carved most of his body parts off. Ned counted his fingers and toes surreptitiously.

'You have one day, Thief-Catcher.' The High Right glared at Ned who had reached a count of at least eight digits. 'Don't let me regret not ordering the removal of your eyeballs.'

Ned heard rather than saw the High Right leave.

His head was still adjusting to being the right way up and despite the leg count, Ned wasn't entirely sure he had active control over his limbs. Standing had yet to be attempted.

A rather loud conversation began filtering through the third best reception room doors, which were ajar.

'I don't care what you fink. I'm going in to get 'im.'

A small, grubby looking child with a mop of straw-like hair marched into the room wearing an air of nonchalance which soon deflated into obvious relief at seeing Ned in one piece. Two Palace Guards peered in, saw that the High Right had finished and decided to mind their own business for once. Palace Guards excelled at minding yours, it was a strenuous part of training: you couldn't be a Palace Guard if you didn't know what your next-door neighbour's aunt had for tea last Thursday.

The small child wasn't a child at all. She was a dirty little sprite with large, hairy ears and a coppery coloured tail just visible from the bottom of her filthy red coat. She peered into Ned's face.

The smell that accompanied her was other-worldly.

'Jenni. A little space.' Ned tried not to breathe.

Jenni huffed, hurt at the not so warm welcome. 'Be like that then. I only came straight 'ere to find you and get you out of whatever mess you're in now.' She leaned in again, utterly disregarding Ned's request for personal space, and looked deep into the bloodshot yet still vibrant blue eyes of her boss. 'Joe said you was scooped.'

Ned pushed himself up from the floor, trying in vain to ignore the incredible smell infiltrating his nostrils. 'Yep. Lucky me.' He staggered a few steps before collecting his limbs and walking towards the door. Jenni capered at his side. 'You need a bath, Jenni. You stink.'

'Been undercover at the docks ain't I?' A few flies buzzed in Jenni's wake. 'Cos we fawt he might be basing 'is operations round that way, right? So I've bin looking for the rose thief ain't I?' She scratched an armpit

5

viciously. 'Came straight 'ere tho di'n't I? When Joe said.'

'Yeah, thanks. What about the docks, what did you find out?' Ned held the third best reception room door open for Jenni and jauntily saluted the guards in the corridor as they walked through. 'Any luck?'

'Just a pile o' shite.'

'Well, I can smell that.'

'Nah, a proper pile of rose shite – that special stuff what makes them grow.' Jenni jabbed her thumb over her shoulder at the Palace receding behind them as they exited through a side gate. 'And it ain't theirs.'

'Whose was it then?'

'Dunno. Didn't 'zactly speak to the owner. There weren't much left, right, and it was in one of them hire when you need a bit o' space like places. You know, the ones Two-Face Bob hires out. It'd dried a bit and that but it was definitely shite.' She beamed up at Ned. 'So even though I di'n't find nobody, I still done good, right?'

Ned nodded, then winced as his upside-down headache kicked in. 'Could be Two-Face Bob is involved, we'll have to have a little chat with him.' He tried to make a mental note to investigate the dockyards further whilst ignoring the hammers in his head.

The unlikely pair walked down Palace Lane, back to Headquarters at The Noose. They did not notice the wide berth the great unwashed gave them, which goes to show that even the down and outs in Roshaven have some standards.

Headquarters wasn't the real headquarters. The official residence of the thief-catchers, over on Justice Heights, burned down in '04 after a nasty disagreement with the Guild of Organised Flame.

It was rebuilt twice before the then Chief Thief-Catcher took the hint and upped sticks.

These days anyone who wanted to find a thief-catcher visited The Noose, a delightful little hostelry that perched jauntily on the edge of the aptly named Black Narrows.

If by delightful you meant grime encrusted walls, floors and ceiling; a barman who'd sooner shoot you than serve you; and a clientele that lacked a certain respectability; then yes, The Noose was extremely delightful. As for the Black Narrows, they were definitely black. Some say it was because that was the only colour of stone left in the quarry, others say it's because all the evil committed in the narrows had stained the streets with blackness. And they were certainly narrow. So narrow, they were a pickpockets' dream. No one went into the Black Narrows voluntarily, unless they were naive tourists or had the misfortune to live there. And if you did live there, no one went out in the narrows at night unless they absolutely had to and even then, they tried to get out of it. Of course, for some, it was part of their professional workload to be in the narrows, especially at night. It was one of *those* places, a tourist honey trap for people seeking danger, and suitable living conditions for those wishing to cause the danger. All in all, it was the perfect location for Thief-Catcher HQ. Anyone who was that serious about needing a thief-catcher clearly had the funds for the job and no one, not even the Guild of Organised Flame, was brave enough to try and destroy The Noose. They'd rather be hung, drawn and quartered.

Reg, The Noose's resident barman - he never, ever, left - nodded in greeting as Ned entered through the concealed side door. It was the shortest route to the rickety stairs that lurked in the rear of the saloon where the gloom was deepest, knee high and thick as treacle in places.

'Anything?' Ned asked. Reg acted as a surly doorman for the thief-catchers, he let everyone in, regardless of whether they were welcome or not, but he was supposed to let Ned know in advance if he let people through when no- one was around. Especially anyone connected with the current Rose Thief investigations.

'Up.' Reg didn't believe in conversation or indeed sentences with more than one word. They were unhealthy and contagious.

The Noose's patrons were of a similar mind except on Thursdays when Yvette von Strunkle performed her weekly show. Then many rich and colourful words were shouted, often hoarsely, by short, hairy men in large overcoats who brought their own peanuts and drank copious amounts of the vilest liquor available.

Ned nodded his thanks and began the treacherous climb. One in five steps were missing and those that remained were so old and rotten that putting any weight on them was risking a broken limb. Ned tried to look at it as a deterrent for time wasters. You had to really want the thief-catchers to climb these stairs. As they skirted the mattress at the top of the stairs, Ned noticed the door to the thief-catcher office was ajar, a shadowy figure visible through the frosted glass. Ned put an arm out to slow Jenni down and went first, a catch spell on quick release from the supply in his spell-caster belt. As soon as he saw who it was. he relaxed.

Bob's two noses wrinkled as Jenni's fragrance filled the office.

The sprite stood behind Bob and stuck her tongue out rudely. The face on the back of Bob's head retaliated by hawking and spitting snotty phlegm at the sprite. She dodged it easily and began to make one of her own.

'Jenni, enough.' Ned plonked himself down wearily in the nearest chair. 'Two-Face Bob, what can I do for you?'

Both faces smirked and spoke in unison. 'It's not what you can do for me, Spinks, it's what I can do for you. For a price.'

'And that is?'

'I know who the Rose Thief is.'

'Yeah?' scoffed Jenni. 'What you got stinking in your warehouse by the dock then eh? We know all about that an' all.'

'Jenni!' Ned leaned back in his chair, putting his battered boots up on the corner of his battered desk before responding to Two-Face. 'Why come to me? Why not report it to the Palace yourself.'

Two-Face Bob walked over to the small window and peered out, looking up and down the street below before turning back to Ned and rubbing his hands.

'Pay me first. Then I'll tell you everything I know. This is a big one right – at least four thousand gold bits.'

'Ha! Four thousand gold... you must be joking. Not even the Emperor has that kind of cash just lying around.'

'*May he live for ever and ever,*' whispered the rear head of Two-Face Bob.

'We already know it's you anyways – wot yer talking about bits? You ain't getting no bits.' said Jenni but Two-Face Bob ignored her.

'I know you got scooped up and I know you've got a deadline.' He jerked a thumb over his shoulder at the sprite who was picking her nails in disinterest. 'I doubt the pixie will be much help to you.'

'Sprite.' Ned corrected him.

9

'What?'

'She's a sprite and unless you have any hard evidence you'd like to leave with the thief-catchers office, get out of my sight.'

Two-Face Bob turned so that his faces could scowl at both Ned and Jenni before he stalked out of the room and banged the door shut.

'Four thousand gold bits.' Ned shook his head. 'You believe that guy?' Moving his head was a bad idea, it reawakened the killer headache he'd been trying to ignore, and Jenni's stink was starting to make his eyes water again. 'You, go get clean. Come straight back and fill me in again on what you found.' He pulled open the drawers of his desk, searching for something, anything that would clear his head. He opted for the half bottle of scrumble he'd been saving for a rainy day.

Jenni clattered and banged in the small bathroom next door while Ned reviewed the case so far.

Chapter 2

A hooded figure darted furtively around the corner of a warehouse. They needn't have bothered. No one was watching and hooded figures were ten a penny down at the docks. It was after all a place for doing things you weren't meant to and as long as you'd paid Two-Face Bob, no one really cared who you were.

The hood slipped into the same rent-as-you-require warehouse Jenni had been scoping out earlier and swept a quick light globe throughout the building. Nothing, not even rats. To anyone else that would've been odd but for the hood it was a relief. They didn't like rats. There was an upturned crate on the floor which would do for a stool. The hood sat and waited. It didn't take long.

A dark shadow began to form in one corner of the warehouse. It grew thicker and coalesced into a figure.

'Report.'

Lowering her hood, the young woman stood and inclined her head in deference to the figure. 'A member of the thief-catcher team has been snooping around the warehouse, Father. But there was nothing here for them to discover.'

'And why exactly is that?'

'I have already destroyed any evidence and, the, um...' She began twisting her fingers together. 'I do not, that is, I have yet to get the red rose of love.'

The shadowy figure began pacing, black eyes glinting. 'And what, exactly, was your task here, child?'

'To steal the red rose of love.'

'And exactly how have you been wasting your time

instead?'

'Um... stealing the other roses.' The woman was now firmly looking at her feet, voice small, shoulders rounded.

The shadowy figure became thicker as it took steps towards the woman. The darkness began to fall away, and a tall, thin man stood before her. He extended one bony finger under her chin and lifted her face to his expressionless one.

'And what possible reason do you have for disobeying my orders?'

The woman stuck out her jaw defiantly. 'Because it's just some stupid love rose. And I never get to do anything for myself. And I thought, I thought...' Her bravado began to quail under her father's stern gaze.

'The artefacts that I send you to procure may not seem important to you, but they are fundamental to my release. Your failure in this simple task is highly disappointing.' He clicked his fingers. 'Perhaps some additional motivation?'

An image began to appear of an older woman in a cage. She was filthy, dressed in rags and her face looked badly bruised.

'Mother! What have you done? Release her at once!' The younger woman made a swipe for the image which dissolved into thin air.

'I will release her when you deliver what you were tasked.'

Glaring at her father, the woman scrubbed her eyes.

'We may have a problem with the slime-ball that runs this place, Two-Face Bob.'

'Go on.'

'He's been to the thief-catchers, informing them that he knows who I, who the Rose Thief is.'

'I am not concerned about those misfits. But I will not have employees defy me. You would do well to heed my lesson here child.' The sorcerer muttered under his breath and crackles of red lightning began to shoot from his hands forming a grey mist.

'What is that?' The woman couldn't help her fascination, this was real power.

'This is a Shadow-Wraith.' Turning his attention to the mist he gave his orders. 'Seek out the man known as Two-Face Bob and destroy him. Return to me and I will grant you your freedom.'

The wraith pulsed in response then drifted through the warehouse wall, intent on finding its victim. Two-Face Bob didn't stand a chance.

'I have little patience for your games, child. You will steal the red rose of love and bring it to me soon. Otherwise, I will dismember your mother and you can take her place - caged, alone, starving, and a suitable playmate for my wraiths.'

The woman's mouth ran dry and she licked her lips. 'I will, Father, I promise. There is something else that may be of interest to you. It's about the Emperor. But I will need some time to fully implement my plan. It requires more rose thefts, as a distraction.'

'I'm listening.' He leant in closer and began to smile as his daughter outlined a plan to not only get him the powerful rose of love but also the keys to an empire full of fae magic.

Chapter 3

Ned perused the Rose Thief case file. On the last day of the spring solstice, an unidentified individual had stolen one of the Emperor's roses. Every week since, on the last day of the week, another rose had been taken. No one had seen anything. No one had heard anything. So far, the Emperor had lost pink for appreciation, white for innocence, orange for desire and yellow for friendship. Blue, black, purple and red remained.

So what? You might think. They were only roses, right?

Prior to being hung upside-down in the spirit of motivation, Ned had been informed that in a fit of pique, some years ago, the Emperor had magically imbued the red rose with the very real meaning of love.

Love, being fickle and hard-won, had seemed far too much effort at the time.

The Emperor, in his infinite wisdom, had sent for the most learned of mages and made them cast a powerful love-spell to tie the tricky emotion down into one place. Subsequently, he now had a thousand and one wives and the fabric of love was interwoven into a delicate flower that bloomed forever. As long as the red rose remained within the Emperor's rose garden, inside the Palace walls and under its mystical protections, everything would be fine. But if this thief stole the red rose without deactivating the Emperor's spell then love would be lost. Not only for the Emperor but for everyone.

Ned sighed. What bloody idiot decides to tie love to a bloody flower? Honestly, flowers are meant to bloom and die. Hell, even love dies eventually. He fingered the empty space on the fourth finger of his left hand absently until Jenni interrupted his thoughts by stomping back in.

'Better?' She twirled, wafting peppermint with the slightest undertone of shite still noticeable.

'Much. Now tell me again what you found out.'

'I found a bit of that jollop wot makes the roses grow. Not much, mind. It were the smell wot got me. I didn't see nobody or nuffink, just the little bit o' muck and I fawt to meself – Boss is gonna wanna know about this.'

'Which warehouse was it?'

'Dunno, one round the back. One of them ones what looks like it ain't been used for a while but one wot gets rented out by Two-Face to all different people. I know where it is though. I can take us right back there, no problem.'

'Did anyone see you?'

'Boss.'

'Right, okay, fair enough. But Jenni, why do you stink so much if you were only looking?'

'Oh well, I went in, didn't I? Had a scout around for fings. On the floor, like. Clues and stuff. Must have been a bit o' residue or summink. There was nuffink there wot you could pick up, but you never know, 'eh? You gotta check it out. You taught me that, Boss.'

'Great, glad to see you picked up something.' Ned's train of thought was disturbed by a blood-curdling scream coming from the direction of the Black Narrows. This in itself was not unusual. Most sounds down the Black Narrows were of the screaming persuasion. There was no immediate response so the screamer tried a different tack.

'It's Two-Face Bob! Eee's been murdered!'

That did the trick.

Soon the Narrows were filled with onlookers – some brought a stool and a beverage, the forward thinkers of Narrow society – others got stuck in the crowd.

The murder alarm had started bonging in the thief-catchers office and seeing as the spell that ran the alarm had a nasty habit of growing ten decibels a minute, it seemed to Ned to be a good idea to get away from that and investigate.

Thief-Catchers were not required to investigate all murders, most were covered by The Guild of Inhumers. There was a monthly newsletter outlining who to look out for.

As long as the correct paperwork had been logged and a receipt issued, everyone knew where they stood. They might not like it but at least they knew about it. The murder alarm somehow knew who had receipts and who didn't. It was spell casting beyond Ned's limited ability, he couldn't even manage the volume control. Although officially a spell-caster, he was severely blocked most of the time and relied on his power well belt to keep him topped up. Plus, it helped to have Jenni around, she did most of the heavy magical lifting for the catchers.

There was a bit of shoving and muttering as Ned pushed his way through the ranks. He didn't have to look too hard to find the murder scene, all he had to do was follow the curious crowd.

A fair number of the shifty looking men in nondescript clothing had come to make sure Two-Face Bob was actually dead. Certain people owed certain things and if his death were true, life had suddenly become a lot brighter.

It only took one look to know for certain. One of

Two-Face Bob's faces stared lifelessly at the smog-ridden skies above, both eyes missing. The other face, which incidentally remained on his head, attached to his body, had eyes popping, mouth open as if to scream, and a terrified look of fear and shock frozen in place. Someone had clearly taken a violent dislike to the man. Looking down at the separated visages of Two-Face Bob, Ned felt a flicker of unease surge in his stomach. It could be because he hadn't eaten in the past twenty-four hours. Or it could be because Two-Face Bob had been to see him less than five minutes ago, claiming intel on the Rose Thief. Ned didn't hold much weight with coincidences. The viciousness of the attack was unusual for the type of murder usually committed in the city of Roshaven. Put that together with Two-Face Bob's extensive protection system of both magical and mundane origin and it was obvious.

'He's been ripped apart by a wraith,' Ned muttered under his breath.

'Care to comment, Spinks?'

Ned turned to his left, his heart sinking at the tall, willowy figure standing next to him. Mariah Neeps was… well, she was a damn fine figure of a woman provided you never wanted to keep a shred of personal information to yourself. Neeps worked for *The Daily Blag*.

'No comment.'

'I'll just elaborate on my warlock theory then. Shouldn't be too difficult. They had a ruckus with one up in Narborough a few months back.' Neeps sucked the end of her recorder thoughtfully as she internally swept through the memorised headlines from her rival news bringer, *The Chronicle*.

'They what?' asked Ned.

But before Neeps could elaborate, Mrs Wicket barged her way through the crowd to stand in front of Ned. Her general shape and appearance were hard to identify thanks to the several flowing capes and feathered hats Mrs Wicket wore when she sallied forth.

She was of the opinion that you can never have too much of a good thing and in her mind capes and feathered hats were the epitome of fashion. She was right if she'd lived a hundred years ago. Still, the capes and hats made her a local celebrity, the one person that simply everyone knew.

The bright orange feather on her highest hat was dangerously close to Ned's eye. He attempted to sidle to the right slightly but was stopped by a podgy hand poking a sausage-shaped finger hard into his chest.

'What are you going to do about my safety, hmmmm?' Mrs Wicket turned her head left and right, to make sure she had a suitable audience. Feathers whipped Ned in the face.

'All citizens' safety is a high priority Mrs Wicket, yourself included. My fellow catchers will be here shortly to seal the scene and a full report will be generated for the Emperor.'

'*May he live for ever and ever.*' The crowd chanted firmly; all eyes fixed on Ned.

With relief Ned saw, out of the corner of his eye, a bubble apparently floating aimlessly along. It was the scene sealer. No one except thief-catchers would be able to pass through and anyone else in the way would be gently pushed out of the sealed zone. The residents of Black Narrows began grumbling but pushed backwards as the bubble descended. They'd all seen more than one scene sealer before. Whilst no one had ever admitted to being trapped half in, half out, the rumour was that the fellow who lived down at the end, past our Marge's boy's girlfriend's uncle's, had indeed been spliced and had to stay that way for two weeks while a crime was solved. When he finally came out his left side was smaller than his right side and his fingernails had turned purple. Ned encouraged such urban myths, if nothing else it made his job marginally easier.

As the bubble completed its descent, the rest of the catchers appeared.

Willow, a green-skinned nymph fed up with life in a tree but addicted to buying young saplings and teaching them the facts of life. Sparks, a firefly highly trained in the art of espionage but let down by his own brightness, and bringing up the rear the new recruit, Joe. He appeared to be a country boy from the sticks, first time in the city. Joe was also meant to be a master spell-caster, though you wouldn't know it to look at him. When Ned had interviewed him, he'd been a little relieved. His own spell casting was hit and miss. Additional training was hard to come by after the last Emperor had outlawed warlocks. It was a fine line. Spell-casters had magic in their blood naturally whereas warlocks had to fight tooth and claw for every single ounce. The snag was that both had to train and in reality, it was fiendishly difficult to tell the difference between the two.

Ned's eyes narrowed as he watched the slightly vacant expression on Joe's face. Neeps was also staring at Joe, but hers was more the look of longing desire.

Ignoring that, Ned considered the fact that the rose thefts had started about the same time that Joe had arrived in the city. But before his brain could explore this thought further the bubble landed over the scene with a loud pop, snapping his attention back to the crime scene in front of him. Sidling out from the penetrating glare of Mrs Wicket, Ned walked through the bubble followed by his team. Jenni waited for them within, it had been her bubble.

Chapter 4

'Willow, I want you to comb the scene. I doubt there will be anything of interest, but you never know. Sparks, it might be worth visiting Two-Face Bob's offices. But go cognito alright? The last thing we need is any more complaints about you spying through windows.'

Willow was already nose to the ground, looking for clues. The firefly's wings drooped slightly at the admonition, before flashing his butt twice at Ned in acknowledgement and zipping out of the bubble towards Two-Face Bob's base of operations in the dock district. Two-Face Bob had always liked knowing who was arriving and who was leaving. It meant the list of likely suspects could be extremely long.

'Joe?' No response. 'Joe – hey, Catcher Joe? Kid, you in there?' Ned started waving his hand rapidly in the lad's face. Finally, he blinked and looked at Ned curiously.

'Sir?'

Ned narrowed his eyes, surely no one was quite that wool-headed? 'I want you to test the scene's resonance. It looks like this was a wraith murder and Neeps thinks there might be a warlock in the city – we need to investigate every possibility.'

It wasn't worth committing a crime in Roshaven unless you'd cleared it with the relevant guild and paid your dues because otherwise, you had the law and the various disgruntled guilds to deal with. Ned was supposed to attend the weekly Guild Leaders' meeting, but the amount of agreed crime depressed him, and he made excuses not to attend as often as he could. If a crime were committed right in front of him, he often pretended not to see the stamped receipts, making the criminal's life as awkward as possible until things got smoothed out. He was a Thief-Catcher after all. But this, this didn't look like the work of any city assassin with a receipt.

'Can't you do it, Sir?' Joe interrupted Ned's train of thought, radiating innocence from every orifice.

'Ere – the boss gave you an order, get on wiv' it,' said Jenni.

Ned swallowed the grin that threatened to take over his face and attempted to look disinterested as his squad did their jobs. Eventually, Willow sauntered over, her tendril-like hair trailing behind her.

'No evidence that I can find, Sir. I even spoke with the weeds between the cobbles. They didn't see or hear anything but between you and me, Sir, their level of cognitive thought is a little basic. It's more like day, night, rain, cold than full descriptions of people in the Narrows.' She huffed a wisp of green hair out of her eyes suggestively. She didn't mean to, that's the way it was with nymphs. Ned fingered the thin bracelet of her hair around his wrist. A protection amulet from Willow against her charms. So far so good but you could never be too careful.

Joe ambled over, a faint sheen of sweat covered his face and his hands trembled slightly.

'Sir, ambience levels are faint and yet there's a narrow spike of power if I concentrate and look through my fourth eye.'

Looking through your third eye was easy, people like Mrs Wicket did it all the time. True spell-catchers had access to fourth eyes and seventh hearing.

'Can you describe the spike?' asked Ned.

'Well,' Joe puffed out his cheeks while he considered which descriptive words would do it justice. 'Spiky. Narrow. Powerful.'

Ned looked up at the sky for a moment before dismissing them both back to headquarters. He waited until they had left the bubble before attempting to centre himself.

'You gonna have a go then, Boss?'

'I forgot you were there, Jenni. A little room please?'

The sprite stood back half a pace. She knew that if anything went wrong, she'd have to leap in and sever the magical connection as well as potentially catch Ned before he hit the cobbles. There was a significant height difference, so it was a matter of leverage and physics and whatnot. Ned took a deep breath and began his exercises.

Closing his real eyes, he willed his fourth open. It hovered somewhere around the tip of his nose, an awkward place when things got itchy. It also made perspective difficult. Ned could feel his own strength ebbing dangerously low and that damned upside-down headache was back, banging louder than ever. He swept his eye over the scene and registered nothing. Looking again, more slowly this time and trying to ignore the muscles spasming in his legs at the strain of remaining upright, he caught the spike. It was indeed extremely spiky, narrow, and thrummed with power. Though faint, it flickered red with flecks of purple. That was a powerful magical signature alright, possibly the result of a warlock. Joe had made out it was only a pale residue. Could Joe really be so gormless that he didn't notice the menace emanating from the power signature? Fatigue washed over him and Ned found himself suddenly sitting on the floor, hard. Jenni had managed to slow his fall

23

from complete spread-eagle to a butt drop. Still painful but slightly less comedic, after all, the bubble was transparent and there was still a healthy crowd of onlookers outside. Including Mariah Neeps. She smiled faintly as she caught Ned's attention.

'Jenni, we've definitely got a magical being, probably a warlock. Tell the others. I'll report to the Palace once I've spoken to Neeps.'

'Yes, Boss. What about the bubble, Boss? We done 'ere, yeah?'

Ned looked down at the eyeless face on the floor.

'Call the city cleaners in. Tell them they'd better do a decent job this time. Last month we had members of the public posting us body parts, it's unhygienic. Leave the bubble till they get here, there might be souvenir hunters.' He eyed the inquisitive crowd. 'Pack of vultures, the lot of them.'

Jenni smoothed her jacket pockets down. She hoped he couldn't tell that she'd half inched Two-Face Bob's brass buttons, but you never knew with the chief. Literally eyes all over his face and probably in the back of his head too for good measure.

'Rightchoya, Boss.'

Ned left the bubble and keeping an eye out for Mrs Wicket's feathers, motioned for Neeps to follow him away from the melee of onlookers.

'I need everything you've got on that other warlock. Even if it didn't make the papers,' Ned said.

'So it is a warlock attack then.'

'I can neither confirm nor deny that assumption. The Thief-Catcher's office, working under the direction of the Emperor - *may he live for ever and ever* - reminds you that it is an offence to stand in the way of the law being processed and we thank you for the excellent demonstration of civic pride in carrying out our formal request to the letter, and within the next hour.'

'An hour! Spinks, you can't be serious? I have other deadlines you know.'

'So do I,' Ned replied grimly as he walked away.

He made it around the corner before staggering to a nearby wall as the remains of his energy ran away from him.

Looking around to make sure no one was about he pushed his hand into the wall hard and willed the collective energy of Black Narrows into his body. It felt slimy, cold and smelt slightly of cabbages, but it got him walking again, hopefully as far as The Noose where he could collapse in private and get something to eat.

Chapter 5

Ned never made it as far as the office. Outside The Noose stood a pair of extremely clean and shiny Palace Guards. They had plumes. They looked highly conspicuous and nervous at being this far away from the Palace. They were eyeballing everything that moved. A rat had been given a serious talking to and several cockroaches were considering how they could better their lives.

'Spinks! You are to come with us and report.' The taller of the two pristine guards hollered, his voice hoarse from shouting at vermin and tinged with relief at Ned's arrival.

'But I've only just come back from the Palace, and I've still got at least twenty-two hours before I'm due to report in,' objected Ned.

'No time. We've got orders. If you please.' The guard gestured for Ned to walk in front of them.

His feet betrayed him by swiftly falling into line and he looked longingly over his shoulder at the sanctuary of his dingy little office and allowed himself to be marched through the streets. Several small children began cheering. Ned glared at them. It had little effect. Quicker than he would like Ned found himself ushered into the Palace's second-best meeting room.

He knew it was the second-best meeting room because the pillars were more decorative, the gold swirly ceiling patterns were more intricate, and several unusual statues languished in various alcoves. The sort of artwork that you have to display because someone very important spent lots of money on it regardless of its artistic merit.

They didn't have statues like that in the third best meeting room. And the floor, this floor didn't have unusual dark stains which meant there was a good chance blood was not going to be spilt but, Ned still felt nervous.

Dignitaries were met in the second-best meeting room. It was opulent and smelled at least seven social standards higher than the one Ned clung to. He felt small and grimy as he stood in the middle of the gleaming floor. The guards left him alone and he tried to wait calmly. There didn't appear to be anyone else in here. He was idly perusing a rather suggestive series of marble statues in the far-left corner when there was a slight cough in front of him. He turned and gulped. The High Left and the High Right had appeared. The Upper Circle was further back. One didn't speak to the Upper Circle. It was best not to make eye contact either.

Oh crap, oh crap, oh crap, oh crap, oh crap! Ned's internal panic monologue had turned on and would not shut up. He tried in vain to look like he knew why he was there and ignore the liquid feeling in his bowels.

'Spinks. Report.' The High Right glared at a spot about six inches above Ned's shoulder. Which wasn't actually that bad seeing as his face looked like it could direct thunderbolts and kill lesser beings on a whim.

'Yes, Sir.' Ned had initially decided to look between the High Right and High Left when speaking but that left him eyeballing the Upper Circle, so he ended up addressing the ceiling. He decided the Palace must have heard about the murder and that's why they'd dragged him back in. They couldn't possibly be expecting him to have made any headway with the rose thefts. 'Two-Face

Bob came forward with some information about the Rose Thief case but before we were able to retrieve said information, Two-Face was relieved of one of his visages resulting in the unfortunate demise of a beloved citizen.' The ceiling really was rather nice - swirly with hints of gold leaf and some archaic runes of protection.

'And?' The High Left interrupted Ned's internal art critique.

'Er... we bubbled the scene of the crime and identified the cause of death as murder by a wraith. We have yet to determine who ordered the kill, but a magical signature was found at the crime scene. A source at *The Daily Blag* revealed details of warlock attacks in Narborough. I have issued a request for all materials pertaining to the attacks to see if there is any correlation.'

'So, you feel you have the matter in hand?' The Upper Circle's voice was clear and sweet. Ned blinked several times as he realised it was a woman. No one would've known under those bulky robes and that ridiculous circular headdress.

'Yes, Sir.' There was a deep silence. Ned tried again. 'Sorry, Ma'am.' It didn't make a difference. You could hear dust falling. He was left to sweat it out for several long minutes before the Upper Circle made a small motion with her left hand. High Left leapt to fill the quiet.

'Whilst we appreciate that catching Two-Face Bob's killer is important, murderous wraiths aside – there has been another theft. The rose of enchantment has been stolen.'

Ned hazarded a guess. 'Enchantment is... blue?'

'Good grief man, are you sure you're qualified to even tie your shoelaces? Purple is for enchantment. We only have three roses left. What the blazes are you going to do?'

Ned drew himself up and refocused his eyes on a particularly complex piece of ceiling decoration. 'It would be extremely helpful to the case if we were allowed access to the Rose Gardens. Perhaps there is some evidence linking the thefts and the murder.'

The Upper Circle walked forward. Ned thought both the High Right and Left moved a fraction out of the way so as not to be in her direct path, but it was so slight he wondered whether he'd imagined the whole thing. The Upper Circle came to a standstill directly in front of Ned. He could smell her perfume, spicy and warm with hints of caramel. It made his skin tingle. Ned dared not look down. Finally, she spoke.

'You and one member of your team will be allowed access to the garden. You will both submit to extensive searches before and after entry. You will agree to be bound by a magical contract to not speak a word of what you see inside. Any evidence you gather must be inspected within the Palace and cannot be removed. Breaking any of these rules will have harsh consequences. Do you understand?'

At first, Ned found he had no voice so he swallowed rapidly and managed to croak out an affirmative, his mind whirling as to what he might see within the gardens.

'Report to the Rose Gate in one hour. Do not be late.' The Upper Circle turned and silently glided away from Ned, across the hall and out through a side door.

The two Highs and Ned let out a collective sigh. A bead of sweat trickled down the side of Ned's face. He turned smartly, retreating the way he'd been shown in.

There was no one outside the second-best meeting room so he began walking towards the main reception area and the doorway out of the Palace. His heart would not slow down and so he gave up on nonchalant walking, breaking into a jog which turned into a flat out run. He burst into the main courtyard at a sprint and had to swerve drastically to avoid a collision with an old man seeking alms. Ned sank to the floor and breathed heavily for a few moments before remembering where he was. Not listening to limbs that screamed in protest he levered himself up and left the Palace grounds.

The bright sunlight outside made him blink rapidly in surprise. It was still daytime. Finally, his body betrayed him, and he was violently sick. Luckily for him, the sticky black vomit plastered the street cobbles and not the Palace courtyard, but it reminded him that he'd been running on borrowed energies and he needed to replenish them now. Somehow, he staggered to The Noose and half fell in the doorway. This was unusual and several patrons turned to stare – normally people fell out The Noose's doorway.

'I got dis.' It was Mortar, a forward thinking troll. Forward thinking in that he had decided rock tasted better than humans and was therefore allowed to live and work within the city. It was more laziness on his part, human bones were small and sharp. They stuck in his teeth and were a devil to pass through his rocky digestive system. If only someone could invent a human smoothie. These days he worked at The Noose as a sort of bouncer. He took people out rather than let them in, Reg preferred it that way as he got to collect a greater variety of coin. Mortar picked Ned up by the ankle and swung him gently as he bouldered over to the rear stairwell. With a practised flip he tossed Ned up the stairs where the expertly placed mattress caught him and deposited him on the floor.

'Thanks Mortar. You're a pal,' Ned croaked.

The rest of his team came out of the office to see what the commotion was. Willow and Joe picked up a foot each and dragged Ned into the room. Once the door banged shut behind him, Jenni threw a massive glowing ball of energy at her boss. It made Ned scream, his back arching off the floor, eyeballs rolling back in his head. Then it was dark, but he could hear voices.

'Jenni, was that absolutely necessary?' asked Willow.

'E looked on 'is last legs to me. I am medical hofficer you know.'

Ned groaned, trying to form words. He couldn't move his arms or legs.

'Don't move Boss, you're immobi, immobli, imbobi, stuck – you're stuck.'

'Jenni.' Ned forced the words through clenched teeth. 'What did you do?'

'A level ten energy 'it. Very sorry I bovvered.'

'No, no, thank you, really. But could we dial it down maybe?'

Jenni scowled and flicked her wrist. Instantly Ned could move. Instantly screaming lances of hot pain flared throughout his body and blackness descended for a second time.

Ten minutes later he came around. There was less noise this time. Willow was leaning out the window, more than likely teasing the moss that liked to grow on the roof of The Noose. Joe had his head in a book and had adopted the ever-popular youthful sprawl position on the floor. It looked effortlessly comfortable yet when Ned had tried in the privacy of his own room, he'd cricked his back and had to spend the next ten minutes looking at the floor before his spine relaxed enough for him to stand upright again. The young had no appreciation of their youth. Ned took a moment to count his fingers and toes. All present. And that crushing pain in his head meant it was still on the end of his neck, more or less. A strong odour swam into being followed by a blurry Jenni.

'Drink this.' She shoved a steaming cup of bright green liquid at him.

The smell alone made him want to empty his stomach of everything he'd ever eaten in his life. He tried to back away but found he was still semi-collapsed on the floor. Before he could do anything about his position, Jenni elevated his head slightly, pinched his nose forcing him to open his mouth for breath and poured the foul liquid down his throat. It burnt the whole way down and tasted worse than it smelled, if that was even possible. Gagging, choking, and spluttering, Ned pushed himself up into a fully seated position and leaned back against the wall.

'What was that?'

'Cure-all. 'and-me-down secret that is, Boss. Better than anyfink out there.'

'Thanks,' Ned replied weakly. 'How long was I out?' His stomach rumbled noisily, so much so it even brought Joe out of his book briefly.

'Ten minutes 'ere or there. Neeps poked her 'ead in and left summik. S'over there.'

Ned eyed the huge packet of papers Jenni was pointing at.

'Right. Willow, get your head out of the lichen. We've got to go through these papers. Joe. Joe. Oi JOE! Go make a run for pizza. Go to Gariboldi's not Garibaldi's like last time. That pizza tasted like mouldy shoe leather.'

'What shall I get?' Joe's face looked the most alive it

had all day. Pizza was a bit of team favourite.

'Green Goddess for me, Joe.' Willow winked at Joe sending his Adam's apple bobbing alarmingly.

'I'll 'ave the fungal surprise.' Jenni shoved several silver bits into Joe's back pocket.

'Get me a large Best of the Rest and whatever you fancy kid,' said Ned.

Joe muttered the list under his breath as he walked slowly out of the room. For a top-level spell-caster, he was sadly lacking in every other area of his life. Ned staggered over to the table and sat on the desk.

'How long since I got back from the Palace?'

'About twenty, twenty-five minutes, Boss. Why?'

'Dammit! Jenni, go catch up with Joe and get the pizzas quick. You'll probably have to give Gariboldi's some assistance. They won't mind, we've got a standard assistance order in place. You need to be back here as fast as you can. We're going into the Rose Garden in less than twenty minutes and I have got to eat something before then.'

There was a loud greasy pop as the sprite disappeared.

'We've been given access to the Emperor's, *may he live for ever and ever*, Rose Garden? The actual garden?' Willow was so excited buds were appearing in places no buds should ever appear. Soon blossom would start spontaneously combusting.

'Calm down, Catcher. I'm taking Jenni, they're only letting two of us in and I need her skill set.'

Willow pouted. 'I have skills.'

'Yes you do and if I need the entire Rose Garden pollinated within five minutes then I will certainly call on your superb talents.'

'What if you want to talk to the roses? They might

33

have seen something, you know?'

'Jenni – sprite – remember? She can do what you can do, more or less.'

Willow's buds were shrivelling and falling off her smooth green arms, which had begun to darken and brown in anger when there was another greasy pop. The alluring aroma of pizza filled the office and for a short while, there was nothing but moans of delight and the smacking of lips.

Sparks entered through the open window and chittered at being left out of the pizza order.

'Here, have some of mine.' Willow placed a piece of greenery on Spark's shelf and he flashed his butt at her in appreciation.

Ned stood up and wiped his hands on his trousers, leaving faint greasy marks, but he was in too much of a hurry to care.

'You lot start going through this paperwork. We're looking for anything on a warlock using red, spiky power. Sparks, you'll have to report to me later. I've got an important appointment. C'mon Jenni.'

Jenni puffed her chest out in pride at being chosen to go until she realised that no one was paying her any attention. They were all so full of pizza they didn't care.

'You'll have to pop us there Jenni, we don't have time to walk.'

She grabbed his arm and whisked him through the distance between the office and the Rose Gate. On arrival, Ned swallowed several times in order to keep his pizza in his stomach. He still wasn't feeling fully recovered from using his abilities earlier. What he needed was a good long sleep and another decent meal but for now, he had access to the legendary Rose Garden.

Chapter 6

The green Rose Garden gate was ajar when they arrived. Jenni and Ned looked at each other for a moment.

'You sure this ain't a trap, Boss?'

Ned shrugged. It was impossible to keep track of the everyday political swirls that happened in Roshaven. Despite the fact that the Emperor was officially in charge of everything, everybody and everywhere, there were still positions of semi-power to fight over. Like the positions of High Left and Right – there had been six of them so far this year. Usually filled by bony men with no hair and large noses, or if they had hair to begin with it soon fell out with the stress of office. The position of the Upper Circle was a strange one. Ned now knew it was filled by a woman but who would give a woman that much power? He considered the others. The Lower Circle was Fat Norris – he looked after trade, well he owned practically every building that housed a crafter or merchant and possibly all of the dockland warehouses as well. He more than likely owned Two-Face Bob. Or at least had. Ned made a tired mental note to look into that relationship as soon as he could. The Stalls was, of course, Madam Silk, the high madam of all the whores in the city. Whoring was not a crime per se; however, indignant wives had been known to cut off rather necessary equipment from husbands who dallied more than they should. It was usually a quiet, private and mostly secretive transaction – after all the Emperor, with a thousand and one wives, knew it was more than his tackle was worth to start sticking his nose into that area of commerce. Women may not have much power in Roshaven but they had enough.

Jenni tugged at his arm, breaking Ned's train of thought. He pushed the gate fully open and a heady fragrance filled his nostrils. This was it. The famed Rose Gardens - he went in eagerly. Narrow pebbled walkways wound complicated paths through elaborately planted rose beds. There were trailing vines decorating romantic trestle arches, bees buzzing, butterflies fluttering and only a slight sour tang to the air from the liberal use of enchanted manure. It made things grow faster but smelt stronger for longer than the usual stuff. Rose perfume made everything feel thick as if you were trying to walk through a cloud. Tinkling water fell from beautiful marble fountains and naked female busts were sprinkled throughout. The different rose colours swirled inward leaving a perfectly circular flower bed in the middle, showcasing the most treasured rose of all. The red red rose of love. Looking at it made Ned feel all warm and fuzzy in places he thought had fallen off forever.

A blue shimmer fell over both Jenni and Ned, the magical sweep checking they had no weapons or spells. At Ned's current energy level, the sweep would be unlikely to even register his spell-caster ability. Jenni glowed orange for a moment and was then cleared as she emptied her pockets. It was a small vial of beetle juice. A delicious tipple in the fae realm but of course no beetles allowed in the Emperor's gardens.

Ned raised an eyebrow at her as she flushed defensively, then threw the vial in the bin nearby.

'I forgot.'

'Walk with me,' a voice commanded. It was the Upper Circle. Appearing from nowhere and swathed in her bulky robes but without the ridiculous headdress.

Ned felt something tickle the back of his mind, she looked so familiar with her dark, square, haircut and heavily kohled eyes. Then he realised what it was. This was the face he'd seen on the imperial seal, the image branded into Roshaven's currency. She was the spitting image of the Emperor.

He nudged Jenni but she was oblivious, too busy sniffing the air and trying to work out the different spells in place. Only a high-level warlock or spell-caster would've been able to make it in and out of the gardens. All warlocks were banned from the city and all magical training was scrutinised heavily, so it was highly unlikely he, or indeed she, was a local. Ned remembered the spiky red power signature he'd felt and shivered.

They followed the Upper Circle through the winding pathways until they reached the scene of the first theft. The swathe of pink roses looked sick. The smell of decay hung heavily in the air as many of the rose heads hung down in defeat, their petals tarnished brown. The soft earth below was littered with petals that had lost the fight and now lay rotting.

'What happened?' Ned asked quietly.

'The theft of one has led to sickness with the others. Here is where the thief made his cutting.' The Upper Circle pointed to a pink rose bush with a blackened stem. It looked like tendrils of poison had spread from the cut down the bush, through the earth and was now infecting the others.

'Something on the blade perhaps,' Ned murmured, leaning in for a closer look. He absently reached out with his ability forgetting his levels were so depleted. Jenni nonchalantly brushed his leg, sending a jolt of power through his body. It made him gasp which he quickly turned into a cough – not too out of place considering

37

the rotten stench that hung in the air.

With that much power raging through his veins he could see the pale remnants of the red power spike like a haze around the rose bush. Looking around slowly he could see faint red clouds hanging over the white, orange, yellow, and purple flower beds. There was no residue for entry or exit, only spikes of power over rose bushes. Ned looked down at the ground, no ley line marks. He looked up – there. So faint it had almost disappeared but there was a shimmer that didn't belong.

The garden was of course open-air. It was located on the far side of the Emperor's Palace, the furthest point from the city. Ned and Jenni had gained access through the garden's gate, the gate itself was located within the Palace. It did not have access to the outside world directly except through its lack of ceiling. Various anti-burglary spells and alarms crisscrossed the open space above the garden and rows of spiked metal thorns and wicked-looking glass shards decorated the circumference. A thief would not be able to climb their way into the gardens. They would have to use magic. Now that he thought about it, they had taken a certain liberty popping in like that. No alarms meant they'd either been observed and reluctantly approved or fae magic wasn't something the Palace defences were equipped to deal with. The Upper Circle followed his gaze.

'Well done catcher, you have found the point of entry. Now tell me something I don't already know.'

'Do you know how we got here?'

'I imagine you walked to the main reception area, announced yourself and were led to the gate.'

'As a matter of fact, we popped here. My sprite knew exactly where the rose garden gate was, so we came right to it. I take it we didn't trip any alarms so not only do we have a suspected warlock with a penchant for roses, but he also seems to have access to fae magic and a map of the Palace.'

The Upper Circle stared at Ned for a long while.

'I want him found.'

'Yes, Your Excellency.'

She looked at him, eyes lidded in thought as if deciding whether or not to execute him and have him replaced with yet another useless lackey.

'May you live for ever and ever?' Ned volunteered. Anything was worth a shot after being looked at like that.

Jenni interrupted them by shoving a handful of mulch up towards their noses. They both recoiled at the intense smell.

'Smells like that uver shite I was telling you about, Boss.'

'The Emperor's rose garden is one of a kind, there are no other mulches in the city specific to our roses. I, that is, the Emperor owns the recipe.'

'Rightchoya.' Jenni winked impishly. Quite difficult for a sprite.

Jenni had balled the mulch up and was bouncing it up and down in her hand. Small flakes of muck were drifting off and catching the faint breeze that danced through the garden. Ned noted with some satisfaction that they seemed attracted to the Emperor's – sorry Upper Circle's – robes.

'I knows what I nose you know? This is the same as that uver stuff and this has been brought 'ere recently. It hasn't squished in with the other lot – see?' Jenni pointed to a faint difference in brown in the soil below.

'So, we have a suspected warlock, replacement

mulch and borrowed fae magic. I imagine this gives you plenty to work with, Thief-Catcher?'

Ned nodded absently; he was thinking about the poison tracks they'd seen earlier. When Jenni coughed and stamped on his foot, he realised he should have replied.

'Yes, right, great. Lots of leads to follow.' He paused then looked directly at the Upper Circle. 'I take it we can gather a mulch sample and discuss what we saw here today, with the rest of the thief-catchers I mean? It will make solving the case difficult otherwise.' Ned cleared his throat, he might as well try and save his neck, while he was here. In for a penny and all that. 'And if it's not too much to ask, Ma'am, could I also have a time extension? We've got about twenty hours left and I'd hate for my torture to pull valuable resources away from catching this criminal.'

The Upper Circle nodded imperceptibly.

Jenni produced a plastic bag from somewhere and put in a sample of the intruder mulch, then the two of them made their way back along the winding pathways to the doorway. On exiting through another blue shimmer Jenni popped them straight back to the office where they walked into a full-blown argument.

Chapter 7

'You didn't even read that file.'

'It can't help us.'

'How do you know? The boss said to read everything on the warlock. I can't do it all by myself.'

'Well, you could always ask that creeping vine we keep cutting back to help you turn the pages.'

'I might ask it to turn you – inside out!'

Ned walked in to find Willow armed with several creepers and pulsing slightly, standing in the centre of a pile of open files while Joe lounged in a chair in the corner.

'What's going on?' Ned glared at the two of them.

'He won't help me read the files.' Willow began explaining but Ned hushed her and looked at Joe.

'Well?'

Joe tried to avoid Ned's gaze and mumbled into his shoes. 'I think I know who the warlock is. I guessed at the crime scene but...'

'What? But what? Speak up!'

'It's complicated.'

'Uncomplicate it. And for Gods' sake, Willow, disarm that greenery!' barked Ned.

Joe smirked as Willow jumped guiltily and let go of the twirling creepers that were beginning to take over most of the office. Without her grip on them, they withered and shrank, snaking out of the window and returning to their usual climbing vine status on the side of The Noose.

'Who do you think it is then, Joe?' Ned asked.

'It's my sister. Twin actually.' He flushed. 'Now you know.'

There was a stunned silence. It wasn't possible for twin spell-casters to exist, one always drained the other of power in the womb. But twin warlocks. They were possible.

Ned tried in vain to pull some power into his wiped caster wells.

'So that makes you...'

'A warlock by birth, yes, but look...' Joe raised his hands in defence. 'I practise as a spell-caster. I don't have any real power anyway. I learned my art the spell-caster way. I'm no threat at all – honest.'

He still hadn't moved from the chair, yet all his dopiness had vanished, revealing a much more intelligent looking Joe. Ned made a quick decision. He had no juice so there was nothing he could do personally.

'Jenni, bind him. Fetch me a truth-catcher.'

Jenni reacted instantly and Joe was lashed to the chair tightly but then she hesitated. 'Is a truth-catcher wot we need, Boss?'

'Yes. Go!' He turned to glare at Joe. 'You lied to me. What else haven't you told us?' Ned was interrupted by Sparks buzzing around his head. 'Yes, yes I know – you haven't reported yet, but can't it wait? I'm having a slight crisis here.'

Sparks flashed twice for no so Ned sighed, made sure Joe was secure and went to find the firefly communicator from the cupboard. He tried to avoid using it in front of other people. He strapped himself into the fake firefly tail attachment. It was rather snug upon the groin area and made things appear... well, made everything *look* a lot more. Once attached, the fae magic that made the translator work started glowing so that he now looked like an oversized firefly with his very own light bulb on his butt.

'Boss, yes Boss. I went to the docks like you said, Boss. Not much there but fish, Boss. Stinks, Boss.'

'Stay on topic, Sparks.'

'Boss, yes Boss. I found Two-Face Bob's office, Boss. Been ransacked, Boss. Nothing left, Boss. His goons were gone, Boss. Just a load of dried dung balls, Boss. Smells like you, Boss. No offence, Boss.'

Ned frowned then remembered the sample they'd collected from the Rose Gardens. Now they knew Two-Face Bob had been involved in supplying the different mulch and had clearly been killed for it. But not his Boss, Fat Norris. So either Two-Face was working a side line and Fat Norris knew nothing about it. Or Fat Norris had hired the warlock himself to murder his own henchman, which to be fair to the big man was unlikely. Fat Norris was more a believer in thug control than magical means - he felt more people could relate to it. And anyway, why did Fat Norris want a load of roses? It didn't make sense. Sparks was fizzing, waiting for Ned to respond.

'Well done, Sparks. Anything else?'

'Boss, no Boss.'

Ned hurriedly removed the translator and placed it back in the cupboard. In the middle of the room, Willow was looking forlorn as she sat in the midst of the paperwork Neeps had provided. Her hair had dropped and looked like it was weeping as it hung around her face.

'Willow – what did you find?'

She perked up at being asked, after all, she had been working hard the entire time and reading wasn't a nymph's strong point.

'Neeps was right, there have been other attacks. Elongoo City lost their collection of shooting stars and Molotov no longer has a wine river – all their grapes were violated. Same red spiky power residue at all the crime scenes. The files are full of speculation about warlock attack but no actual evidence of who or what.'

'Right, and this red power signature, that's what we saw today at Two-Face Bob's murder. And again in the Rose Garden.' Ned glared at Joe. 'It seems like this warlock is probably Two-Face Bob's murderer as well. Looks like your sister has some serious explaining to do.'

Before Joe had the chance to respond the door crashed open and Jenni came through with the Palace's truth-catcher. It was the Upper Circle. Wonderful. Not only did Ned not have time to protect Joe, if he decided he was going to, now he had to contend with the bloody Emperor herself, standing in The Noose!

'Er.'

It wasn't Ned's best conversation opener, but it seemed to do the trick. Joe sat bolt upright in his chair, eyes widening and all pretence of being self-confident had vanished in an instance. Sparks was hovering by his shelf, butt flashing in excitement or possibly fear. Willow had gone a nasty shade of puce, which, considering she usually had a greenish tinge about her was rather unsettling. Jenni looked extremely pleased with herself.

'I fawt you'd want the best, Boss, so I got 'er.' She jabbed a thumb up at the Upper Circle who stood demurely in the doorway, her circular headdress obscuring any of the tell-tale features Ned had seen earlier. He decided to play it safe.

'Welcome to TCHQ your roundness. Thank you for

coming so promptly. If I could just have a word privately?'

'There's no time for that.' The Upper Circle's voice was so melodious Ned's eyes narrowed slightly, she sounded far too calm. 'I am the truth-seeker and I shall seek what truths are hidden. Is this the boy?'

Ned nodded mutely and Joe looked scared half to death. He was pressed as far back into the chair as possible and looked like he would break bones to pass through it if he were able.

'Don't you see it?' he whimpered.

Ned shook his head then caught a strange whiff of something. It smelt like the enchanted mulch they'd seen in the Rose Garden, only worse. He checked his boots – nope, not him. Jenni smelt unique but this was different, he was sure this wasn't her. He squinted at the Upper Circle and noticed something out of place, there – the soil which had floated away on the breeze landing on her robes in the Rose Garden was still there but now it had coagulated into a large muddy patch. Tentacles seemed to be waving back and forth and was that... an eye? Ned muttered an apology as he leant forward to inspect the muck closer and brushed the Upper Circle's arm. Instantly he was flooded with power, he felt like he'd run ten thousand miles and could easily run ten thousand more. His heart was thudding in his chest and every sense was heightened. The mud splat still stank but now he could see the spiky red power running through the whole thing. It was also emanating a slight grey miasma and had leached all the colour from that part of the Upper's robe. Ned acted without thought and snatched the robe off the Upper. He prayed for sensible clothing. He was slightly disappointed.

Instead of diaphanous trousers and belly tops in

sheer fabric that he always supposed nubile young women in the Palace wore, she was dressed in plain yet close-fitting dark trousers and tunic. It left nothing to the imagination, but the imagination still had to work pretty hard as the nondescript clothing took away any femininity she might have had. The Upper stiffened at the loss of her cloak but her circular headdress remained undisturbed. Now that the cloak had been removed the mud stopped pretending to be mud and started to fizz loudly. Ned dropped the clothing in alarm and the magic mud dissolved a hole in the cloak. The brown muck transformed fully into bright red gunk with even more tentacles questing for nearby prey. It was so acidic that the air burnt making everyone's eyes sting and the backs of their throats tingle. The blob was a little too zealous for its own good and quickly eroded the floorboard, falling through to The Noose below. There was a sharp yell and then a lot of swearing.

Ned and Jenni ran out the door and hurtled down the stairs, speed carrying them over the dodgy parts of the staircase. The red goo had evolved once more, this time into a mist that was rapidly leaving The Noose through the wall. It was taking bits of the wall with it. A bright light shone into the dingy corners of the pub making it look even more filthy and rundown. Loyal patrons blinked in surprise then turned back to nursing their drinks. Reg threw a vile look at Ned.

'Extra.'

Ned nodded mutely and he and Jenni returned slowly upstairs, Ned thinking furiously. It must have been some residual warlock magic awakened due to its proximity to Joe. Thank the Gods he hadn't taken the lad with him to the Rose Garden - who knew what might have happened?

When they got back into the office, the Upper Circle was sitting in front of Joe, who had his eyes closed and face screwed up in pain. There was a soft glowing nimbus of power around them and Willow was idly plaiting her hair, trying not to look in wonder at a truth-catcher at work.

'I see you started without me.' Ned wondered if he could stall for time. 'There's no need. New evidence has been brought to light...'

The Upper Circle interrupted. 'It was the least I could do. You saved my life so now I'm returning the favour.' She was focusing intently on Joe.

'I hardly think questioning Joe is saving my life.'

'What if Joe is not his real name? Did you know that his mind is full of a compulsion web? It forces him to follow someone – what else does it make him do? Did they put it there or was it someone else? These are all dangerous questions we must get to the bottom of – if he is connected to the Rose Thief, I want to know why he's stealing my roses!' The Upper Circle realised her error and tried to speak more calmly. 'I've not seen a web like this before, it extends deep into his psyche and can't be removed without killing him. But perhaps it will provide us with a direct link to the thief.'

Ignoring Ned, her power flared, making a crackling noise and shooting out blue sparks but before she could do anything Ned sent a bolt of his own magic directly into her ear. It made her gasp in surprise, dropping the spell she'd been weaving.

'What are you doing?' she hissed, turning on Ned.

'I'm not letting you murder one of mine.' Despite the magical sparks flying, Ned refused to back down.

'I wasn't going to murder him, at least not intentionally.' The Upper Circle smoothed her trousers. 'I

47

was merely going to send back a powerful jolt to the person behind that compulsion.'

She turned back to complete her spell, but Joe had vanished. So had Jenni. Ned tried to look as innocent as possible, helped by the fact that Willow was stunned. Her mouth gaped and tendrils started growing out. She quickly bit them off and started blushing, but the effect helped Ned to consolidate his surprise.

'What have you done?' he yelled.

'Me? What did you do?' The Upper Circle rounded on him once more, her usually calm eyes flashing in anger. 'Where did you send him? I know you re-fuelled, I felt your clumsy touch and allowed you some power as thanks for your service. Where is he?'

Jenni began whistling innocently in the corner of the room. The Upper Circle frowned. She hadn't been there before.

'You,' she began and whirled to confront the sprite. Big mistake. Jenni started to grow, becoming not only taller but wider, uglier, and smellier. Soon she filled the corner of the room and the ceiling began to creak under the strain of her towering mass. The Upper Circle let out a scream of frustration and swept out of the office. In the next instant, Jenni was back to normal size although her extra-large smell lingered.

'Where's Joe?' asked Ned.

'Safe. In the glade, innit – bawling like a baby but 'e'll be awright. Momma K will look after 'im.'

Ned winced. Momma K was unique. Her version of looking after could be something as simple as a hot meal and a bed for the night. More often than not it involved some kind of mental or physical test as she helped you realise the solution to a problem you did not know you had. Most people avoided Momma K. They were happy being ignorant of their character flaws. Ned had been to see her several times. He was not overly keen to return. He always ended up wanting to stay.

Chapter 8

Leaving Willow and Sparks to man the office, Ned took Jenni with him to go and see Momma K. Jenni had offered to pop him there but Ned's body already felt like it had been through the washer, the ringer and left to dry, pegged out on the line in a gale. He felt the walk would do him more harm than good, but he needed to clear his head a little. Plus, there were a few power wells on the way and now seemed like an excellent time to replenish. His stomach rumbled.

'Can we go via Aggie's?' Ned didn't bother to check if Jenni was following. At the thought of one of Aggie's warm cinnamon spiced bread twists his feet had made up their mind, that was the way they were walking no matter what.

He clocked some Palace Guards looking highly conspicuous on a nearby corner, out of uniform but in the cleanest street garb he'd ever seen. Let them follow him, he wasn't going to tell them anything they didn't already know. Aggie's was the best bakery in town.

There was, as expected, a queue out the door – it was nearly the end of the day, so portions got generous and more often than not the beggar children left with double their own weight in odds and ends. Aggie was a waste not kind of baker, more interested in taste than appearance, so every scrap of dough was worked and baked. It made her creations unique and much loved. Ned squeezed through the doorway and waited by the counter for Aggie to notice him. She had, as per usual, a cloud of flour permanently circling her, like her own personal brand of halo, strangely her usual cheerful demeanour was gone. This was a cross and snappy Aggie. She started to swear about folks cutting the line, then she saw who it was.

'Hmpf. Cutting it a bit fine, aren't we?' She lobbed a cinnamon twist at Ned's head. A sharp eye and a hint of power-assisted catch reflex meant that it landed in Ned's hands and did not sail through the window.

'Everything alright, Aggie?'

'Everything alright he says – as if he didn't know.'

Ned frowned. He didn't.

'Who do you think gets my special spices in for me?'

Ned shrugged.

'Two-Face Bob of course, and he only went to see you about the Rose Thief and now he's dead.'

'How do you know that?'

'Just because I bake by profession does not mean I can't read or talk to my other customers, thank you very much. I'll have you know Two-Face was very partial to an Apricot Spigot.' Aggie looked daggers at Ned, making him edge back towards the door.

'We're looking into it, Aggie, I swear.' She didn't look impressed. 'I'll make sure your spices come through I promise.'

'I'd take your promise on good faith if I didn't already know that the Upper Bloody Circle has threatened to close everything – yes everything – until the Rose Thief is caught. That means no wagons, no shipments and no air drops. We will be cut off from the outside world. Tell me – what am I supposed to do if I run out of sugar? Can't bake without sugar, can I?'

Ned was shocked. He let Aggie's tirade wash over him and he tried to process what the Emperor had threatened. Trade was the lifeblood of Roshaven,

51

without it everything would start falling apart. And this was all over some stupid flowers. The Rose Thief hadn't even stolen the magically endowed one yet. Could this be about something deeper? If only he had time to figure it out.

'I didn't know that Aggie – but we're on the case. We'll get to the bottom of it as quickly as we can, I promise.'

'Don't bother coming back until you do. I can't afford to give it away anymore.' She turned, resolute, preventing him from making any kind of comeback.

The cinnamon twist tasted like ashes in his mouth as he walked away from the bakery. He was too hungry to throw it away, but he doubted whether he'd ever eat another one, especially if this case didn't get solved soon. Jenni followed in his wake, for once blissfully quiet.

Ned stopped at one, then another power well trying to draw as much as he could into his own storage belt. Touching the Emperor had recharged him, but it felt like foreign power. It skittered under his skin. At least the power wells never ran dry. When Roshaven was originally built, magical ley lines were used to their maximum potential – it was why the Druids happily existed within the city walls, the natural power of the city hadn't been paved over. Each well was located over a nexus point and access was freely available to all spell-casters. Some Guild or other had tried to capitalise on charging for access but the fae who lived in the city soon changed their minds and no one else felt inclined to see their innards draped artfully across the city walls anytime soon.

Walking in silence they made their way to the heart of the city where a small garden was well kept. It wasn't much of a garden, more like a patch of grass and a small sapling. It looked lost surrounded by the cobbles and rooftops of the city. It was the only gateway left to Momma K's realm though, the next one was a four day ride out towards the River Whine – it never stopped moaning. Ned looked around for the plainclothes Palace Guards, but they'd disappeared. He must have lost them at Aggies. It didn't matter, they couldn't follow through here. He motioned for Jenni to open the gateway and she hesitated.

'Boss – she's not 'appy wiv you. Says you forgot 'er birfday. I ain't saying you did or you never but...' She shrugged as if to say rather you than me.

Ned swore softly under his breath. He quickly patted his pockets to see if there was anything worth gifting Momma K. His hand closed over the broken watch he'd been carrying around with him. It would have to do; he hoped no other clever young buck had tried the same trick. Momma K liked novelty.

Jenni grabbed hold of the air around the sapling and twisted it somehow, it was difficult to watch as the sky started to bend and then rapidly expand. Ned tried not to follow the landscape as it flew past his head. He'd made that mistake the first time he'd come and had ended up being rather ill on some delightful looking toadstools. At the time he'd prayed fervently that no one lived there. Now he knew better, sprites didn't live in toadstools – brownies did and there were none of those in Momma K's kingdom.

Ned took a deep breath and strode towards the bright lights in the forest glade ahead, somewhat to the left of the horizon. Momma K was entertaining, he could make out the strains of lively music and the lights were flashing blue, green, red and yellow. Either that or it was some kind of new-fangled torture device, either one was likely and, in actual fact, it was probably a combination of the two. Momma K liked to multi-task. The music got louder and deeper as they got closer. It felt to Ned that it vibrated in the pit of his stomach. It was making his teeth hum uncomfortably. As he began to think his eardrums might blow, the music stopped abruptly, and the light changed to soft purple. Momma K knew he had come. As Ned walked around a rather stout pumpkin, he saw Joe passed out on a pile of lettuces. The young lad appeared to be breathing and was otherwise unharmed so he'd have to wait until Ned had placated Momma K. Ned spread his arms wide, fixed a grin on his face and yelled happily, 'Momma K – how you been?'

A diminutive ebony coloured sprite with waves of silver hair spun elegantly on one leg, her petite body framed by two gloriously patterned silver and black slender wings. She held out a hand to stop his progress.

'Oh no ya doh. Ya doh no jus' walk in me kingdom like dat. Tell me ya did no jus' walk inta me kingdom like dat.' She shook her head and waggled her fingers at him.

'Momma K, you know I got love for you.'

'Ya best show it. Words is words, dey ain't showing me no love.'

'I stopped time for you.' Ned offered his broken watch and held his breath as the tiny figure came forward and scrutinised his gift.

'Whaaaaat? Ya stop time fo' me? For lil' old me?' She graciously took the broken watch and tied it around her waist. 'Oooooh ya did good boy, ya did good.'

They walked together past a row of giant strawberries that glittered slightly in the sprite-light.

'How's things, Momma K?'

'Can't complain, can't complain. But me hear ya got problems, boy. Big, spiky, red problems. Me can no keep him here.' Momma K leant in and stroked Ned's hand gently. 'Me can no change wha' dat boy got. Ya gonna have ta see if ya can push it out of him and it ain't gonna be pretty.'

They both regarded Joe who had now woken up and was looking mournful. He was idly twisting a piece of grass around and round his fingers ignoring the sprites cavorting nearby.

'What do you suggest?' asked Ned.

'Find a body of water and drown him,' replied Momma K.

'Drown him?'

'Ya want to try and get dat power out of him, ya got ta kill him. Best way back to life for humans is ta be drowned. Dey come back seven times out of ten.'

'Seven times huh? Not sure I like those odds.'

'Ya don't got to like 'em, ya just got ta make 'em.'

'True.'

The two of them stood there nodding, regarding Joe for a while until Momma K decided she was bored and drifted off. All thoughts of Ned and Joe were firmly pushed out of her mind as she decided what kind of flower to use for her next baking project. These weren't always edible and were rarely safe for human consumption.

Ned looked around for Jenni, she was kissing a frog. He sighed. Ten to one the frog was a prince from some far-flung land who had upset the sprites. He watched to see if a transformation was going to occur. The frog waggled its toes and hopped off. Clearly just a frog then. Jenni spat loudly.

'Snails.'

'We've got to drown Joe.' Ned told her.

'Okay, Boss. Ocean or lake?'

Ned sighed. Either option was problematic. If they went to the lake they had to contend with The Lady, a water sprite with an excessive algae disorder. She cleaned the lake constantly and the only way she could do that was to filter it through her body. After several complaints, she'd reversed orifices and now the cleaned water streamed out of her eyes instead of elsewhere, giving her the nickname of Piss-eyed Nellie. It streamed out of her ears, nose and mouth too, but this was still considered to be more hygienic than the previous route. It did, however, make understanding her a little difficult. Everything was rather watery. Piss-eyed Nellie didn't like being interrupted and would more than likely have an episode if they tried to drown Joe in her lake. It looked like it would have to be the ocean.

Once Ned cleared it with the mermaids. He still owed them. They bailed him out at the interspecies poker game to the tune of anything they wanted to be named at a later date. It wasn't the most comforting price to have hanging over your head especially when you wanted another favour. The mermaids would be able to resuscitate Joe provided nothing went wrong. Ned would have to get them to cash in their debt first and then drown Joe.

'We'll go to the ocean, Jenni. I've just got to pay Pearl first.'

'You sure that's a good idea, Boss?'

Ned shrugged. It looked like he didn't have much of a choice.

'Couldn't we do it inna baff?'

'I'm fairly sure it needs to be a natural body of water – it'll have to have plenty of natural resonance to draw out the compulsion web within him.'

They were now standing over Joe, who gave no acknowledgement of their presence and merely continued to twist the grass around his fingers. Jenni took him by the hand, and he bobbed up to stand like a marionette. He followed her rather bonelessly out of the glade and back through the portal to the tiny patch of grass in Roshaven. Ned was right behind them and looked wistfully over his shoulder as Momma K's kingdom winked out of sight. One day he'd get to stay for the party, and he didn't think he'd care much if that meant he could never come home.

Chapter 9

'Jenni, pop into the office and let Willow know what's happening. I'll meet you at the Dead Pier.'

She nodded and vanished. Ned took a good handful of Joes' shirt, and began walking. Joe followed without a murmur. Whatever Momma K had done to calm him down was working, a little too well. They arrived without incident although there were a few odd glances from passers-by. Ned looked around and realised Joe was levitating slightly and consequently was being pulled along like a human-shaped balloon. He didn't know if that was left over Momma K magic or warlock juice reaction. It didn't matter, they had arrived at the Dead Pier.

Skulls hung at jaunty angles along railings made of femurs and tibias. Some of the skulls were painted blood red, others black but most had been bleached white and were highly polished. They all had deep, dark, empty, eye sockets and grinning teeth.

The Dead Pier was a place to pay tribute to a loved one. Back in the day, it had been respectful to leave a bone behind. Indeed, the original wooden construction of the pier had been overlain with lashed together ribs, leg and arm bones so many times, it was hard to tell whether any wood remained. It was considered far too provincial these days to simply add to the pier with any old bone, instead, only skulls were left behind. At All Hallows, one lucky custodian had the honour of ensuring that all the skulls were strung across the width of the pier with candles flickering within them, creating a most atmospheric effect. The Emperor had allowed the pier to remain because it was a huge tourist attraction and he, she, charged heavily for guided tours. *The things idiots will part cash for,* thought Ned, as he eyed a tourist crocodile winding its way down the far end of the pier.

Jenni was already back and standing by the Drop-Off, the traditional spot to talk to the mermaids, not that they often bothered to reply. The world of land was boring and way too bright for their eyes to handle too many trips upwards.

'I'll speak to Pearl first. Have you got him?' Ned passed his human balloon over to Jenni. She looked rather odd as Joe towered over her but at least Ned knew her grip would be like iron and if the lad came to, Jenni could deal with any magic the other warlock might decide to channel through Joe.

Ned sighed and took his boots and socks off. They were good boots with bootlaces that sort of matched and only one small hole in the right heel which was rather comforting on wet days when his sock became gradually soggier and soggier. It made him feel alive and in tune with his city. He gingerly dipped a toe in the water. It seemed to swirl around his foot and suck hungrily at his toe before he hastily lifted the foot out. It didn't take long for Pearl to appear. A large, dark brown seal poked its head out of the sea. The seal looked bored already. This wasn't a good start.

'You owe me.' A female voice came from the seal.

'Hi Pearl, good to see you too,' replied Ned.

'When are you paying?'

'Er, now?'

'Then you'd better get in.'

Ned shot a glance at Jenni who grinned encouragingly. He took off his thief-catcher coat but left everything else. If the mermaids intended on drowning him, then being naked wouldn't make any difference and if he got into difficulties trying to swim fully clothed then they would help him out. He hoped. He left his portable power wells where they were, he might need them. Ned carefully sat down on the edge of the pier ready to make his own way into the sea, but Pearl had become impatient. Morphing her seal flipper into an arm, she grabbed his foot and pulled him inelegantly into the drink. He landed with a smack and felt the sting of saltwater. Thankfully he'd taken a deep breath, but the look on Pearl's face was anything but friendly.

Underwater she was gorgeous. Everything you'd ever dreamt a mermaid should look like and more. Golden blonde hair that floated seductively around her head, large blue eyes and beautiful porcelain skin, perfectly rounded breasts with rose-tipped nipples inviting you closer and the most mesmerising turquoise fish scale tail you've ever seen. Light danced over the scales in shimmering patterns and whorls. It was enough to make you forget to hold your breath. Ned drew some power from his wells and forced his neck to grow gills. It burnt like hell and the first gush of water through the new breathing system made him feel like he was drowning in acid, but this was the best way to interact with the mermaids. You never knew how long you would be down here, and air supply had a nasty tendency to run out.

'Why have you shamed me so?' Pearl sounded upset.

'Shamed you?' Ned asked.

Pearl lashed her tail rapidly through the water. 'You have left payment a long time.'

'I apologise. Things came up – the city needs my help.'

'Are you saying we aren't part of the city?'

'No – yes – I mean, of course you are. An important part, but there have been thefts and murders that took my attention away from payment.'

'Are we worth that little to you?'

Coldness emanated from Pearl as all the colour and sparkle leached out of her and bleak sadness overtook. If Ned hadn't been previously spell-cast against mermaid charms it was likely that he would have drowned out of pure misery – a common mermaid ploy. When she realised it was having absolutely no effect, Pearl tried a different tack and let her power shine. She was now the most colourful mermaid; the most curvaceous woman Ned had ever seen. Her hair grew even more luscious, her face glowed like the most beautiful face in the world and her breasts – Ned shook his head feeling drunk and disorientated.

'Pearl, just tell me what I owe.'

She pulled back the glamour somewhat as Ned tried hard to look anywhere apart from straight ahead. Half-naked women were highly distracting. It had grown darker and darker - without realising Ned had been slowly sinking to the bottom of the harbour. He narrowly avoided getting skewered on the mast of an old sunken ship before his heels touched the sandy bottom with little puffs.

Pearl swished her tail, making the clouds of sand dance around his feet and named her price.

'I want to be on the team,' she said.

'You want to be a thief-catcher?' Ned was surprised.

'Yes. I want it authorised by whoever the highest power is now.' Keeping up with who ruled Roshaven wasn't a mermaid's strong point. When you live forever and can't leave the ocean, who sits on a throne inland isn't that important or interesting.

'Why do you want to be a thief-catcher?' Ned asked cautiously.

'You're always coming to me for help, so I want to be recognised as a valued member of the team.'

'Right.'

'You might think it's amusing but this means a lot to me, Ned. You should be thankful I don't want anything else – like your liver.'

Ned tried to smile but he knew mermaids enjoyed eating human offal. The undertakers kept them in fresh supply but there had been killings in the past. The past that wasn't actually that far away. It had been a mermaid murder investigation that Ned had come to Pearl for help with, leading to high stakes in the interspecies poker game. Now, it looked like he owed her thief-catcher status. He shook his head in disbelief.

'Fine, welcome to the team.'

Pearl grinned toothily. 'I want proof of authenticity,' she said.

'As soon as I get back to the office, I will get you a badge, a copy of the rules, and enter your name in the ledger.'

'That's it?'

'That's it.'

'Ohhhhh,' Pearl squealed in happiness and spun around him so fast that Ned lost his balance and fell in slow motion onto his butt. He couldn't help but grin at her happiness. If only everything was that easy.

'What was it you wanted, Boss?' Pearl was grinning at him from ear to ear which would have been lovely if it hadn't revealed her extremely sharp, shark-like teeth.

'Er, right, I want you to drown someone and then bring him back to life.'

'No.'

'C'mon Pearl, I know you can do it. You saved me.'

'Those were specialist circumstances and anyway it's against the code.' Pearl was all business now; her glamour had finally relaxed, and she looked like an ordinary woman. Half-naked with a tail and still fabulously gorgeous, but at least Ned could concentrate on changing her mind instead of shutting up his libido.

'What if I told you it was top level thief-catcher work and we needed you to help us crack the Rose Thief case?'

'So you'd be asking me as my boss? This would be my first official job?'

'Yes, exactly.' Ned was silently praising any and all gods currently listening that Pearl's payment had been to be a member of the team.

'Well,' she swished her tail seductively. 'I guess that means I can't say no.'

'Excellent.'

Ned swam up to the surface and tried to shout to Jenni, but gills make talking coherently difficult. He had to splash the surface of the water hard in order to get her attention and then mime her throwing Joe in. They gathered a rather large audience as Jenni mischievously pretended to misunderstand what Ned wanted. It's not every day you see a semi-floating man being held in place by a small sprite, the head of the thief-catchers soaked to the skin bobbing about in the bay and an extremely attractive mermaid in seductress form happily giving any and all a right eyeful. Eventually, a half-brick skimmed Ned's shoulder followed by the still vacant Joe who seemed to float at the surface for a long time before gradually, gradually, sinking beneath the waves. Ned dived down in time to see Joe fully wake up. There was mass panic as he gulped in water, panicked further, thrashed, gulped in more water, panicked some more and all the while his eyes were fixed on Ned, pleading him to save him.

The thrashing and swallowing and panicking seemed to last for a lot longer than it should have. Pearl shook her head.

'He can't drown.'

'Whaddya mean he can't drown?'

'Don't ask me – he's your warlock – shouldn't you know better?'

'Huh?'

'Oh, for goodness sake! Warlocks can't drown. Their type of inborn magic means they can't die by natural elements. Surely you knew that?'

Ned shook his head. He'd hadn't actually known warlocks couldn't drown – so much for this plan. He swam down to the half-brick and untied the rope connecting it to Joe who immediately lashed out strongly as he swam up to the surface and kicked Ned in the face. A red mist began pooling in front of Ned's face as his eyes watered in pain.

'Badtard brode by nobe!'

'Get out of the water, Boss.' Pearl's teeth were back, sharp talons had grown out of her fingers matching the razor-sharp prongs projecting from her tail along its length. *Fabulous*, thought Ned, he had awoken her bloodthirst. Pearl pushed him away from her hard, up towards the surface. Ned was surprised at the force then saw more mermaids rapidly approaching in the distance. He fumbled with his power well and willed the gills away. The sharp pain in the middle of his face was joined by a burning agony in his airless lungs and the acid-like burning feeling on his neck. As he broke the surface Jenni scooped him out with an air spell of her own – just in time. Talons swept for him as he left the water, multiple fins circling below. Blood streamed down his face as he regarded a rather wet and bedraggled Joe on the pier. Ned fell to the floor with a wet plop and watched the red droplets splash the bones below him. It made them look even more macabre.

'A liddle help?'

Jenni tutted and waved her hand, the blood stopped pouring and Ned tried a few nose twitches.

'Aargh!' Still broken.

'I don't do bones, Boss – too 'ard.'

Ned tenderly felt his face. A size nine possibly nine and a half, steel toe capped with reinforced heel. All because he'd tried to drown a fellow in order to save him. Some people had no gratitude. The two men regarded each other for a moment. Ned spoke first.

'Look, I'm sorry I tried to drown you. We were trying to get the compulsion out of you. Break your connection to the warlock.'

'I'm sorry I broke your nose. I was trying to break your face.'

'Well, at least you're honest about it.'

Jenni hopped from one foot to the other. 'Er, Boss – drawing a bit of attention 'ere – shall we go 'ome?'

'Yes, Jenni. Let's.'

She popped them all back to the office in The Noose. Sparks started buzzing around in a highly distressed state as soon as they appeared, and Willow stared in fascination at the bloody mess on Ned's face.

Ned waved at Sparks. 'Can we get a Druid, please? I'm in pain.'

Sparks flashed his butt in agreement and disappeared. Ned sank down into his chair and regarded

Joe who was sat sullenly on the floor by the window.

'I think you've got some explaining to do, kid.'

But before Joe could say anything Sparks exploded back into the room, butt flashing, wings whirring and followed by at least a hundred of his friends and relations. Ned sighed, clearly Sparks had sent out a distress signal. Well, if nothing else there would be plenty of light for the Druid to fix his nose when they arrived.

A few moments later Kendra poked her face around the door frame - she was nervous. Druids weren't often the most liked of the medical profession, due to a highly popular book called *Why It Isn't Safe To Be A Virgin*. There were many reasons, but the one that most people found acceptable was that otherwise, Druids would sacrifice you. The fact that there had been no human sacrifices for hundreds of years was neither here nor there – the issue was that Druids were known for it. A firmly established fact they could do nothing about. History was history, after all. Kendra had tried valiantly to break this taboo by announcing to one and all – via the local rag – that she was a virgin and had no plans to sacrifice herself anytime soon. All that had managed to achieve was a rather large postbag of suggestive mail every Wednesday containing various offers of deflowering and other rather less poetic suggestions. Now Kendra tiptoed around – going out in public was asking for trouble. She never knew who might try to throw her to the ground and have their wicked way with her. There was a young blacksmith down in the Iron Quarter that Kendra wouldn't say no to, but it was hard to communicate that and avoid the other hopefuls, so she stayed indoors and only came out for emergencies.

Taking one look at Ned's face she took out a packet

of blood moss from her medicinal pouch and softly asked for some boiling water. Jenni conjured up a tea kettle and bowl and Kendra began steeping the moss and brewing a tonic. When the moss was a soggy mass, she pressed it on Ned's face and waved her hands in a complicated pattern. The relief was as intense as the pain.

'I can't do anything about the wonk I'm afraid but if you drink the tea it'll stop the pain from coming back before the bones have realised they've been healed.' Kendra passed Ned a cup. 'Judging by the ferocity of the attack, I'd drink the tea.'

Ned sniffed it warily. It smelt like unwashed socks.

'Best to down it in one.' Kendra smiled and added some mint to sweeten the flavour. She watched him force the drink down. 'How would you like to pay for our services today? We are short a few attendants at tonight's power vigil if you'd like to stand in. Nudity is a requirement, but the dancing is totally optional.' Kendra's face was so open and sincere that Ned didn't have the heart to say no.

Chapter 10

There was a hesitant knock on the door and Fred, a Palace Guard, entered holding an embossed envelope addressed to Ned. It looked expensive with gilt edging and fancy scroll work.

'Just put it on there.' Ned gestured to a towering pile of paperwork stacked next to his desk. It was unclear as to whether it was being supported by the desk or whether it was holding the desk up. Most of the furniture in the thief-catchers HQ was non-existent and what they did have had seen better days a hundred years ago.

'I can't.' Fred looked faintly embarrassed. 'It's an imperial announcement. I have to announce it.' He swallowed nervously. 'There should be a fanfare, but our Brian is feeling under the weather and I've only got to page one on how to play the trumpet. It just tells you what bit goes where.' He was on the brink of tears now. 'I wanted to do it proper like but... me mam is going to be so disappointed... this was me first...' He trailed off, gulping, furiously trying not to cry.

'Never mind lad, first times are always tricky. If you like we can pretend the fanfare was the best we've heard.' Ned was trying to be kind, but it was difficult when Jenni was sniggering in the corner.

'Oh, thank you, sir, that would be grand. The best you say. I'll tell our Brian; he'll be right pleased. He's on chapter four you know.' The young guard was beaming at everyone in the room having quite forgotten why he was there in the first place.

'The message?' prompted Ned.

'Message? Oh yes! The message.' Fred fumbled with the envelope. 'Ahem. While you were paddling in the sea another rose has been stolen. In light of your flagrant disregard for the Emperor's wishes, *may he live for ever and ever*, and the obvious protection of a dangerous criminal – er – I hereby announce you have failed to solve this case. Your time is up, and you will be hung by your feet until... you... are... dead... er... look, sorry about this – I'm just the messenger, you understand?'

'Is there anymore?' Ned asked.

'Oh yes. Shall I carry on?'

'Please do.'

'Right... hung... dead... heels... ah yes.' The guard refocused. 'However, given that you are the only semi-efficient thief-catcher in Roshaven, the Emperor, *may he live for ever and ever*, has decided, in his infinite wisdom and grace, that you shall have what's left of your life to solve this crime. Should you find the Rose Thief before the red rose is stolen then you may keep your... er miserable existence – sorry, I'm just reading it... um yes that's it. Just a list of his eminence's titles which I can read if you like? No? Ah okay. Well then. Cheerio.'

As Fred left the room everyone turned to look at Ned.

'Looks like the countdown has been lifted so I suggest everyone go home, get some rest and we'll attack this again in the morning. Kendra, we will come to the circle. Midnight, yes?'

Kendra looked rather confused but nodded slowly. Ned smiled at her and ushered her out of the door politely but firmly before turning to address the others. 'Anyone else who wants to come along is welcome, but I won't make it an order.'

'But Boss,' Willow looked close to tears. 'He said

you were going to hang?'

'Only if we don't catch the thief and I intend to so there's nothing to worry about.' Ned hoped he sounded more confident then he felt. 'You will be coming home with me.' He jabbed a finger at Joe who was looking rather worse for wear. 'See you all in the morning, team.'

Ned didn't wait for anyone else to protest. He hefted Joe to his feet and began pulling him out of the office with him. Jenni followed with a shrug. When she didn't return to Momma K's she usually slept in Ned's garden – it was a wild, overgrown place where she could torment pixies and gnomes to her heart's desire. There was also rumoured to be a particularly nasty brownie that Jenni was determined to conquer so the evening looked to have some kind of bright side. Willow watched them go, dead leaves falling from her hair to the ground without her realising. Once she decided the rest of the catchers were gone and they weren't coming back, she shuddered and climbed out of the window. The lovesick moss and lichen swarmed, making a soft carpet for her to lay on as they rippled across the roofs towards the small city orchard. It wasn't the best orchard she'd ever been in but since Willow had started visiting, the yield had trebled and there was an interesting Old Pippin who'd known Willow's grandmother. Sometimes it was comforting to be around what you knew and right now Willow needed root, trunk and branch to comfort her. Sparks stayed in the office. He was too buzzed to go outside right now. He'd attract all the wrong kind of attention with a butt that bright. Several of his friends and relations had stayed after Ned had been treated and it looked like there was going to be shindig or at the very least a hootenanny. A firefly's social life was electric.

Chapter 11

'What exactly are you going to do with me?' Joe demanded.

'Nothing much.' Ned shrugged. He was tired and wanted to catch a few hours shuteye before his presence was required at the Druid circle.

'Don't you want to question me further?'

'I will. Tomorrow.' Ned's quiet confidence unnerved Joe who began biting his fingernails in earnest.

They walked the rest of the way in silence, Jenni bringing up the rear and humming tunelessly. Ned's place was an extremely narrow house tucked in the corner of Wide Street, looking like an apologetic leftover. Which it was. The builders had been so keen to fit the houses to the name of the street that they had forgotten to measure twice and cut once and ended up cutting twice and not measuring at all. Consequently, there were an awful lot of extremely wide houses on Wide Street, which was fine for the huge families that occupied the various abodes. It did, however, leave a rather embarrassing gap on the corner where Wide Street joined High Trees Mall. There had to be a building there, it was part of the plans, so the builders had shoved leftovers together. It was a house full of character, and draughts, and oddly shaped rooms, and a wonky roof, but Ned felt right at home there. He had more space than he knew what to do with, thanks to the unusual shape.

Ned felt that relaxing, soothing balm in coming home - the one that makes cups of tea made there feel better than anywhere else. His body ached all over and he felt more tired than he had for a long time. Forgetting for the moment that he'd promised to attend the midnight vigil; he was looking forward to a hot bath and a comfortable bed.

'Ere Boss – do you want a wake up call for midnight?'

So much for that fantasy. Ned nodded wearily and kicked his boots off into the corner. He gestured for Joe to make himself at home while Jenni laid traps at all the doors and windows. Joe watched her curiously.

'It's so you don't escape,' Ned explained.

'Right. Because she thinks I *want* the Emperor, *may he live for ever and ever*, to catch me and kill me.'

'You don't need to say that you know.'

'What?'

'The ever and ever bit. I'm pretty sure the emperor is a… not as powerful as he'd like us to think.'

'I thought, you know, that we get fined or something if we don't say it.'

Ned smiled a small, sad smile and went to see if anything had miraculously appeared in the cupboards during the daytime. They were suspiciously full. Jenni was being nosy, seeing if there was anything for her.

'Is this your doing?' Ned asked her.

'Nah - it's Momma K. She saw the 'ole mermaid fing and felt bad.'

'Well, give her my thanks – looks like we are actually eating tonight.'

On closer inspection, a takeaway might have been a safer bet. Momma K's tastes were eclectic at best. There were sugared ants and grasshopper brittle, some slug jam and wasp honey which was sharper than the bee variety. She'd sent through some worm sausages and snail burgers together with a huge hamper of what must have been every leaf variety in her grove. Possibly some of it was safe to eat but Ned didn't want to take the chance. Fortunately, there were also some edible things like the elderflower tonic water and the mushroom quiche. Once you'd crunched a few sugared ants they weren't half bad and the berries from the forest more than made up for the beetle cheesecake. It was the mandibles sticking out that put Ned off. Jenni was ecstatic, all her favourites and she hadn't had to do any of the cooking. She ate until her stomach extended outwards as far as she stood upright. Joe stuck to the berries and nuts, not even trusting the mushroom quiche which Ned had to admit did have an odd aftertaste, but he was so hungry he was past caring. He'd make sure he never found out what the recipe was.

It was a few minutes to eight by the time they'd finished with dinner. Ned took out his pipe. It was one of his favourite post-work pastimes to sit and smoke in the calm of an evening after a busy day. Today had certainly felt like a marathon. His head wreathed in cloud rings, Ned shut his eyes, just for a moment, and felt that blissful feeling when sleep carries you away before you even realise what has happened.

An extremely loud and raucous rooster cawed inside his head. At least that's how it felt. His pipe lay on the floor where his sleeping hand had dropped it and Jenni lay snoring on the table. The remains of a few last treats were scattered around her. There was no sign of Joe. Instantly Ned was fully alert, ears straining to hear past the usual creaks and groans of the odd house. Movement – there. Relief coursed through him; Joe was in the bathroom. He was still here. Ned leaned over and poked Jenni in the back. She rolled off the table and plopped on the floor.

'Ow.'

'You awake?'

'Nghhfrgr.'

'Good. We've got to go to the Druid Grove. I owe Kendra.'

Jenni yawned loudly. Her jaw popping and snapping before finally closing as she sat up and stared daggers at her boss.

'I ain't dancing.'

'Me neither.' It was Joe, stood in the doorway. He looked different, more alive than before. Ned realised what it was. Now that everyone knew he was a warlock and he didn't have to try so hard to fit in, Joe had dropped his camouflage. He looked taller, more intelligent and a good deal more dangerous.

'I've decided I want to tell you everything so we can stop my sister before love is lost.'

'How very noble of you. Bit busy at the moment.' Ned swung his feet into his battered old boots and looked for a warmish cloak. 'You coming?'

'To a midnight power vigil? Try and stop me.'

A knife sang through the air and thunked into the wall behind Joe's head, his ear throbbing with the close shave it had had.

'You will not steal power. You will not desecrate a holy place. You will not shame the office of thief-catcher in any way.' Ned wasn't even looking at Joe who had lost a little of his composure and was stammering promises to behave. 'Let's go. We don't want to be late.'

It was getting close to a quarter to midnight, so they had to hurry through the streets to the standing stones circle on the east side of the city. The Druids would have liked it to be more central, but politics had been too strong at the time of erection and if they hadn't dug their heels in both metaphorically and actually, they would never have got the grove in the east side. Mystical stones were heavy and took a lot of lugging. Besides, they were established now and generated a tidy income for the Emperor from tourists who wanted to know whether this stone circle was more or less blood-splattered than they imagined. You know what Druids are like.

The streets were virtually empty. Except for the beggars because you never know, right? Besides, drunks with anything left were usually generous. And the thieves, because, you know, they have a code of honour and are meant to work the late shift. And the assassins, who were only practising because if you ever did see them, then you knew you meant enough to someone to have them pay to kill you. And the ladies of the night because if they didn't come out at night then they were faced with a complete social identity crisis. And the hawkers, who did a brisk trade from the tourists looking for some after-hours excitement. And every other Tom, Dick and Bloody Harry, who you wouldn't want to meet in a dark alley after hours. It was rumoured that Harry's blood was cat, but you never could be certain, could you? In essence, it was like every other bustling night in Roshaven.

Gradually others began heading towards the Druid stone circle in a sort of furtive, circling pattern. People would walk past the entrance in ones or twos, slow down to stare inside for as long as possible without actually going in, and then continue on their circuit. Some of the spectators were peeping Toms – George and Jack, actually – but others were first-timers feeling too nervous to go in and some were waiting for their mates to join them. Ned sighed heavily. He could do without this tonight, but a promise was a promise and Kendra had done a bang-up job with her healing. Joe looked around with interest as they crossed the courtyard and entered the stone circle. Some of the newbies followed in their wake trying to look anonymous in the small crowd.

Kendra was waving enthusiastically. It made certain things move in a rather pleasing way. Joe moaned slightly as Ned barked a laugh.

'Just think of dead bodies. Or if that floats your boat consider Mrs Wicket in the altogether. Everything will behave itself don't worry.'

Joe was turning redder and redder and trying not to look. The problem was there were naked people everywhere so in order not to look he'd have to crane his neck to look up at the sky and then he'd probably start bumping into things, the thought of which made him even redder still. Jenni took pity on him and cast a small spell. It made everyone's bits and pieces look like a blur. Everyone was still naked, and Joe's Adam's apple was still bobbing up and down excessively, but at least he could look where he was going.

Ned bowed slightly at Kendra as they came close. 'Evening Kendra. What's the ritual tonight?'

'Oh, you know, the usual. A moon blessing for the city and a small sacrifice. The Emperor, *may he live for ever and ever*, has requested a power vigil in order to catch the Rose Thief.' Ned rolled his eyes. Kendra mistook his meaning and gave a tinkly laugh. 'I know, don't worry, we all know the thief-catchers will catch the thief but maybe a little bit of positive thought will help? Sorry to rush off but I'm on newb alert tonight. Just get comfy and find your places. See you later.'

She darted off, gathering nervous looking people from various nooks and crannies. There were many stammers and blushes as she efficiently began helping them undress and get ready for the evening's events.

The High Priestess was chanting by the entrance, a standard secrecy spell – a bit like the one Jenni had cast on Joe. The people outside could still see into the grove, but they could only make out blurred shapes and now that everyone had arrived, no one would make it through the entrance barrier either. There would be no latecomers and no surprises. A good thing when everything is hanging in the breeze. Ned stripped off and shook his head ruefully at Joe who was hanging onto his undergarments fiercely.

'No one will judge you; this is a safe space.' Kendra was back with her string of newbies. 'Why don't you all stand together on the other side of the altar?' They looked and realised that it offered a modicum of screening from the rest of the group and there was a swift march over. Ned stood next to Kendra, at ease and seemingly not bothered by anything. Just because he'd taken some free spirit pills before he left his house, didn't mean he wasn't concerned about being seen, mentally weighed up and measured. It meant that there was no reason to get all gnarly about it, man. He was in the perfect state of mind for a Druid service.

There was little for the onlookers to do. The High Priestess was hurtling through the incantations and the proper Druids were channelling all their inner energy and focus. The reason they allowed visitors and newbies was so they could use their energies as well. It saved on time and made those attending feel like they'd been part of something as their vital life force was drained from their bodies. It sounds worse than it is. That vital energy is replenished as people sleep - a lot of energy goes to waste normally. It tends to be the source of dreams and nightmares, so if you fancy sleeping like the dead, get yourself down to a Druid Circle and offer up a bit of life force. It also makes a pretty light show as newbies tend to be bright and colourful and old hands darker and more sinister. They know what goes bump in the night.

The final ritual of the night was the power vigil. It required everyone to focus hard on the Rose Thief and his capture. Visualisation was key and indeed the smell of roses started to fill the air. Ned peeked at Jenni who wore a mask of innocence. But it seemed to buoy the group up who began chanting, low at first and then louder and louder – 'Catch the thief, catch the thief, catch the thief.' It seemed to Ned that the energy was hardening at the centre, near the altar where the High Priestess stood. It was getting brighter and brighter, smelling stronger and stronger of roses and yet something dark was revolving in the centre of the altar. Faster and faster until Ned realised it was a figure. He shouted a warning, but it was too late, the warlock manifested in a blaze of spiky red power and Joe fell to his knees with a scream, clutching his head.

'You rang?'

The voice sounded powerful over the sudden silence, but the Rose Thief wasn't really there. The figure had no depth and it was impossible to see its face. It was a magical projection. Ned's heart began slowing and he took a step closer to get a better look. There was something about the manifestation that tickled at his brain. If he squinted hard and tried to look past the shadowy figure Ned thought he could see columns in the background. Very familiar columns. The ones from the third best interview room at the Emperor's Palace. Ned knew them intimately.

Chapter 12

Panic ensued. Everyone was milling with gusto. The power vigil had broken, and the warlock had disappeared once the magical focus was gone but not before draining every magical item in the vicinity. The only person who seemed to be unaffected was Jenni. Nursing a killer headache, Ned tried to file away that piece of information, it seemed like it might be important. All the Druids were flat out on the floor, some had nose bleeds, others concussion, but most were beginning to rouse. All except the High Priestess. There was a small crowd gathering around the naked, prone woman. Kendra checked for signs of life, her hands trembling as she touched the still body. There was no breath. There was no heartbeat. There was no aura.

'She's dead. He killed her.' Her words were met with stunned silence. No one knew where to look or what to say. One of the acolytes with limited power had recovered enough to begin ushering people back to their clothes and saw to it that extra blankets were provided. After pulling on enough to be decent Ned grabbed a couple of blankets and brought them over to Kendra who remained slumped on the floor by the dead woman.

'She was my mentor – she was everything to me.' She raised her tear-stained face to look at Ned as he wrapped the blanket around her. 'What will I do now?'

'Carry on. That's all you can do.' Ned gently covered the High Priestess.

Jenni, now fully dressed, bought over a steaming cup of something. 'This'll perk ya, Kendra. Drink it – do you good.' She shoved the cup into Kendra's hands who accepted it automatically and raised the cup to her lips. After the first sip made her splutter and cough, she suddenly gripped it tighter and drank it down.

'What was in that?' Ned wanted to know whether he should have one.

'Stuff, but not for you, Boss, you need a clear 'ead.'

Kendra was starting to droop again but she somehow managed to pull herself together enough to grab Ned by the arm fiercely.

'Promise me you'll catch that warlock.'

'I will. I promise.'

Kendra nodded, then fainted dead away and Jenni motioned for a few young Druids nearby to pick her up and take her into the inner sanctum.

'Do you fink you can, Boss?'

'Hmm?' Ned was putting his jacket and boots back on.

'Find the warlock?'

'I've got a good idea where to start.' He marched over to where Joe lay on the floor, passed out by the look of things. Ned kicked Joe's foot and was rewarded with a groan, so he hauled the young man up to sitting and slapped him, hard. Joe sprang to life.

'What? What's going on?'

'That's what I want to know.'

'I can't... she'll kill me.'

'Then you won't be the first. Put some bloody clothes on. Jenni – call the others in, we've got a confession to witness.' Ned waited until Joe had scrambled into his trousers and shirt then grabbed him by the scruff of the neck and began to walk out of the grove. By now the privacy magic had faded away and there was a large crowd of people outside. Shoving Joe in front of him,

Ned used him as a human shield to push through the throng. There were a few complaints here and there but when they caught sight of the thunderous face of the thief-catcher they soon shut up. It helped that Ned was frantically drawing power back into his spell-caster wells. Little crackles of lightning were actually rippling across his body. For once he didn't seem to be blocked in any way. Clearly, anger focused him well.

They reached HQ in no time and Willow was climbing back in the window as they trooped in. Sparks was already on his shelf.

'Jenni, seal the room. Sparks, set the recorder. Willow, bind him to the chair.' There was a flurry of motion. The spells Jenni weaved were thick and fast, the air practically humming as all the entrances were closed and six different kinds of wards put into place, preventing anyone from coming in. Sparks retrieved the power supply for the ancient recorder that sat in the corner of the office. No one liked using it because it was heavy, noisy, and awkward to move. It always recorded the truth, even when no one was speaking it and it absolutely could not be tampered with. This was a good thing, in theory, but when the interviewee was thinking about what to have for dinner instead of answering the interrogators' questions the recorded file could end up somewhat unintelligible. Ned was fairly sure he'd be able to keep Joe focused. Fear was a wonderful motivator. Willow had encouraged nearby vines to wrap around Joe who was sitting dejectedly in a chair in the middle of the room.

'Talk,' ordered Ned.

'What do you want me to say?' asked Joe.

'Tell me why you are claiming to be a common spell-caster and not admitting to being a warlock. Tell me why the brother of a powerful warlock is pretending to be a thief-catcher at all. Tell me why your deranged sister is playing at being a thief.' Ned's face was dark with anger. 'How many other innocent people have you killed in this sick partnership of yours?'

'Hey - I am a common spell-caster. My twin sister got all the warlock power. I've had to train and train and train to get where I am. Just because the warlock blood in my veins prevents me from drowning and stuff, I am not, nor have I ever been, a warlock.' Joe was red in the face and shouting. He took a breath and continued more calmly. 'I came here to join the thief-catchers in an effort to keep an eye on my sister and stop her from doing something she would live to regret. I don't know why she's in the Palace – we're not exactly talking. I've never killed anyone, and I don't plan to either.' He closed his eyes for a moment. 'I am deeply sorry for the death of the High Priestess and I will do everything in my power to help you. By now my sister will know where I am. I've avoided her attention so far, but she will come and find me. It won't be long. There's nothing you can do to stop her from getting to me.'

'Why would she want you?'

'I amplify her power. So I try to stay away. But she knows where I am now.'

'We'll see about that. Jenni – are we snatch proof?' asked Ned.

'Only if they ain't my lot.'

'Speak to Momma K, then, see if you can swing it so that it's not worth taking this particular job. Willow, I need your grapevine network to be in constant touch – anything that moves out of place I want to know about it.' He regarded Joe solemnly. 'I have more questions.'

'Fine.'

'Why is your sister stealing the Emperor's roses? What could she possibly want with some bloody flowers?'

Joe gulped. 'I don't know, I really don't. It doesn't make any sense. The other roses are just flowers. If she was going to steal roses for magical means, all she'd need is the red one. That's where the magic is.' His voice took on a pleading note. 'You have to understand I don't keep close tabs on her. I try to stay as far away as possible, to be honest. But we're bound by our magic and usually I only manage to stay away a maximum of a hundred-foot radius. I can't get any further.'

'But you've been with us, what, a few months now?'

'Which means my sister has been here, in the city, planning.'

'And you have no idea what her eventual plan is?' Ned did not sound convinced.

'I think, I mean, maybe, she wants to kill love. Why else would she want the red rose? The rest is just... having some fun, I guess.' Joe trailed off. He really had no idea why his sister was doing what she was doing.

Willow was in tears and began stroking the various plant life that had gathered around her in consolation. 'Why would she want to kill love?' she sobbed.

Joe tried to shrug. 'I don't know. She got dumped by this bloke and she didn't take it very well, but it feels like it's more than that. I said at the time I thought she was over-reacting and she kinda flew off the deep end. Ever since she's been thwarting relationships. I didn't think anything of it until we came here, and I found out about the enchantment on the red rose. I mean who puts that kind of spell into play?'

Ned couldn't help but nod in agreement. He caught himself and continued with the questioning. 'Why murder Two-Face Bob? He was obviously involved, helping your sister in some way.'

Joe shook his head. 'I don't know. I don't think she did. She's never had the strength to release a wraith before - I didn't even know she knew how to do things like that. It's really not her style.'

'But killing the High Priestess is?' Ned's retort was sharp.

Joe turned pale. 'You have to believe me; she's never done anything like that before either. Do you know how much power it takes to drain someone magically? There's no way that was her.'

Jenni piped up. 'E's right, Boss. S'tricky. Gotta 'ave a fair amount o' juice for summink like that.' She had been listening intently, as had all the catchers.

Ned sighed. 'So what, you think someone else is pulling your sister's strings? Doesn't sound very likely to me.'

'I don't know. I'm sorry. I just don't know.' Joe slumped in defeat.

Everyone was quiet as they absorbed Joe's confession. Ned checked the recorder, Joe thought he was telling the truth, no lies. He clicked the recording machine off. Joe broke the silence with a cough.

'Er, Boss – do you think I can get unvined? They're a bit tight.'

'No. Willow, keep Joe tied up will you, please. I've got somewhere to be.' Ned turned to go and then stopped abruptly. 'What's your sister's name?' he asked Joe.

'Amelia. But she's not a fan, prefers Mia.'

As Ned left the office, Jenni fell in step with him.

'What's the plan, Boss?'

'Did you notice? When the warlock appeared at the vigil? In the background, she was in the third best

84

meeting room. She's in the Emperor's Palace. Something else is going on here and I mean to find out what.' Ned glanced back at the office door. 'Look, is he secure in there?'

'As snug as I can manage. I'm good, Boss, but even my magic ain't totally unstoppable. If she really wants 'im, she'll get 'im.'

'I want you to stay here then, keep an eye on the place. If I'm not back in an hour don't come looking for me, keep the team safe, alright?'

Jenni looked up at him soberly before giving a quick, sharp nod and disappearing back the way they had come. Ned walked slowly towards the Palace. Clearly, Joe's sister had infiltrated the Palace in some way but how exactly? Was she masquerading as a servant? Or had she done something to the Emperor? It all felt very fishy and Ned was determined to get to the bottom of it. He wasn't having some warlock destroy the delicate balance that Roshaven had developed with its unique take on crime and payment. It worked because everyone followed the rules. More or less. Everyone knew their place. Ned didn't care much about the loss of a flower or even the loss of love. It was an inconvenient emotion and one of the main reasons why the thief-catchers had such a high turnover. People kept falling in love and their new spouses suddenly didn't appreciate the all-hours, all-day approach required by the role of thief-catcher despite knowing all about it when they were courting. But Ned did care about his city and he wasn't going to let anyone saunter in and destroy it.

Ned realised that he was walking in shadow. The bulk of the Palace loomed over him. He cut left and headed towards the kitchens. It was the safest way in.

Chapter 13

'What did you do?' Mia asked in a shaky voice as she tried to get up from the floor. 'What was that?'

'That was me taking advantage of an opportunity you were clearly too blind to see.' Her father's projection looked rather pleased with himself. 'You should be thanking me. The death of a High Priestess is a small price to pay for the amount of power I was able to extract.'

'Power? What power?' Mia shook her head, trying to clear the fuzziness from what had happened. 'I just wanted to surprise them at the vigil, not murder anyone. How did you do that?'

The sorcerer sneered down at his daughter. 'You are not ready to learn such arts, child.' He spat the last word at her in disgust. 'At times I wonder whether I chose the right offspring to assist me with my endeavours. You show increasing weakness.'

'I don't understand,' Mia frowned. 'You used me as a power conduit? How?'

'A familial link can be a powerful thing, child. It is, after all, your connection with your twin that amplifies your gifts when you are together. I assume you felt his presence at the Druid Grove?' The sorcerer glared at her, as though challenging her to lie.

Mia nodded reluctantly, she had been hoping to avoid mentioning Joe's nearby presence, but her father just nodded to himself.

'Using your flesh and bone bond to me,' he continued, 'I can channel through you and gather power.

But don't worry, I left you enough to finish your tasks here.' He paused again, looking around the room. 'I take it you have acquired the red rose by now. Is the takeover complete?'

Mia was standing now. She tried to hide her inner panic by walking over to a nearby table and pouring herself some wine.

'Not exactly,' she murmured.

'Are you confessing your failure, child?' The sorcerer raised a hand threateningly. 'Do you require further motivation?'

'No! No, there is no need. I have managed to evict the Emperor from the throne but there has been a complication.' She took a long swallow of wine. 'He, or rather she, has barricaded herself in the left wing of the Palace. With all the wives and servants. There is some kind of magical shield in place that I have yet to break.'

'Yet to break or unable to break?'

'I have been busy, organising a stasis box to carry the rose away from here. Otherwise, we run the risk of destroying love, for everyone.'

'There is no need for a stasis box. Just bring the rose to me and I will consider letting you have this pitiful kingdom to do with what you will.'

'But love...'

'But what? The emotion has power, true, but you should never let love control you. You would not have had that incident if you had not let love affect you.'

Mia flushed but kept quiet.

'I do not like how long it has taken you to get to this point, child. You should have crushed the Emperor like the flea that he, or apparently she is. She does not best you, does she?'

'Father, please. She has some power, but nothing I

can't handle. I was just caught off guard, that's all. She cannot hold out in there for long. I have forbidden the kitchens from making any food. I will break down those wards.'

'See that you do. I want my rose. I have wasted enough time indulging in your whimsy.' The sorcerer looked into his distance at an object Mia could not see. 'It is almost time for my captivity to end. I will not accept any delays or excuses.'

Mia inclined her head. 'No, Father. Of course not.' The room felt empty. She looked up and let out a breath she had not realised she was holding. He was gone. If she had not mentioned the Emperor's masquerade to her father in the first place, she could have been finished here by now and the red rose would not have vanished from under her nose. Instead, now she had to try and break some kind of old-world magic, get rid of the true heir to the throne and find a missing flower. All to help her father free himself and add another puppet kingdom to his collection. Mia sighed. It would be worth it in the end. When she could be free of him and take her mother, and Joe, somewhere remote, safe. Away from all this.

Chapter 14

Ma Bowl ran the Palace kitchen. No one could remember her real name or if they could they weren't talking. She had been known as Ma Bowl after an incident involving a certain beloved mixing bowl one of the Emperor's wives had taken a shine to. Normally Palace staff allowed the Imperials to have whatever they wanted but as a young kitchen maid, Ma Bowl had protested loudly. The Emperor's father, *may he live for ever and ever*, had been so taken with her devotion to crockery that he had allowed her to keep it and encouraged her promotion. The young kitchen maid was now the Head Cook and her bowl sat on a shelf near her stool where she could oversee everything happening in her domain. The bowl might stay on the shelf, but it was scrupulously cleaned daily and absolutely no one was allowed to use it. Ma was sat on her stool in her usual position when Ned poked his head into the kitchens. It was quiet. This was unusual. There were no delicious smells wafting, no bread baking, no saucepans bubbling.

'What's going on, Ma?'

She regarded him balefully. 'The Emperor, *may he live for ever and ever*, has decreed that no one eats until the Rose-Thief is caught. I sent everyone home. It was too much for the younger ones, they didn't know how to stop peeling potatoes. I suppose I should take that as a comfort.'

'No one is allowed to eat?' Ned was incredulous. 'That's going a bit far, isn't it?'

'His Eminence is in a rotten mood. He has sent all

his advisers away. All the little kiddies are locked in the nursery and the wives have been sequestered. They're not happy, but no one has the nerve to speak up. He is raging in the upper corridors. The High Right was overheard telling the High Left that he'd never seen him in such a temper.'

'Why are you still here?'

'I don't know where else to go, besides I need to be ready to prepare a snack should it be required.'

Ma Bowl looked distraught. Ned considered going over to comfort her, but he didn't want to get side-tracked. She would start talking about how much Ned reminded her of her late husband and would then start reminiscing. Last time she'd spent four hours describing the ins and outs of their pantry at home. Apparently, the late Mr Bowl had been a keen pickler.

'Do you know where I can find the Upper Circle?'

Instantly Ma Bowl's demeanour changed. She bristled with dislike and huffed a little.

'I don't know why you want to talk to that hussy.'

'It's an ongoing line of questioning. Can you help me?'

Ma softened. 'Of course I'll help you, Ned. You know, you remind me so much of my late husband Derek...'

'She would be?'

'Fourth floor. Left wing,' Ma sniffed. 'She's got the whole floor to herself, but I don't see why someone like that should have so much space. They should give it to someone who actually does a lick of work around here.'

After thanking Ma, which involved a rather floury hug and the acceptance of some forlorn looking baked goods, Ned set off for the fourth floor. The corridors were eerily quiet. Usually, there would be servants scurrying. The servants of the Emperor were very good at scurrying – it was a natural talent to those families who had served the Palace for generations. It boiled down to being able to hurry from job to job without actually doing any work or being caught not doing any work and ferrying that all-important servant currency – information. Ned had hoped to chat to a few maids on his way to the fourth floor but there was no one around. There weren't even any guards. Everywhere he looked he could see evidence of neglect building up. Plants were withering in their plant pots. Mirrors had lost their gleam and the shiny brass knockers on the doors were tarnishing. Everything seemed duller and colder. But the things that bothered him the most were the spiderwebs. There shouldn't be any spiderwebs in the Palace. Those maids that weren't on scurrying duty would have been on cleaning duty. Huge webs hung in darkened corners and the further Ned travelled into the Palace the bigger the webs became. Thankfully there was no evidence of the creatures that would live in such webs, but as soon as Ned thought that thought he started to consider where they might be. His skin began to crawl so vigorously that he had to stop and scratch all over five times before he made it the left-wing door on the fourth floor. At one point he thought an actual spider was sitting on his shoulder and he screamed. It was clearly a loud scream as it broke the illusion, no giant webs and no spiders. Just someone having a bit of magical fun. Worryingly, absolutely no one came running to investigate. Ned didn't know whether to be thankful or more concerned.

The large doors that led onto the left wing were firmly closed and ice cold to the touch. Ned's breath curled out of his mouth. He dipped into his spell-caster pockets to give him the juice to see what wards were in place. It was a 'go-away', a rather good one. Ned definitely felt like he would rather be anywhere but here. He pushed against the door and it swung noiselessly open. He shivered as he went through the doorway. It was like walking into another world. For one thing, there were staff bustling - that's one up from scurrying. Warm lamps were lit, and the smell of cinnamon hung in the air. As Ned walked along the corridor he glanced into a couple of the open doors. They all seemed to lead into one large room where what looked to be the thousand and one wives of the Emperor were gathered. They were doing whatever it was that large groups of women do together. Gossip and laughter hummed in the air and several of the young male servants were blushing furiously.

Ned felt relieved that the warlock wasn't holding all the Emperor's wives hostage, but he was also slightly confused as to why they were all here. No one seemed remotely bothered at his presence, so he continued walking down the corridor until he reached a door ajar at the end. He knocked twice, then went in, not quite expecting what he saw.

The Upper Circle was sitting on the floor playing with a kitten while the High Right and High Left were suspended upside down from the ceiling. They didn't look at all happy about it and were struggling to keep their robes from obscuring their faces and showing everyone their nethers. Ned held his composure, just, because the High Left was losing the battle and an extremely red, spotty pair of bloomers were coming into view.

'Thief-catcher! Caught anything good lately?' The Upper Circle dissolved into giggles and it took a few minutes for her to collect her composure. 'Can I kill Joe yet?'

'Erm, no, Your Eminence.'

'Caught onto that one as well didn't you? Ah well, couldn't hide it forever. Bet you'd love to know who's fathering the kids, hmm?' She tapped the side of her nose but missed it by a few inches and then went cross-eyed trying to find the end of it.

'Have you been er... celebrating?'

'You could say that. I mean, why not celebrate a coup you can't uncoup. It's better than crying over spilt kingdomness.' The Emperor's eyes filled with tears. 'Don't make me cry! I'm in charge, I say there will be no tears.' She wagged an unsteady finger in Ned's general direction.

'Why are the Highs up there?'

'They didn't appreciate my choice of wine.'

Ned gently wove a fall-and-catch spell and unhooked the one keeping the Highs stuck to the ceiling. They tumbled gently to the floor and murmured their unsteady thanks. The kitten went over to investigate and see whether there would be any food from the newcomers while Ned shouted for coffee into the corridor, not caring who carried out the order.

'We can't just sit here and give up. The warlock is trying to rid the world of love and I reckon that wouldn't be a good thing. I'm sure between us all we can figure out something. Clearly, you have some power left.' Ned said encouragingly as he looked at the Emperor who was wiping her runny nose on a rather grubby looking sleeve.

'Well, yes, I've got a bit but it's here in my wing. Hereditary resonance. Ingrained in the walls. I can't take it with me, and the warlock knows that so she's not coming in here and I'm not going out there.'

Ned nodded to himself and started thinking aloud.

'What we need to do is to find the man who jilted her – see if we can't force some kind of reconciliation or at least an apology. Maybe that will stop the warlock from destroying the last rose.' He frowned. 'Why hasn't she?' Surely there is nothing in her way now if you are all in here.'

The Emperor was giggling hysterically.

'Someone else has stolen it!' She collapsed in laughter, tears streaming down her face. 'I have no idea where it is.'

The Emperor went back to playing with the kitten who had returned to her while Ned took stock for a moment. It seemed that every time he got a toehold on what the hell was going on someone changed all the rules, again.

'When was it stolen?' Ned asked.

The Emperor didn't reply so Ned looked at the Highs for some assistance.

'We don't know precisely.' The High Left looked extremely embarrassed. 'It must have been within the past day or so.'

'Right, but the warlock did steal some of the original roses, didn't she?'

'We believe so, yes.'

Ned nodded - something was missing, things didn't add up. If the warlock was the Rose Thief, why hadn't she started with the rose of love instead of taking the others first? If someone else was already planning to steal the love rose, then who killed Two-Face Bob? He obviously knew what was going on as he had supplied the special manure. Unless the warlock had been acting out, a woman scorned and all that. Too bad for Two-Face. Ned tried to summon up some sympathy but found he didn't care. The High Priestess on the other hand –

that was murder. That she would pay for, this warlock who was messing with his city.

'I'm going back to HQ. Are you alright here?' Ned asked.

The two Highs forced smiles on their faces and loudly confirmed all was well as they walked Ned out of earshot of the Emperor.

'You have to do something,' hissed the High Right. 'We can't stay here indefinitely – the Emperor isn't safe. People might start finding out that he's not who she said she was, he was, is... the point is everyone knows the Emperor is a strong man who leads his city empire with dignity and honesty. Everything would fall apart if people found out he's a woman! I mean, the very idea.'

Ned stared at the High Right in silence and he had the decency to look away. 'I think we have bigger problems than who finds out the Emperor is a woman. Keep everyone in here, you seem to be protected for now. I might have a way to get rid of the usurper, I just need to find someone. I'll report back as soon as I can.' Without waiting for a reply, Ned left the same way he had entered. He was fairly sure the lack of staff was a deliberate ploy by the warlock designed to make intruders feel brave and therefore willing to explore, but Ned was feeling decidedly disinterested in the whole bloody affair. He'd been working this case hard, trying to find out who the Rose Thief was and now that he had finally got to the bottom of it there was another thief who no one knew anything about. Everything was screwed up. He barely noticed walking back through the kitchens and forgot to say goodbye properly to Ma Bowl – an action that would come back to haunt him several months down the line when he popped in to pay his respects and received a short, sharp, whack round the lughole with a metal spoon. It drew blood and got infected, but that is another story. Ned let his feet take him back to the office without thinking about it. There had to be something he'd missed.

Chapter 15

Ned finished telling his team what he had found out at the Palace. There was a long silence. Sparks didn't talk anyway but even he could not think of anything worth flashing his butt about. After watching everyone's reaction, Ned noticed how sheepish Joe was. He had dug his feet into the floor and was turning them nervously and kept shooting covert glances up at Ned.

'Is there something you'd like to share, Joe?' asked Ned.

Joe blushed and stammered. 'No, n n n n nothing.'

But he couldn't hold his composure with the whole team glaring at him, especially when Jenni started cracking her knuckles at him.

'Okay, fine, I know where the love rose is.'

Ned snorted. 'Let me guess, it was you who stole it.'

'Not exactly.' The ends of Joe's ears began to turn pink. 'Well, sort of. I told Mia's ex I could get it and suggested that it might be a good idea for him to take it away from here before she did.'

'You stole the rose? When? How?'

'Wot? 'Ow did you steal the rose?'

Sparks had gone mad, flashing his butt left, right and centre.

'Quiet!' Ned shouted to make himself heard. 'Enough! Joe, are you seriously telling me that you've already stolen the red rose? And that this whole time you've known where your sister's bloke was?' He ran a hand through his hair. 'You didn't think it was worth sharing this with the rest of the group?'

Joe gulped. 'You have to understand, it's a matter of trust.'

'Yeah, as in you ain't got any of ours.' Jenni was scowling.

Joe looked around at the hostile room sadly. 'I don't want anything bad to happen to my sister.'

'It's a bit late for that,' muttered Ned.

There was a subdued quietness until a loud fart rattled the room. Everyone immediately looked at Jenni who, feeling it was some of her finer work, took a small bow.

'Tell me, who is this jilted lover?' asked Ned.

The vine holding Joe loosened a little. Willow was absorbed by the story, forgetting to maintain the mental lock.

'I can't tell you, I'm sorry.' Having worked his hand free Joe clicked his fingers and vanished.

'What just happened? You were supposed to be holding him! I thought you said no one was getting in?' Ned yelled at Willow and then Jenni.

Willow flushed and avoided Ned's gaze, but Jenni stared right back at him.

'I did, Boss and they 'ent. You never said nuffink about people leaving. You gotta be spific.'

Ned scrunched a piece of paper on his desk into a tiny ball, trying not to scream out loud in frustration.

'Have we thought Joe might be lying to us?' Willow spoke softly and began weaving the loose vines into a complex basket.

'No – really? You think?' Ned was unable to keep the sarcasm from his voice.

'I mean, what if he's the lover?' Willow refused to look directly at anyone.

Jenni was scowling again. 'Wot? 'is sister's lover?

That's sick, innit.'

'No – you might be onto something there, Willow,' said Ned. 'What if indeed. Sparks, get me Joe's recruitment file.'

There was a short flurry of action as the file was found and then emptied on the table. A moment of silence followed as each piece of information was sifted through. There wasn't much – a mug shot, confirmation thief-catcher papers from the Palace and an empty space on the next of kin paperwork.

'Guys, we have to fill this stuff in better,' Ned complained.

Everyone avoided making eye contact. Ned had been the one to complete the paperwork this time. He peered closer at the mugshot. There was something in the background, something familiar. It was Neeps' head and the corner of *The Daily Blag* newspaper building. He could tell because of the large amount of pigeon droppings - the birds were attracted by the printing chemicals. Something about eating it made the pigeons act crazy and then crave more ink. Excessive consumption of a particular ink colour would begin infusing the pigeon feathers, a little startling when the ink was blue or red. The real problem was the lethal toxicity, but by that time the pigeons were too addicted to care, and the city milliners enjoyed working with the excellent plumage.

Ned stood up abruptly. 'Let's go, Jenni.'

'Where to, Boss?'

'*The Daily Blag*. Willow, Sparks, stay here and if anyone comes asking, boot 'em.'

Willow was very pale, and Sparks had stopped flashing. Neither of them owned any boots so they were unsure as to what was expected from them, however, whatever it was they'd do it. Ned and Jenni thumped down the stairs, only to be met by Palace Guards trying to block their exit from The Noose.

'The Emperor, *may he live for ever and ever*, demands a report, Thief-Catcher.'

'Tough.' Ned pushed past and stalked out. Mortar held the guards back till Ned was out of sight. He felt angry. Angry that Joe had escaped. Angry that they had missed a big clue under their noses. Angry that the whole thing was over a stupid flower. When they arrived at *The Daily Blag,* all the shutters were drawn, and it had an air of closure about it. Jenni licked a finger and pointed it towards the building.

'Glamour.' She flicked her wrist expertly. The facade fell away revealing a ground floor level window that blazed with light and noise. It was coming from the small accommodation rooms Neeps had on site. It sounded like an argument. Ned carefully pushed the unlocked front door open, looking out for any magical booby traps.

'Why did you come here?' Neeps' voice was shrill.

'I told you, I need your help.'

'I'm not helping you again. You put me in danger – I could've been killed harbouring this for you.'

'But you weren't.'

'It's more dangerous than I'd like. Did you see what happened to the High Priestess at the Druids' Grove? Completely burnt out, like that.' Neeps snapped her fingers.

'Neepy, come on – don't be mad.'

'Neepy?' Ned and Jenni mouthed at each other in surprise. They crept down the hallway towards the source of the voices.

'Oh, I can't stay mad at you, but you shouldn't be

here. What if your sister finds you?'

'She's more interested in finding the missing rose.'

'But that's here too!' Neeps paused. 'It is beautiful though.'

Ned and Jenni peeked through a chink in the door. There on the table was a huge pot containing the spelled red rose of love. It shimmered slightly and its heady perfume filled the air.

'It's okay, Boss, I know you're there.'

Joe and Neeps turned to look at the doorway. Ned feeling slightly miffed, strode into the room determined to put an end to whatever it was that was happening.

'I'm arresting you for the theft of the red rose of love. I assume you have the other roses in your possession?'

'Er no – I'm not the Rose Thief, Boss. I told you – Mia stole the roses, not me.'

'You expect me to believe you when one of them is staring me in the face.'

'Okay, so not this one, Neeps stole this one. But it's alright. Brogan will be here soon; we can give him the red rose. He can take it far away from here or give it to Mia and profess his love. Maybe, if we're really, really lucky she'll leave with him and life can get back to normal.'

Ned snorted. 'I'm not letting her leave with that magical rose. Besides, she's wanted for murder. On two counts.'

'I told you that wasn't her, I know it wasn't.' Joe tried to defend his sister.

'Huh. Even if I believed you, which I don't, what about the whole 'where she goes, I go' spell?' asked Ned.

'I do. Go where she goes. So, I'll be out of your hair too.'

'What is he talking about? You're leaving?' Neeps

clutched Joe's arm in alarm. 'Can I come with you?'

There was an awkward pause followed by a loud banging at the back door. Joe looked relieved.

'Just a minute,' he called.

Ned watched, eyes narrowed, as Joe went to the back door and let a huge man in. He filled the doorway. Over six-foot-tall and broad chested with large, muscular arms. He had thick, black hair and brown eyes twinkled in his handsome face.

'I hear my girl is causing trouble.'

Ned sniggered; he couldn't help it. Before long tears began rolling down his face as he tried to keep the giggle fit inside. He wheezed a breath of air but couldn't stop a bark of laughter from escaping. Like most things that occur inappropriately, it spread like wildfire. Jenni was already grinning from ear to ear but now she threw in a deep belly chuckle for good measure. Neeps tittered behind her hand whilst the goliath that was Brogan guffawed loudly. Only Joe remained unmoved. He stared at the others in disbelief.

'This is serious, you guys.'

Peals of laughter rang out.

'I mean it, we need to figure out what to do.' Joe stood there looking so pathetically miserable that it didn't seem quite so amusing and when a tear rolled down his cheek the giggles turned into coughs and a lot of eye contact avoidance as the others stamped their mirth down.

'Shall I make some coffee?' Neeps was the first able to speak. Not waiting for affirmatives, she went to the small kitchen next door and began brewing.

Brogan levered his bulk down into the nearest chair, Jenni perched on the table. When Neeps returned with beverages everyone was still fairly red faced but the giggle fit had passed.

'Right, who is this guy then? Joe?' Ned took charge, someone had to.

'Well... Brogan and Mia were dating about three months ago.'

'We were in love, mate. It were beautiful,' Brogan said, misty-eyed.

'Yes, well, it didn't stop you from getting caught inflagrante with that horse-mistress from up the hill, did it?' snapped Joe.

'She was expressing her thanks.' Brogan shrugged, a crooked smile on his face.

'Naked.' Joe didn't sound impressed.

Ned perked up, this sounded interesting.

'It's their custom.' Brogan was grinning.

'Pretty sure turning up naked in your bed chamber with a variety of aphrodisiacs is a little bit more than simple thanks. Even their wedding ceremonies are consummated fully clothed. On the back of three horses. Don't ask.' Joe flung up a hand, forestalling Ned's question on the mechanics of such a thing. Ned huffed a little, he'd been hoping for a diagram.

'Brogan, you broke my sister's heart.' Joe paced up and down the room. 'Clearly Mia wants everyone to feel the pain and loss she felt, is feeling. That must be why she's trying to steal the rose of love.'

'If that's your theory, why did you infiltrate the Thief-Catchers with some cockamayme story?' Ned was annoyed and feeling a little foolish. 'If you'd just come to me in the first place, we could have sorted all this out by now.'

Joe looked sheepish and dug his foot into the floor. 'I didn't know exactly where she was – what her plan was. I wasn't completely sure she was even after the rose. The thing is a bit of a joke – among the magical community, I mean. Who puts love in a rose?' Ned was nodding in agreement then caught himself and glared at Joe who hurriedly carried on. 'Look, the locator spell works both ways. If I get too close to her, she knows where I am and she's a lot stronger than me.'

Jenni was chewing idly on a brass candle stick holder and nodding. 'Yeah. S'probably the jilt wot done it. Powerful boost to magics is deep emotional pain.'

'Does she know you're here? In this building?' Ned wondered if they were safe.

'I'm not sure, to be honest. But more than likely, yes. Although, she knows I'm not much of a threat to her, magically speaking.'

Ned did not feel remotely comforted. 'Let me make sure I've got all the facts. You broke her heart.' He pointed a finger at Brogan, then swung it over to Joe who flinched at its attention. 'She ran here, you followed whilst doing your best to keep as far away as possible. How did you even know she was going to steal the roses?'

'I didn't, I swear. I joined up with you figuring that you'd be the first organisation to hear of anything out of the ordinary. I just wanted to keep an eye on her. I didn't know she was going to try and overthrow the Emperor.'

'She's done what?' Neeps looked appalled. She was a staunch imperialist.

'The Emperor is fine.' Ned reassured her whilst Neeps whispered *may he live for ever and ever* under her breath. 'I spoke with her, er, him today. Yesterday. Recently.' He scratched his head. 'What day is it today?'

Everyone ignored him. Brogan looked thoroughly nonplussed, as if he had absolutely no idea what was going on. Which to be fair, he didn't.

'I don't understand. Mia is pretending to be a man?'
Brogan asked.

'Wot it is, right, is this. Basically, she fawt 'e 'ad the
power but she didn't know 'e wos a 'er and then fings got
slippy when they all buggered off into their wing and
now she's got nuffink, not even the 'ighs but she's still
pretending to be 'im. Obvs she found out about the roses
and her 'art is bleedin' and whatnot so she must 'ave took
to stealing them for fun, mebbe, not knowing it wos red
for luv – which is bloody ridiculous 'sidering – anyway
now she knows, she's done away with 'im, but not really
cos we knows she's 'im and 'e's safe so there's nuffink to
stop 'er from getting the red 'cept they've got it 'ere and
no one but us knows – right? S'easy really.' Jenni leant
back with an air of pride at being able to succinctly
explain everything in one breath.

No one spoke. Ned could actually see the cogs of
Brogan's mind turning, his hamster running at full pelt.
This could take a while. He decided to change the
subject.

'Why was Mia stealing the other roses in the first
place? Surely she must have known that the red one was
the enchanted one.'

'I don't know.' Joe sounded a little frantic. 'Probably
because she heard the Emperor loved his rose garden
more than his wives.' Joe shrugged as if this was the last
of their worries. 'She stole the most beloved swines from
the last town she passed through. The bacon was
excellent.'

'Can we please say the honorific correctly? He
deserves our respect, don't you think? For ever and ever?
It's not difficult, is it?' Neeps' eyes were bugging as she
circled the edge of hysteria.

'Well, whatever the reasons behind it at least we've

stopped her for now.' Ned gestured at the rose on the table. 'It's warded here, right? Right?'

Joe was decidedly intent on the far corner on the room, whilst Neeps looked at the rose, at Joe and back at Ned. 'No one knows it's here though, do they?' Her voice sounded shrill. 'I mean, it'd be the last place they'd look, right?'

There was a loud hammering, on the front door.

'Palace Guard – open up.'

Chapter 16

'You had to say it didn't you, Neeps? Jenni – if you please?' Ned spoke in low, urgent tones so as not to alert the guards that underhand things were afoot. Palace Guards were mostly idiots but every now and then someone who could think joined up and made everyone's life a misery. As long as it wasn't Geoff at the door, they'd be fine.

Jenni touched the pot with the rose in it and it disappeared. Brogan whistled in appreciation. 'I could use a gift like that.'

'I'm sure you could, but for now, let's try and pretend we are all innocently meeting up for an innocent conversation about innocent topics.' Ned said, looking at the people in the room. Brogan radiated insolent charm and cracked his knuckles cheerfully. Joe looked pale but resolute, he came to stand with Neeps. She was as white as a ghost. Lovely. Absolutely no guilty consciences on show here, then. The door banged again.

'Open up!'

Ned took charge, again. Someone had to. He opened the door. 'Geoff, how are you?'

'Spinks – already here? Something fishy going on is there?' Geoff tried to look past Ned, to see who or what else was hiding.

'How do you mean?' Ned tried radiating innocence. It was worth a shot.

Geoff sneered. 'That Neeps. She was at the murder scene, wasn't she? And at the Druids' Grove. She has access in and out of the Palace. It's clear she's the Rose-

Thief. By the power vested in me by the Emperor – *may he live for ever and ever* – we're here to arrest her. It's okay if she resists.' Geoff eased his sword out of its scabbard.

'I thought those were supposed to be ceremonial.' Ned was beginning to worry.

'I can make it very artistic,' Geoff said. 'I've been practising.'

A figure peeked out from behind Geoff and gave a small wave. It was Fred, the guard from earlier, the one who had bought Ned's *if you don't catch the thief you'll hang* message. Difficult face to forget.

'Fred!' Geoff snapped at him. 'Don't engage with the suspects.'

'So I'm a suspect now, am I?' Ned tried to play for time. 'How do you know I wasn't following my own line of enquiry? After all, a clever man like you made some interesting deductions.' Geoff's chest swelled in pride. 'Pity they're all wrong, but that's what comes when puffed up bits of toy soldier try to do a real job. You're not a thief-catcher. You'll never be a thief-catcher. Now go back to the Palace and guard an empty piece of wall. There's nothing here for you.' It was a gamble, Ned didn't want to annoy Geoff but at the same time, he knew that they knew they shouldn't really be here and that they were stepping on the jurisdictional toes of Thief-Catcher territory. The reason everything worked so well in Roshaven was because everyone had their own little piece of pie and fiercely protected it. If you tried to steal someone else's you might find your own taken from underneath you. Much better to hold to your own stuff with an iron grip. Fred began tugging on Geoff's sleeve urgently.

'He's right, Geoff – we shouldn't be here. We don't

have jurisdiction.' He looked apologetically at Ned. 'I'm only here because our Brian is still under the weather.'

Ned nodded in sympathy and started to close the door. He thought he'd convinced them, but the door juddered to a stop. Geoff's boot was in the way.

'No, I don't think so, Spinks. We're coming in, imperial order.' And Geoff pushed past him into the house. Fred followed, mouthing sorry at Ned.

Everyone was still in the room. There was no sign of the rose, just the merest hint of perfume in the air, but when Geoff saw Brogan, he turned pale and backed away, stammering apologies.

'Sorry, everything seems to be in order. Nothing to worry about, sorry. Routine checks you understand. Sorry.' He tried to back out of the room but in his haste, he tripped over Fred who was blocking his way and knocked him down. Being on the floor didn't stop Geoff. He resorted to crawling on his hands and knees, backwards down the hallway. It wasn't until he reached the door that he finally stood up and ran out the door. Ned offered Fred a hand and pulled him up.

'Thanks,' said Fred. 'I'd better go see if Geoff is alright. The new Emperor - *may he live for ever and ever* - chose him specifically for this task.'

'How do you mean, Fred?' Ned was instantly suspicious.

'Well, he's different now. The Emperor, I mean. Crueller. Harder. I'm guessing there was a Coo. One of his sons or something. I mean it's still imperial blood right and we've still got one so that's okay. Isn't it? I haven't told anyone. Well, except you, just now. But you won't say anything, will you? Until it's been properly announced. I'm sure it will be. You think so, don't you?'

'Alright, take a breath, Fred. Best keep it to yourself

109

for now, eh? What exactly did the new Emperor say to Geoff?' asked Ned.

'Thanks.' Fred breathed a huge breath in and exhaled noisily. 'I don't know what he said. He just called us all into the third best reception room. I've not been in there before, it's quite nice.'

'And?'

'Oh yes, well, we was all lined up and I thought oh gawd it's an inspection and I haven't polished me breastplate and me plume is crooked. It takes a lot of polish you see, and we have to buy our own and I've been helping out me mam look after our Brian. On account of him not being well.'

Ned tried hard not to show his frustration, but he could feel his patience running short. 'Then what happened?'

'The Emperor, *may he live for ever and ever*, walked up and down our row. He stopped to look at a few of us, not me thank goodness, on account of me breastplate. But he looked at Geoff for a long time and then pressed a finger to his head. We all thought it was odd. The Emperor never touches us. I mean, we usually never, ever see him. Geoff said afterwards it was like being chosen for a higher purpose, he said he was filled with the secrets of the universe, but we all thought he was being daft. Do you think he was filled? Is it catching?'

Ned reassured Fred and walked him out of the building. Feeling relieved the guard trotted off back to the Palace. Geoff was probably already back and if he was lucky there might be a couple of chocolate digestives left from the night shift.

Back inside, Neeps had turned on Brogan. 'He certainly seemed to know you.' She was talking shrilly, spots of red in her cheeks.

'Never seen him before in my life,' replied Brogan cheerfully. 'Probably just my reputation. It's pretty big you know.'

'It wasn't that. Joe's sister did something to Geoff.' Everyone turned to look at Ned. 'She obviously knows that you'd try and do something, so she's made some early warning systems. You can bet your life she knows Brogan is here. I think we need to speed up our plan. What is the plan?'

'Well,' Joe flushed. 'Me and Neeps were going to have a brew and maybe a packet of those special jammy ones, sit down and talk about it. Then you came in. Then Brogan. Then the guards. And the rose appears to be gone. So maybe it isn't our problem anymore and we can just have the brew?'

Jenni clicked her fingers and the rose reappeared on the table. She looked at Joe in disgust. 'Can't you even see a glamour? It were right in front of yor face. It weren't even a decent one.'

Joe shrugged as Neeps placed a plate of biscuits on the table. No jammies.

'Will Mia see you?' Ned turned to look at the human mountain tucking into five biscuits at once. He was oblivious to everything else. People in his line of work didn't often get to sit down for tea and biscuits. He was secretly hoping there might be some cucumber sandwiches, crusts cut off, and a slice of juicy fruit cake. A barbarian can only live in hope. Brogan finally realised everyone was looking at him.

'What?' Crumbs sprayed everywhere.

'Will Mia see you?' Ned repeated.

Brogan shrugged. 'Depends.'

'On?'

'What kind of mood she's in.' Brogan smiled

wistfully. 'Love or kill. It's what I like about her.'

'Excellent. In that case, I think we should just go to the Palace.' Ned looked around at everyone. 'If she refuses to see him then we've lost nothing, she already knows he's here.'

The others nodded doubtfully at Ned.

'Who we going to see?' Brogan asked as he tried to decide between a custard cream and a garibaldi.

Ned ignored him.

'Jenni, can you pop all three of us back to the Palace?'

The sprite cocked her head to one side and pursed her lips. 'Mebbe, but e's got wards. Can't do nuffink with wards.'

Brogan had decided on the custard cream and was actually paying attention this time.

'I've got the finest wards around. Protect me from one in five warlock attacks.'

'One in five? That doesn't sound like good odds.' Neeps was making notes, she couldn't help it. Anything could make a good story in the right nest of truth bending and the paper hadn't done anything on barbarians for at least a week. This could be an opportunity to show their biscuit loving side.

'It might not be but it's better than no odds at all.' Brogan shrugged. 'Besides most warlocks are pansies so just knowing I've got 'em stops attacks. Most wards bounce back you see.'

'Bounce back?' Neeps was intrigued.

'Oh yeah. Act as a shield. Funny to watch – there was this one time, over in Vorland - or was it Worland. Anyway, it was North. And me and Slippery Eel were doing this job right, some treasure or something. Or was it a virgin rescue? Anyway – point is, one in five, every time.'

Everyone nodded politely as Brogan decided to eat the garibaldi as well. Barbarians.

'Right, c'mon. Let's go. We might as well get it over with.' Ned stood up.

'Get what over with?' Joe looked confused.

'Storming the castle,' replied Ned. 'Brogan, you can bring the rest of the biscuits with you, I'm sure Neeps won't mind.'

She shook her head as the barbarian tipped the rest of the plate into a side pocket of his leather jerkin. 'Are you going Joe? She is your sister,' Neeps asked.

'I... I... that is, she's not very... um.'

Everyone was looking at him and Joe gave a nervous giggle, wondering whether he could get away with not going. No one spoke. The silence stretched on, awkwardly. Brogan began work on a couple of chocolate hobnobs that had been hiding at the back of the biscuits but were now at the top of the pile in his pocket. His jaws munched loudly. Joe shifted foot to foot, all this pressure was making him need a wee. He could feel Neeps' eyes burning into him.

'Alright, alright. I'll come with you. But I'm about as much good as a chocolate teapot.'

'Chocolate?' Brogan licked his lips in anticipation.

'Why?' Ned felt suspicious. This boy had the potential to be one of the strongest spell-catchers, sorry warlocks, he'd come across for a good long while. And yes, he was a bit dense when magic was right under his nose. And alright, he hadn't seen Jenni's glamour, but he did escape interrogation in The Noose. Ned had measured his power when he joined the thief-catchers, he had been impressed at the time, but truth be told, he had yet to see anything significant. It would be useful to

113

have more reliable power on their side.

'It's Mia. She nulls my magic. It's a twin thing.'

'That's alright if she nulls you then you null her.' Ned felt relieved.

'Erm... not quite. I amplify her. Again, a twin thing.'

'Amplify? Are you kidding me?' Ned had had enough. 'Fine. Stay here. Hide the rose from the Palace Guards, they might come sniffing around again. Jenni? Let's go.' And without waiting to see whether Brogan was following Ned stormed out of the house. Twins! And warlocks! And bloody magic roses full of love! He stomped down the street, Jenni capering beside him.

'Cheer up, Boss. Could be worse.'

Brogan lumbered up to join them. 'Where are we going?'

Ned hunched his shoulders into his cloak and strode onwards. He was finishing this lovers' quarrel tonight once and for all. Then he was going to go sleep for a week and get back to his normal thief-catcher life.

Chapter 17

When they reached the Palace, lights blazed from every window. There was a sea of plumed helmets guarding the front.

'This way,' muttered Ned as he took them around the back to what he hoped was the relative safety of Ma Bowl's kitchen. It was dark and cold as he pushed the door open. Ma Bowl was nowhere to be seen. All the ovens were still dead, there was still no food prep on the tables, still no delicious smells wafting and as Ned checked the shelf, even Ma Bowl's bowl was missing. This was not good.

'C'mon. We need to find the Emperor.' He gestured for the others to follow.

'Which one, Boss?' asked Jenni.

'At this point, I don't care.'

Brogan ambled along behind them, oblivious to the dark mood Ned had sunk into and blithely ignoring the looks Jenni was shooting at him. All in all, being a typical Barbarian, large, hulking and stupid. The Palace felt wrong. Even when John the Boring had been Emperor there had been more life in the corridors than this. They reached the left wing on the fourth floor without incident and as before, there were no staff around. The *Stay-Away* wards on the doors of Left Wing were still strong, resonating decay and danger ahead, invoking a massive desire to turn around and walk away fast but Ned was past caring. He pushed open the doors and a warm light spilt out over them.

'Wow.' Brogan blinked in surprise at the brightness,

a huge grin sweeping over his face as he took in the chambermaids, the scullery maids, the junior cooks, the maids in waiting and best of all the thousand and one nubile young wives of the Emperor. 'This is my kinda place.'

'Focus! We are here to patch things up with your girlfriend, remember? Not get you, and us, into more trouble.' Ned gave Brogan a little push to get him walking again. It was like trying to move a building. Brogan looked down at Ned in amusement before striding off in front of him.

'Jenni, go with him, please. Keep him out of trouble, if you can. I'm going to find the Upper Circle. Hopefully, she's finished being drunk.'

Ned was in luck. She had finished being drunk. Now she was being hungover. Which was a lot worse. The High Left and Right were cowering behind an overturned chaise-lounge which looked like it had seen better days. It was smoking in several places and one of the legs had been blasted clean off. There was the sound of painful retching from the corner of the room as a heap of stained satin revealed itself to be the Upper Circle. The retching made her head clench which then pounded even more painfully than before, making her feel even more annoyed with having been drunk in the first place. She swore loudly and threw another fireball at the unsuspecting furniture. It sizzled as it hit its mark and died out. Ned noticed the two Highs had several buckets of water nearby and had clearly been dousing furniture to prevent further damage and any danger to the rest of the court.

'Your Worshipfulness?' Ned approached cautiously.

'Shhhhhhh. Whisper, Spinks, whisper. The devil is inside my head and he is dancing.'

Ned whispered. 'I've found the pretender's boyfriend and brought him to the Palace. Hopefully, he can patch things up and the two of them will be on their way.'

'You did? You really did that? For me?' There was some dry heaving and groaning. 'Show me, show me.'

Ned helped the Upper Circle to the doorway, resting her against the frame. He scanned the crowd and closed his eyes in disbelief for a moment when he found Brogan. 'He's there, over there.' And he pointed to the Barbarian who had three different wives sitting on his lap, another feeding him grapes, another massaging his neck and several more flocking round him with wine and various tasty morsels.

'That? That...barbarian is her love? No wonder she's angry – I don't blame her. Owww my head.' The Upper Circle staggered away from the doorway and sank to the floor. She closed her eyes and adopted a foetal position on a pile of nearby cushions. Ned waited a good five minutes before attempting to interrupt her. The smell emanating from her was rather pungent and he was fighting his own urge to hurl. He coughed.

'Er... do you know where she is?'

The Upper Circle groaned before sitting herself up slightly and looking blearily at him.

'Who?'

'The Emperor.' Ned corrected himself hurriedly. 'I mean, the false usurper.'

'She's in the throne room torturing Ma Bowl.'

'Torturing Ma Bowl? Why?'

'Because,' the Upper Circle took a deep breath. 'She refused to make a quinoa salad with pomegranate jus and chia seeds to go with a kale, spinach and alfalfa sprout smoothie.'

'I'm sorry – what?'

'Exactly. I don't even know what half of those things are. She asked for miso soup last night. Who wants to eat misery soup?'

Ned wanted to joke that the Upper Circle looked like she had but thought better of it. It would be a lot easier to close this case with his head still attached to his shoulders. Ghosts did not make it far in public law and order enforcement. Something about the inability to handle iron chains.

'Right, well. I'll take the boyfriend to her and see if we can't solve this little mess, eh? You just... er... stay there and feel better, okay?' He winced at the patronising tone his voice had taken on, but it was too late, the words were out of his mouth. He waited for the explosion.

'K,' she snivelled. Who would have thought the Upper Circle, let alone the Emperor would ever snivel?

Ned eased away from her, it looked like she was falling into an exhausted coma. Hopefully, she would sleep through the sour belly and continual pounding headache and awaken to the charms of cotton wool mouth and slightly quieter jackhammers in her skull.

'See that she gets plenty of fluids – non-alcoholic this time.' Ned spoke to the Highs on his way out.

They nodded miserably. This was not how they had been expecting to spend their officeship. One of them, Ned couldn't tell the difference between the two bony men without their accoutrements, signalled for a handmaiden who scampered away to get jugs of water. Ned marched over to the Barbarian.

'Brogan. Hey Brogan.' Ned was being ignored. 'Oi, Barbarian!'

Brogan turned his head lazily in Ned's direction and waved a languid hand. Jenni stood in his line of sight and cracked her knuckles loudly. She said something, Ned didn't catch it but somehow Brogan was standing ramrod straight, radiating compliance and looking half surprised at the smart salute he whipped across his forehead. A lesser man would have suffered a concussion.

Satisfied, Ned nodded. 'Let's go,' he said.

'Where to, Boss?' asked Jenni.

'The Throne Room.' Ned looked down at Jenni. 'She's got Ma Bowl. She's torturing her. I want you to get her out of there, bring her here or somewhere safe. Wherever she wants to go.'

Jenni looked up at Ned in amazement.

'She's doing wot?'

'I know Jenni, it's not right.'

'I'll bloody 'ave 'er. Sod the flippin' rose of wotever. S'not right to 'urt the 'elp.'

'I'll deal with Mia.' Ned glanced at Brogan who was marching perfectly alongside them. 'Well, we will. If whatever you did to him wears off in time.'

'I didn't do nuffink.' Jenni wiggled two fingers in her ear vigorously while muttering under her breath. Brogan sagged from alert recruit to barbarian hulk. But he made no comment and avoided any kind of eye contact with Jenni, whatsoever.

They walked the rest of the way in silence, seeing the occasional blast hole and singe mark signalling that Mia had been expressing her opinion about something or other. The two Emperors were really very similar when things weren't going their way. When they reached the Throne Room the door was ajar. Ned motioned for the other two to stay back while he peered around the door to see what was going on. He nearly fell over as Jenni pushed between his legs to take a look and was then unable to straighten as Brogan leant his bulk on him as he too had a good look. So much for being sneaky. They needn't have worried. Mia was far too busy showing Ma Bowl a large chest, the contents of which were not visible from the doorway.

'So you just soak 'em and they grow?' Ma Bowl sounded highly suspicious.

'I'm telling you Ma dried porcini mushrooms are the way forward. They'll add another level to your risotto – no question.'

'That's the rice thing, right?'

'Yes, that's it. You will try it, won't you?' Mia hopped from foot to foot. 'Ooh, you are going to have a taste explosion. There is so much I have to show you. I mean, you know about cashew nut butter, right? It's out of this world and as for smoked tofu, I mean – if you can't get it then the other stuff will do but it's worth going the extra mile for.' Her head whipped around as the door finally creaked and moved, Ned staggered, but thankfully, the others withdrew meaning he didn't fall into the room entirely.

'Thief-Catcher.'

'Imposter.'

'Really? Are we going there? Why don't you bring out the rest of your little crowd? I see you have your filthy imp behind you.'

'Sprite.'

'What?'

'She's a sprite and she doesn't take lightly to being called names.'

Mia coloured slightly. Even she knew that it probably wasn't a good idea to pick a fight with Jenni. Not in such a confined space. You would need a couple of oceans between you to really be able to flex your fighting muscles and stand a chance of coming out the other side alive.

Brogan finally entered the room looking like a fine hulk of a man. Somehow in the last ten seconds, he had managed to oil his muscles. He was grinning as he strode straight into a magical forcefield. It was so strong he actually bounced off, with only his cat-like reflexes stopping him from falling on his butt.

Unaffected by the forcefield, Jenni popped over to where Ma Bowl was standing, trying not to be too obvious as she poked through Mia's chest and put a couple of items in her voluminous apron pockets.

'C'mon, Ma – I got someone who needs one of your pies.' And before Ma could protest Jenni had popped her away.

'Damn fae magic,' muttered Mia, fussing with her hair and smoothing her stolen Emperor robes over her hips. 'What do you want, Brogan? Last time I saw you, you seemed busy and extremely preoccupied. I'm fairly certain I told you I never wanted to see you again.'

'Honey, it was all a misunderstanding. It wasn't my fault. I woke up and they were already there. I didn't do anything to encourage them.'

'Them?'

The atmosphere in the room dropped by several degrees and Ned could see his breath huffing into the room. It had also become darker as if the candles were too depressed to burn brightly anymore. In fact, Ned felt that the best thing for him to do was to go and find a knife and cut his wrists. Preferably in a warm bath a long way away from here where no one was likely to interrupt. As he turned to leave, his attention was drawn by the collection of rose plants in the corner. He continued to swivel back the way he had been facing and drew some power from his wells. Just a glamour. A bloody strong one.

'Mia, darling. You're the only one for me.' Somehow Brogan had a red rose in his hands and was holding it out to her.

Ned frowned, was that THE red rose? How did it get here? More to the point, how did the bloody barbarian get hold of it?

'Well, you're not the one for me.' Before Ned had the chance to react Mia waved her hands in a complicated pattern opening a vortex in the middle of the room. The magical ward fell away and Brogan and the rose were pulled through the swirling portal to another dimension before Ned could shout stop. As soon as the Barbarian had passed through, the portal closed, and the light and warmth returned to the Throne Room.

'Did you have anything to add?' Mia looked coldly down at Ned who felt that at that precise moment there definitely wasn't enough room between him and her.

'Where did you send him?' He inwardly cursed his own curiosity.

'Nowhere nice.' A faint smile played around Mia's lips. 'Do you want to join him?'

Ned was edging backwards. He stammered a negative and then thought *bugger it*. He turned and legged it down the corridor. He kept expecting lightning bolts or fireballs to follow him but there was nothing. He made it back to the fourth floor in record time and leant panting on the doorway, ignoring the keep away wards. After having witnessed Mia open up a portal to another dimension, he did not think keep away wards would do much good if she decided to come a-knocking.

As he entered the large hall, a thousand and twenty-one sets of eyes stared at him accusingly.

'What? What happened?'

Joe came forward, his face a picture of misery. 'It's gone. The rose is gone.' He wiped his snotty nose on his sleeve which had clearly been used many, many times before. 'And the Palace Guards came back to take Neeps. I think she might be hurt; I couldn't stop them. We have to do something, Ned.'

'Brogan took the bloody rose and your beloved sister just sent her ex-boyfriend and it to an alternate dimension so right now, I'm all out of somethings.'

Chapter 18

Ned felt like all the life had been punched out of him, his energy levels sagged and so did his legs. The floor seemed much closer than before and extremely comfortable. As he folded downwards Joe also dropped to his knees, his face wet with tears.

'What a jessie,' thought Ned. 'Crying over a girl.' And then everything went black.

He was brought round by several aromas. One was Jenni – you don't forget sprite. The others were a sour tang and meat pie – not together precisely but mingling. Ned's stomach couldn't decide whether it was a good or a bad thing.

'What happened?' he asked.

'You passed out, Boss. How'd you feel?' Jenni leant over him in concern.

'Fine, let me up.' Ned staggered to standing and his stomach rumbled. 'Is that meat pie still around?'

'Yes Boss, 'ere.' Jennie shoved a plate into Ned's hands. It was filled with pie, a Ma Bowl special. It lasted about five seconds and Ned's belch reverberated through the wing. There were a couple of claps from the far end.

'Right, Jenni, let's get out of here. Back to HQ.'

'What about Neeps?' Joe hovered at Ned's elbow.

'We'll think of something, lad.'

'And what about my Emperorship?' demanded the Upper Circle, who was also nearby.

That explained the sour tang thought Ned. He turned to face her. 'That, Your Worshipfulness, is your problem. We were assigned to solve the theft of the Palace's roses

– which we have done. It was Mia – er, do you have a last name, Joe?'

Joe nodded. 'It's Green.'

'It was Mia Green. She stole your roses.'

The Upper Circle planted herself in Ned's path. 'Aren't you supposed to catch the thief?'

'Not today.' Ned was resolute. He wanted out of the Palace. He wanted to check in with the rest of his team, have a pint of something indescribable in The Noose, go to sleep for a week and then he'd decide whether they could catch the thief in question. He stepped around the Upper Circle pulling Joe and Jenni in his wake, leaving her standing there, speechless. The group descended to the ground floor and left the Palace without being stopped by anyone. There were more guards milling around outside, but none of them seemed to know what to do about people leaving. Their orders were clear about people trying to come in though. That wasn't allowed.

When they arrived back at The Noose, it was eerily quiet. For once there was no one in the pub. Not even Reg. Ned frowned but decided it was a problem for another time. As he wound his way carefully up the stairs, he could hear sobbing.

Pushing open the door carefully he was surprised to see Willow in a heap on the floor. She had lost all her greenness and was decidedly naked. Joe's Adam's apple began to bob alarmingly as he took in the scene and dashed to Willow's side. Ned went to a chest in the corner of the room. He was fairly sure there was some kind of clothing inside, or at least a blanket – ah, there. It looked, and smelt, like a horse blanket, but at least it would cover her up. He draped the blanket round Willow managing to avoid copping an eyeful. He lifted her gently to standing and guided her over to a chair. She sat, hugging the blanket around her and lifted her tear-stained face to the others. Even her eyes had changed. Now they were grey.

'It's gone,' she said, in a small voice.

'What has, love?' Ned asked gently.

'Exactly.'

'Sorry? I don't understand. Where's your green gone, Willow?'

'It went with love.'

'You mean you gave it away to someone? Can you do that?'

'NO!' Willow shouted. 'Love, it's gone. There's no love anymore. I'm a nymph. A child of love and nature. Well, they've split and now I'm just human. And I hate it!' She dissolved into tears again.

Ned ran a hand over his face. Not only had Mia stolen the imperial roses, usurped the throne, introduced a meat and two veg chef into clean eating, sent her boyfriend and the red rose of love to an unknown dimension, but now, apparently, she'd also managed to lose love.

'If love is gone, why don't I feel any different?' Joe was prodding his chest and taking the opportunity to sniff his armpit surreptitiously. It didn't work, everyone noticed - they always do. And if you can smell an unsavoury smell, you can bet your life everyone else can.

'I guess you must be newly infatuated or something,' Ned hazarded a guess. 'Love's hold is strong in the beginning, it will take a while before that fades away. In normal circumstances, I'd say about a month. That's when you find out... well, that's probably why anyway.' He turned back to Willow. 'C'mon, love, let's get you sorted out. You can't stay here – you should go home.'

'I'm a nymph. I live in a tree. But without my powers, I'm just a long-haired naked woman sitting on a branch in the freezing cold.'

'Right, er... I know, I'll take you to the Druids. They know all about nudity and hair.' Ned smiled encouragingly.

Willow shrugged. She let him lead her out of the office and down the stairs. Joe followed behind.

'Where do you think you're going?' Ned didn't want to babysit a love-struck warlock as well as deal with a de-nymphed nymph. Then he realised Jenni was missing. 'Jenni? Jenni!' There was no answer or sign from the diminutive sprite. 'Look, Joe, stay here and keep an eye out for Jenni. And Sparks for that matter. I'll be back as soon as I can.'

Joe looked disappointed, he was looking forward to the nudity and the hair, but he nodded reluctantly and traipsed back upstairs. At least he could pretend he was in charge and sit in the big chair.

Ned held Willow's hand and led her through the streets to the Druid Grove. There were a few catcalls on the way. A significant amount of leg was showing from beneath the blanket, but on the whole, the streets were quiet. Ned felt uncomfortable. Wasn't it market day today? Admittedly with everything that had happened he was not exactly sure what day of the week it was, but privately Ned thought the market decided to spring up on most days ending with 'y'. There was always someone hawking something. Usually, it was rubbish, but whenever you strolled through without any money, you always saw something you liked or had been looking for for ages, yet the next time the market came and you did have coin, nothing. And there was no way the sellers sold that much merchandise in one small town. Ned had a hard time believing the marketeers made any money at all, but then commerce had always seemed like a foreign language to the lad with the city in his bones. Walking the streets was soothing to Ned's soul. So why did he feel irritable? Why would he rather be anywhere than here? He tried to focus on the sobbing girl beside him, but to be honest, he was beginning to not care what happened to her.

'Ow!' Something kicked him in the shin, hard. He looked down but there was nothing there.

'WHERE ARE YOU GOING, BOSS?' shouted an unseen person.

He knew that voice, it was Jenni. But there was no one there. He drew on some power from his well belt and tried to concentrate. Jenni's overall shape began to shimmer in front of him. Abruptly she snapped into being.

'Boss! 'ow could you?' she demanded.

'How could I what?' Ned felt slightly bored. What was he doing again?

'You stopped believing in me. Ain't I real to you no more?'

'You're the one that disappeared on me.' Ned picked at a fingernail. 'Anyway – do you know where we're going?'

Jenni kicked Ned again.

'Owww! Would you quit it? What did I ever do to you?'

'You forgot 'bout me. 'Oo is that anyway?' Jenni jerked a thumb at the naked girl walking alongside them.

'It's Willow – she's lost her nymph. I'm taking her, taking her... we're going to... somewhere. I can't remember. Doesn't seem important anymore,' replied Ned.

They all walked along in silence. You see, without love, you stop caring. Love fuels your passions and interests. It makes you care about people and things, sometimes highly irrationally. If you take love away then people become forgetful and aimless, nothing seems to matter anymore. Chefs stop cheffing. Florists stop flowering. Parents stop parenting. In short, no one cares about anything anymore.

There was a giant smashing noise to the left of them as a brick landed in a shop window. Ned looked on as two men climbed in, disappeared from view then scrambled back out, each holding a handful of jewels. He felt a slight unease. Wasn't he supposed to do something about things like that? He needed to get rid of this naked girl first. Willow – that was her name and he was taking her to the Druids. He felt like he was waking up from a dream.

'Jenni! Where have you been?' Ned asked in surprise.

'Right 'ere Boss.'

'Oh. Sorry. I must have missed you. What did you do to me? I feel...different?'

'Nuffink. Just added some fae magic to your well is all. Gave you a bit o' passion. Seems like you needed it.'

'Yeah.' They walked together in silence, Willow shuffling along beside them. 'Hey, Jenni - why is it affecting Willow like this if you're alright?' Ned asked.

'I fink its cos she's nature right, and I'm straight fae. Most people don't know the difference.'

Ned nodded but he wasn't entirely sure he knew the difference either. 'I think we're in trouble, Jenni. Love has only been missing an hour or so and look at how badly we've been affected. We've got to do something.'

'You're not wrong, Boss. Let's get rid of the dead

wood first, eh?'

They rounded the corner and arrived at the Druid Grove. It too was eerily quiet.

Chapter 19

'Where is everyone?' whispered Jenni. They entered the courtyard, avoiding the magical death mark that still splashed some of the cobbles. Only visible to those who cast, it was a stark reminder of the tragedy that had befallen the Druids. Ned found he didn't particularly care, he just wanted to make sure he didn't walk through it with his boots. They were a devil to clean at the best of times and trying to get rid of magical splashback was time consuming. Although, he wasn't trying to impress anyone, so it didn't matter what he looked like. Come to think of it, it probably didn't matter whether he turned up for work or not, there was a good chance that no one would notice the difference. After all, no one cared about Roshaven anymore. Why would you? It was dirty and smelly and broken and... an immense wave of nostalgia washed over Ned. It was his home and he, he, he felt something for it. It was warm and a bit tingly, but he wasn't sure what it was. Ned looked down to notice that Jenni was standing on his foot.

'Any particular reason?' Ned asked, wriggling his toes.

'Just 'minding you of love, Boss.' Jenni looked up at him hopefully.

'What's that then?'

Jenni scratched her head. 'It's that fing wot makes you all googly inside. You know, that fing?'

Ned shook his head and then his boot. As Jenni moved off his foot, the warm feeling went away, and Ned felt a little emptier than before. 'I think you'd better stay close Jenni, losing this love thing is having a bigger effect than I thought.'

Willow had stopped in the courtyard - she looked deep in thought. But a sort of empty-headed nothingness of thought rather than an I'm-having-a-coherent idea kind of thought. Ned poked her gently and she swayed a little but did not move. He waved his hand across her face and she didn't even blink.

'Got another one, eh?' A cheerful voice rang out across the courtyard. Ned turned to see an extremely fat nun waddling over to them. 'Hello dears,' she said. 'I'm Sister Eustacia. Can I help in any way?'

'Why hasn't the sadness affected you?' Ned felt highly suspicious of this do-gooder.

'Between you and me, I haven't the faintest idea.' Sister Eustacia chuckled a happy, burbling chuckle and beamed at all of them. Ned almost smiled back; she was rather infectious.

'Fae blood,' Jenni spat on the floor. 'She's a halfer.'

'Halfer?' asked Ned.

'Yeah – either 'er ma or pa was fae and did it wiv a 'uman. 'appens. Don't see 'em much.' Jenni turned her attention to the smiley nun. 'You got any powers?'

'Just faith in the lord, my dear.' Her smile slipped slightly as she glanced around the courtyard. 'Faith that seems to be seriously lacking elsewhere but I will keep the flame lit. Shall I put her with the others?'

'The others?' Ned was reluctant to leave Willow

where she was, but he wasn't sure he trusted nuns or people who smiled this much.

'Come along dear, I'll show you.' Sister Eustacia took Willows' arm and gently tugged her to get her moving. Willow shuffled along quite happily and even managed to work her legs to step down the stairs into the inner hall.

Ned and Jenni followed, looking around. Ned had never been this far into the inner sanctum of the Druid Grove before. He thought he ought to be interested and excited at the possibility of seeing some of the secrets of the universe, but he actually felt mildly annoyed. Why were these women making him do things when all he wanted to do was go home and sit in his pants? Preferably for several days. Jenni put her warm, slightly sticky hand into his. Some of the indifference left him but not as much as earlier when she had been standing on his foot.

'It's getting worse, fast, Jenni. We've got to think of something.'

'Here we are, dears.' Sister Eustacia gestured to a room off to the side of the main hall. Inside were about a dozen figures, most standing still and staring into space. One or two bumped aimlessly around. An air of general wretchedness hung over them all. There was no spark of life or happiness in the room. Even the colours looked like they had been leached out. Sister Eustacia gave Willow a gentle push and she moved into the room as far as this small amount of momentum allowed. 'She'll be safe in here dears, until whatever this is goes away. Any idea when that will be? Only I should be getting back to the Nunnery. I came for the student exchange program we've been running. An effort to improve relations between the Lord our Saviour and the heathen masses.'

133

She giggled. 'Only don't tell them I called them that, they'll think I haven't been paying attention.'

Ned gazed at her with barely concealed indifference. Jenni kicked his shin but even that only earned her a vague glance, not even mildly tinged with disgust. Jenni made a snap decision. It was probably the wrong one, but she had to do something. Grabbing his leg, Jenni popped them back to the Emperor's throne room. Sister Eustacia blinked in surprise, then shrugged. *Fae*, she thought.

Before the Emperor pretender had chance to react, Jenni found the trace magical signature from the portal through which Mia had sent Brogan, reopened it and threw herself in with Ned bobbing along behind. They landed with a thump on black sand, wind howling around their heads, Brogan nowhere to be seen.

'Where the bloody hell are we, Jenni?' Ned had to shout over the tempest. 'It looks like the back end of beyond. What did you do?'

'It's close, Boss. It's the middle of nowhere. I fawt we'd go get that rose fingy.'

'I can see it's the middle of nowhere but where exactly are we.' Ned asked again crossly.

'Er... the middle of nowhere, Boss.'

Ned looked around. Black sand crunched underfoot, and a black sky hung overhead but there were no stars. There didn't seem to be any light anywhere and yet Ned was able to distinguish the difference between the ground and the sky. The black was showing off its shades and without the colours of the rainbow interfering, it was doing an impressive job. The only distracting thing was the wind. It was still howling around their heads. Ned hunched into his jacket as much as possible, but it didn't do much good. High winds were practically non-existent in Roshaven, despite it being a seaport. The ships seemed to glide in and out of the harbour. No wind meant the delightful odours of the place remained unmixed. You could tell where you were by closing your eyes and following your nose. Of course, if you closed your eyes in the Black Narrows you would probably never open them again. A wave of homesickness flooded Ned and he struggled to fight back the tears. The rational part of his mind was berating him heavily for being close to weeping like some big softie. He sniffed loudly.

'Where's Brogan gone, then? Is there some place else, other than the middle?'

'Not sure, Boss, never been 'ere before. Summik's sorta glinting over there.' Jenni pointed off to the left, but Ned had something in his eye and couldn't see clearly so he nodded and strode off in that direction. They walked for several minutes. Nothing in the landscape changed. Time and distance stretched out in front of them as Ned thought about all the people he was probably never going to see again. Ma Bowl with her delicious chicken soup, Aggie with her cinnamon twists, Sparks who had gone missing and was probably dead somewhere. Poor little delightful Sparks. Ned had never shown his full appreciation for that bug and now he never would. He couldn't hold them back anymore. His shoulders shook as he wept and wept for all his friends left behind, all the people he was never going to see ever again. For his city.

'Er, Boss? You alright?'

'Yep.' Ned's voice was a little high-pitched.

Jennie peered up at him and saw the tears. She calmly put her hand in his and waited a few minutes.

'Jenni? Why are you holding my hand?' Ned's voice

sounded back to normal, although his other hand and sleeve were rather wet after having wiped his face dry.

'There's a Great Sadness 'ere, Boss. S'affecting you.'

'And not you?'

'Nah. I don't get sad, I get even. S'alright, I fink we're nearly at the shiny bit.'

Ned focused his attention on the horizon in front of them. The small hand in his was making him feel much better, at least now he could see out of his eyes. There seemed to be a lumpy shape sitting next to a shimmering pool. As they drew closer the lump revealed itself to be Brogan, who was bawling his eyes out. He did not stop crying as they approached, he didn't even seem to notice their presence. At his feet was the shimmering pool, more of a pond really - it did not look that deep.

'Jenni?' Ned asked. 'Has Brogan made that pool out of his tears?'

'Looks like it, Boss. I fink this is where the sadness is coming from.'

Ned looked around, there was nothing else but more sand and horizon as far as the eye could see, in all directions. Without any distinguishing characteristics, they looked like they were still slap bang in the middle of nowhere. He looked down at the barbarian weeping in front of him, a mere shell of the man he had met earlier that day.

'Brogan? Hey Brogan, buddy! It's me – Ned. Remember?' He shook Brogan's shoulder.

Brogan managed to lift his head and half shrugged in response before a terrifying wail of grief burst out of him. Ned sat himself down next to the large man and attempted to put an arm around the giant muscle and barbarian armour.

'There, there, mate. There, there. It's going to be

alright.' Although how exactly, Ned wasn't sure.

Jenni had let go of Ned's hand and instead, she was sitting on Ned's knee which felt a lot weirder than Ned was happy to admit, but if it stopped him from feeling the Great Sadness, then he was happy to go with it. She extended a grimy hand to Brogan's arm and immediately his sobs lessened, and shudders wracked his body as he brought his grief under control. Eventually, he was able to speak.

'What are you two doing here?'

'Looking for you,' Ned replied. 'How are you feeling?'

'She banished me, she don't want me no-more. She sent me here to nowhere and she don't even care.' Brogan dissolved back into tears. The others waited as he collected himself. Again. Jenni produced a grubby hankie from who knows where and Brogan blew his nose loudly. She told him to keep it and he tucked it into his breastplate with a small squelch.

'Where's the rose, buddy?' Ned wanted to try and put everything back where it was. Starting with that bloody rose.

'I dunno. I got here and it's all dark and empty and stuff. I saw the rose on the floor and thought I don't want to be anywhere near that thing. I started walking. I walked for days and days and days. How long have I been here?'

'Couple of hours.'

'Oh. Well, felt a lot longer.' Brogan picked up a handful of sand and let it trickle back down through his fingers. 'I decided to sit down. And I thought about everyone I was going to miss.' He pointed at the pond of tears as if seeing it for the first time. 'Did I do that?'

'Yep.'

'Huh. I miss her, you know? And she sent me away.' Another wail this time but not quite as loud or as wretched as the one before. Ned and Jenni waited patiently for it to subside. 'What am I going to do?'

'The first thing we're going to do is find that bloody flower and then we're getting the hell out of here.' Ned sounded far more confident than he felt.

'Slight problem, tho', Boss.'

'What is that Jenni?'

'We don't know where the rose is.'

'Yes, I'm aware of that. We'll just have to pool our collective talents and find it eh? Between the three of us – shouldn't be a problem.'

Chapter 20

It had been hours. Or minutes. Or days. The difficulty was that they had no frame of reference, no distinguishing mark to try and orientate themselves upon. They were literally nowhere, plus everything looked the same. Every time they tried to separate and cover more ground Brogan and Ned soon became overwhelmed with grief, unable to do anything other than weep. There were now three pools of tears in the sand which might have been a useful point of reference except for the fact that once you had walked away from the pool it ceased to glimmer and was absolutely no help whatsoever. They had to walk along in a line, holding hands.

'Anything?' Ned glanced along the line. Jenni scowled and Brogan shook his head. It all looked the same. Ned stopped walking. 'There has to be a better way. We must be missing something. Jenni – any ideas? Please tell me there's a magical solution.'

Jenni was drawing shapes in the sand with her toes, she shrugged, paused then snapped her fingers and looked up with a grin. 'Yeah! Boss – I got it. We've gotta find luv.'

'Isn't that what we're trying to do already?' Brogan

looked confused. More so than usual.

'Yeah, but no. We gotta find our luv. Wot's inside us. Wot we luv the most.'

The two men stared at the sprite. She bristled under their scrutiny. 'Wot?'

'Find our love?' Ned was incredulous. 'I thought love was lost. I thought that was why we were in this whole mess in the first place.'

Jenni kicked piles of sand, trying to find the right words. 'Yeah, but it's your own luv you've gotta find, not everyone else's. That will lead us to the rose, I fink.'

'Can you show us what you mean, little sprite?' Brogan asked.

Jenni nodded and motioned the two men to come and stand closer to her. When they were within touching distance, she stood one foot on one of theirs and let go of their hands. Sadness washed over the men, but it was manageable, they didn't feel the need to dissolve fully into sobs, yet. Jenni closed her eyes and concentrated, her brow furrowed, whispering words under her breath. She cupped her hands in front of her as if she was holding a ball. Nothing happened. Ned's nose started to itch, and Brogan began picking his teeth. Minutes ticked by and still nothing happened. Then Ned noticed there was a faint pinkish glow emanating from Jenni's hands, it got brighter and brighter until there was a glowing pink ball of energy fizzing slightly in her palms. She grinned up at them.

'I found mine – watch.' And she threw the ball out into the nothingness. It arced up and gradually disappeared from view.

'What's supposed to happen next?' Brogan looked wistfully into the distance at the pink glow that was gradually fading.

'Wait for it.' Jenni had puffed out her chest in pride.

They waited. Still nothing. Minutes ticked by and the silence grew more and more uncomfortable. Jenni started biting her nails. Gradually they became aware that there were small pink globules twinkling in the black sand, stretched out in a line in front of them.

'C'mon. Let's go.' She grabbed their hands and stopped standing on their feet, tugging them forward. The heavy sadness lifted somewhat, and they all followed the pink blobs that stretched into the distance.

'Will these take us all the way to the rose?' Brogan sounded out of breath. Barbarians clearly were not as fit as they would like people to believe. That muscular body was probably achieved with magical potions, stinky herbs and prayers to backwater gods. None of this working out lark that was sweeping the play centres at the moment. Personally, Ned didn't see the point of paying to stand in a room and lift heavy things when you could quite as easily go get a job and do the same for free - not even for free - you would be getting paid. And those people who liked the track were just as bonkers. People actually paid money to spend time walking the indoor track that snaked the length of the largest play centre in Roshaven. It was about a mile long and could fit three people abreast comfortably provided you had worked out a who-went-first order when going through doorways. And a slipstream option for people who wanted to run past. When the track had first opened it was a total free for all, but after several nasty collisions and one rather heated bout of fisticuffs, the play centre owners had decided to make the track one way. They ended up reversing it on Tuesdays and Thursdays because people like a change. Ned didn't get it. Walk around Roshaven. It had miles and miles of well-worn streets that could tell a tale or two. In fact, some of the older streets did speak, late at night to those whose boots could read cobble. Ned had liked spending his night shift hitting the streets. Only very, very occasionally did they hit back.

'Nah.' Jenni pointed to where the blobs seemed to end. 'They'll take us this far; rest is up to youse two. You gotta find your luv.'

Looking behind him, Ned couldn't see any pink blobs at all. Apparently, once they passed one, it lost its usefulness and disappeared back to wherever it had come from in the first place. Unless of course, the whole thing was one of Jenni's pranks. She was a sprite, after all.

'Do you have a way out of here when we find the rose, Jenni?' asked Ned.

'Nope.' She still sounded cheerful.

'Well, I'm not going next. Brogan – where's your love?'

Brogan looked down at the rapidly disappearing pink blob at his feet and cracked his knuckles. 'I don't know how to do visual... visual... looking.'

'Just fink 'bout wot luv means to you, the rest will take care of itself,' Jenni explained.

'K.' Brogan seemed to have shrunk into himself, he looked less bulky and squatter as if the weight of the entire world was pressing down upon him. 'I guess I love wine and women. More wine than women. Truth be told there's only ever been one woman for me. I don't know why I ever messed things up as much as I did. I guess I was frightened.' He looked to Jenni for reassurance. She squeezed his hand encouragingly. 'I was scared she would leave me. Why would someone like that want to have anything to do with someone like me? I'm not a

142

clever man. I've magically enhanced myself to keep up with the pack. It's a risk, I know, but the ladies seem to like it, so you think it's worth it in the end.'

I knew it, thought Ned to himself. *Next thing you know he'll be admitting to never having heroed anything before.*

'I'm only a barbarian by look. Never done me own quest or nothing. Too nervous to take on the big stuff and no one will touch me with the little stuff cos I look too imposing. Probably should've held back on the enhancements but what are you going to do? It was after I did them that I met Mia. She was wonderful, she glowed with life. I didn't think I stood a chance, but she noticed me at a party and spoke to me. I'll never forget her first words to me. She said, *'Oi lump – move out of the way.'* Such a beautiful voice, like honey mixed with treacle or something.'

Ned stopped listening. Brogan went on and on extolling his beloveds' virtues until a tiny pink ball started to form in the air in front of him. At first, he didn't notice, he went on describing Mia's perfect fingernails and the delightful way she would clip him around the ear when he forgot to put the milk in her tea before the hot water. He had to remember so much to be with her it was hard work at times but in the end, completely worth it. As he finally stopped speaking, the pink ball had fully formed and was pulsing gently in the air.

'Frow it,' urged Jenni. 'Not too 'ard, you don't wanna shatter it.'

Brogan gently cupped his hands around the ball and executed a textbook underarm lob. The orb sailed through the air, weeping droplets as it flew out of sight.

'C'mon. Let's follow 'em. S'your turn next, Boss.' But

Jenni didn't take their hands this time. In fact, she had not been holding them since they stopped for Brogan to find his love. Ned realised he didn't feel so sad; a measure of contentment had come back into his life. He still felt as though he could quite happily bawl his eyes out but at least now he knew he was not going to dissolve into tears right this instant and he was quite looking forward to getting one step closer to home. They all jogged along, lost in their own personal thought clouds. They did not notice the gathering storm behind them. To be fair it is hard to notice anything when you are not actually looking at it but at least one of them should have taken note of the prickling feeling between their shoulder blades and then glanced round to look. They all thought it was sand.

Like before, the pink globules stretched out over the black sand, lighting the way. Without any change in the landscape, it was difficult to tell whether they were actually making any headway or whether they were going around in circles. One rock would be nice, a small change in the flatness and a distance gauge. Ned was beginning to feel concerned. It was his turn next to let the love in. But that story happened a long time ago and he had absolutely no desire to re-hash those painful memories and anyway, that was a love lost, not a current love, so surely it wouldn't do any good. Besides, no one likes to dwell. It's one of the major evolutionary leaps' mankind has made. Dwarves, elves, pixies and the like, they cling on to the past, always moaning about how much better it was and the fact that our ancestors still owe them fourteen silver bits from that time when they needed help. Fae-folk. Ned realised he was feeling angry, he looked across at Brogan. No, he still had that stupid lovesick look on his face and his globules were still going strong. Jenni was looking at Ned out the corner of her eye as if she knew something was wrong but had no inclination to get involved. He scowled at them both and hunched his shoulders. Stupid bloody place to end up chasing a stupid bloody flower for a stupid bloody emotion. Love – ha! What is it good for? Absolutely nothing.

The storm whipped itself into a wild frenzy in appreciation of Ned's black mood. Still no one had noticed the towering inferno building behind them, but the sand had. It was trying to run away. Finally, Jenni realised that the sand was undulating under her feet, making walking a little easier as each footstep glided a little further. It was a bit like skating. Brogan hadn't noticed anything, he was still intent on his blobs and Ned, well he was in a black mood. It matched the cloud behind them. Jenni stopped and turned slowly around. She gulped at the huge storm brewing. It was rage and hurt and pain and probably certain death. What was Ned carrying with him?

'Er, Boss? I fink we need to get a move on.'

'You don't say?' snapped Ned.

'Boss! Look behind ya.'

Ned turned and shrugged indifferently. 'It's a cloud, Jenni. They happen.'

'Can't you feel it, Boss? S'like anger and pain and 'urt all rolled up. S'not happy. I fink we should run.'

'Why bother, we're all going to die here anyway. Have you seen any drinking water or food? This is hell and we are stuck here.'

'Boss – you don't believe that?'

Brogan had stopped walking; he had come to his last globule. It was pulsing paler and paler. He looked up at the other two in concern. 'I think it's going out. What do we do now?'

'Boss – you gotta find your luv,' urged Jenni.

'It's overrated,' snarled Ned. That's when the storm hit. A blanket of pitch fell over them as the enormous cloud rolled carelessly onwards. Ned could not see anything. Not even his hand in front of his face. Finally, something that matched his mood. He sat down. There was no point in moving, this was it. This was the end. He could hear the others shouting for him in the storm. Let them waste their energy. They were never getting out of here. Never getting back to Roshaven.

At the thought of his city, Ned's heart panged. He thought of his battered old chair in his rickety office at the top of those death trap stairs. People didn't make workspaces like that anymore. It was the type of place that built real job commitment. And The Noose. Oh, The Noose was a rare hostelry indeed. Reg might pretend he was indifferent to everyone and everything. but Ned knew how much those monosyllables cost him and how much he had paid the Guilds in order to stay at the top of the Black Narrows. It was home. The blackness around Ned lightened slightly, becoming midnight black instead of pitch. It was subtle but if you knew what to look for you would see it. Jenni and Brogan missed it and continued to stumble through the darkness.

Ned thought about his favourite loop of the city. He started at The Noose, of course, the heart of the place. A brisk hike through the Black Narrows – you didn't want to go too slowly otherwise you would get mugged, but you also didn't want to go too fast, otherwise you risked getting shot at for acting suspiciously. It was a react first, ask questions later kind of place. But it had real character, it had nuance. Some of the Narrows had not had a murder for nearly a week and you could still get a cuppa from some of the older residents. They appreciated the concept of thief-catchers even if they were most likely on the list of wanted thieves. Once you exited the Narrows on the west side it was a slow loop round Piss-Eyed Nellie's lake. If you could ignore her, which to be fair, most people could, it was an enjoyable walk with a bit of nature sprinkled here and there. A lot of woodland folk who had moved to the big city liked to live around the lake. You had to be mindful of where you stepped – it could be someone's house in that toadstool. Momma K had extended a little protection over the community, but it still came under city rule and Ned liked to make sure everyone was getting along. Pixie fights could be catastrophic.

Ned didn't feel quite so angry anymore. He thought about the trolls that lived down Quarry, they carved out their homes and shared what limestone they didn't eat with the masons of the city. Luckily the seam was deep, or so Ned had been told and the troll population was small. Reproduction was a highly complicated affair involving a lot of igneous. Hard to find this far from the volcanic region of the South. Trolls were lazy and on the brink of extinction, but Ned knew that Calcite and Magnetite were thinking of making the pilgrimage. There was even talk of twins. That would be interesting. Then of course, there was Momma K's small grove slap bang in the middle of the city and the Druid Grove further east. It was funny, so many different races and religions in one small place. Roshaven should have been a powder keg ready to explode, but everyone sort of rubbed along together.

Jenni and Brogan could see Ned now - the blackness had begun to lift. The huge cloud was breaking up and drifting apart. They hung back, something telling them both that now would be the wrong time to speak. Ned had his eyes closed and his fist clenched, tears rolling down his face but that wasn't what kept them back. He was glowing bright pink. All over. Jenni had never seen anything like it. She had not realised her boss had so much love inside him.

Ned's mind swept on, taking in all the twists and turns of his city walking past the Emperor's Palace and even feeling a stab of fondness for Her Imperialness. It was his city and it was suffering from the Great Sadness. No one cared anymore. He couldn't leave it like that - he had to do something. Ned opened his eyes and jumped to his feet. Without knowing how he scooped all the pink energy from his body into his hands, making a huge ball and then he flung it into the distance as far and as hard as he could. The orb didn't travel far, instead, it hung in the air and grew and grew and grew until it became a love portal.

'Shall we?' Ned extended his hand to Jenni who curtseyed, badly, grabbed Brogan's codpiece and together they all walked out of nowhere.

The rose of love remained behind in the black sands. Its magical power spent.

Chapter 21

The throne room was dark and cold, fake Emperor Mia nowhere to be found. Brogan dropped to his knees and dry heaved. Thankfully they had had nothing to eat in the middle of nowhere otherwise it would have sounded and smelled a lot worse. Ned felt queasy watching him.

'Let's check out the fourth floor, that's where everyone else was last time I was here.' Ned swallowed a few times to settle his stomach and led the way. The corridors were still deserted, still looking forlorn. There were dust balls gathering along the skirtings and the mirrors were dulled, silver was tarnished, and lights dimmed. No one had been doing the housekeeping. Their footsteps rang loudly and echoed through the hallways. Ned let out a sigh of relief when they reached the fourth floor, lights were still blazing through the cracks of the doors and the go-away spell was still repelling although not as powerfully as it had been. They walked through the doors into a wall of sadness.

No one was actually weeping; they had already passed through that stage. Everyone was sitting still, stuck in a funk, indifferent as to what was happening or what would happen to them. People were not eating or drinking, talking or interacting in any way. The trio walked to the side reception room, Ned hoping that the Upper Circle had stayed put. He didn't fancy trying to look for her while everyone was so miserable and unhelpful. He had to get Brogan to help him push the door open, it felt like there was something in the way. It was the High Right – or possibly the Left. Ned always had trouble telling them apart when they were not wearing their ceremonial robes and even then, he often needed a clue. The other High direction was slumped in a chair by the fireplace. There was no immediate sign of the Upper Circle but there was a heap of blankets in the corner that appeared to be breathing. Ned walked over and nudged it with his toe. It groaned.

'Found her, I think.'

'She's gotta find 'er luv Boss, then we can start spreading it out. Shouldn't take long. S'natural emotion.'

The two of them started digging through the pile to find the Upper Circle and a sour smell began wafting upwards. Clearly, the Upper Circle had not bothered to wash since the results of her hangover.

'Jenni?'

'Yes, Boss.' She waved an arm and a bathtub filled with hot water appeared by the fireplace. The two of them dragged the Upper Circle out of her nest. She appeared to be catatonic.

'Er, I think you'd better do this bit, Jenni. You know, propriety and all that.' Ned's ears were turning pink.

Jenni grinned and shooed him away. Ned turned his back and went over to where Brogan was sitting talking to one of the Highs. He seemed to be having some kind of effect, the High was at least looking at him. As he grew closer, he could hear Brogan talking about his love for Mia. There was a pause and haltingly the High began to speak.

'Her name is Molly. Everyone said she would never make it. I rescued her, you know. She likes to sleep in my bed. On my pillow. Her tail makes me sneeze.' Slowly the colour started to come back in the High's face – not that there was much to begin with, but it went from the grey-white of someone near death to the sallowness of someone who spends all their time inside. His eyes became brighter and he looked more awake and alert. Taking in the scene around the room he stood up hurriedly. 'Where's Left?'

'Right,' said Ned, he had thought so. 'Over here, in this chair.'

'He keeps an ant farm.' The High Right bristled under the twin stares from Ned and Brogan. 'We talk about our pets. We do have interests you know.' The High Right stalked away and started talking gently to the High Left. At first, there was no difference, but slowly the Left began to respond. Within five minutes his normal off-white colour was back, and he was also talking animatedly, hands waving in the air.

'Okay, so now we have to do the rest of the city,' muttered Ned. He had wandered over to the bathtub to see how Jenni was getting on, forgetting for a moment that the Emperor was naked. He flushed bright red when he saw her bare knees sticking out of the tub. Who knew the Emperor had such beautiful knees? 'I, er, thought I'd come and see how everyone was getting on.'

'She's mostly clean now, Boss, but she still needs to find 'er luv. Why don't you talk to 'er?'

'Me?'

'Yeah. I'll go find Ma Bowl, get that lot going.' Jenni sauntered off gathering up Brogan and the two Highs with her. The door clunked rather loudly as it shut behind them. Ned gulped as the knees disappeared back into the bath suds and a dripping wet, mop top of a head appeared. Thankfully all other pieces were still covered in thick, white, bubbles but to be on the safe side Ned focused on the far corner of the room. He could feel himself blushing hotly.

'Thief-Catcher?'

'Yes, Your er, Eminence?'

'Why am I in a bath? Why are you here? Where is everyone?' She began to cry. 'Why do I feel so sad?'

Ned cleared his throat.

'You stank. I found my love. They're off doing theirs and now you've got to find yours. I think that's everything.'

'I need to get out of here.'

Ned looked around desperately for some help. There was none. Then he spied a big fluffy towel and grabbed it, gratefully holding it out for the Emperor, shutting his eyes tight. There was a wet sucking noise as she stood up. Ned could hear water trickling off her body. He felt rather hot around the collar. She stepped out of the bath and into the towel which Ned automatically wrapped around her. He stood with his arms around her as she leant into him. She smelled much better than before and was delightfully warm. They stayed that way for a few moments until there was a small cough from the doorway. It was a lady-in-waiting with a pile of new clothes. The two of them sprang apart, the Emperor gathering her towel around her as Ned fled for the door, cheeks beetroot.

Outside it looked like everyone was finding their love. There were a lot of happy tears and laughter, life was bleeding back into people and the room. Children began running and screaming, as they often do when extremely happy, and maids began cleaning. Things were getting back to normal.

It was definitely the Emperor who appeared at Ned's right hand.

'Thank you, Thief-Catcher.'

'Er, yes, Your Worshipfulness. It was nothing. Happy to help.' There was a long pause. 'Um, what did I do?'

The Emperor smiled and glided away. Ned's knees felt weak and his heart was racing. Oh no. He didn't have time for that. He had a city to save and a usurper warlock to deal with.

'C'mon Jenni, let's go help the other catchers. This lot can roll out to the streets. We'll meet in the middle.' He strode off, not waiting to see whether she was following him. His ears were burning, and he could hear ladies in waiting tittering.

The streets were still quiet and The Noose empty when they got back to HQ, there was no sign of life from the office, but Ned hoped the others had stayed where they had been left. Traipsing up the stairs he thought about how he was going to help Willow, Sparks, and Joe find their love. The office was cold and dark but there was a heap of hair on the floor. As Jenni and Ned entered the hair moved, revealing Willow – her face still puffy from crying. For some reason, she had returned from the Druid Grove.

'What are you doing here, love?' Ned was concerned. Had the Druids kicked her out or had she just gravitated back to a place of safety? Willow ignored his question and stared at him with lifeless eyes.

'You came back then,' she said dully. 'Don't know why. Nothing here but misery.' The hair descended back to the floor.

Jenni waggled her fingers at the various lamps and

candles in the room. Everything came on at once including a roaring fire in the grate. Ned didn't think there had ever been a fire in the grate before. He decided to ignore the obviously magical aspects as the flames danced in hues of orange, purple, and green. As it became warmer and brighter in the office Joe was revealed to be slumped in a chair in the corner. He appeared to be asleep or possibly dead. He could wait. There was no sign of Sparks, his shelf was empty.

Ned hunkered down to where Willow was lumped on the floor. 'C'mon Wil – you've got to get up.' There was no response, so he delved in to find an arm and dragged her up to standing. She swayed a little, head bowed, hair still covering her face. Ned gently gathered her into his arms, closed his eyes and began stroking her hair, murmuring to her. Several minutes passed before he noticed the sweet smell of floral perfume in the air. Opening his eyes, he saw a sea of green, flowers blooming all over the place and tendrils getting into places they had no right to go. Ned jumped, then yelped and quickly untangled himself.

'I feel better.' Willow whirled in a cloud of green, scattering petals and leaves all over. 'Thanks, Boss.' She leant in and gave Ned a chaste peck on the cheek, then ran to the window and started reacquainting herself with the rooftop mosses and lichen. They needed cheering up too.

Ned thanked his lucky stars for the hair bracelet Willow had given him, it was back to being bright green again and hopefully at full strength. There seemed to be an awful lot of high-quality nymphing going on. He turned to regard Joe. His chest was moving so at least he was alive.

'Any ideas Jenni?'

'Yep,' she grinned and popped. A few seconds later she returned with a snivelling Neeps in her arms. She plonked her down on the floor next to Joe.

Ned was surprised. 'What did you get her for?'

'They're a fing ain't they?'

'I don't think so, Jenni.'

'Oh. I'll take 'er back then.'

'Well, maybe it's worth a shot, eh?' Ned felt bad for Jenni.

'Whaddya fink then? Make em hold hands or summink?'

'May as well.' Ned grabbed Joe's arm, extending a limp wrist while Jenni did the same with her human. It was a lot harder than you might think to get two disinterested hands to find each other and then hold fast. 'Might need a little binding.' Jenni nodded and muttered something under her breath then let go of Neeps. The arm sagged but the hand held fast. Ned did the same and Joe's hand hung weirdly but stayed clasped tight to Neeps. 'Now, all we need to do is wake them up and get them to express their undying love, for er... each other.'

Jenni apparated two glasses of water and upended them. There were twin gasps and swearwords, a good sign for a couple that might last a long time. Joe and Neeps looked at each other.

'You're alive, I thought, I thought...' Neeps used her free hand to tenderly move a stray hair away from Joe's face. 'Are you okay? I tried to find you, but it was so hard to think or move. I'm so sorry. What happened?'

Joe seemed unmoved. He stared disinterestedly at her.

Neeps was still on her own personal love high, laughing and crying at the same time. 'I'm okay, it's okay.' She looked up at Ned and Jenni. 'They took me to the Palace and left me in a side room. I didn't know what was happening or where any of you were. I just knew I was so miserable I couldn't do anything.' She breathed in deeply.

'You might want to release their hands, Jenni, they'll probably need them before long.' He frowned at Joe who was still unresponsive, then turned to regard Willow's lushness hanging out the window. She was trailing vines. He nudged one with his foot until it was touching Joe's leg. Colour seemed to bleed back into him, and the life sparked in his eyes once more.

Ned smiled to himself. 'Thought so,' he murmured.

Jenni had been watching and nodded in approval. Willow turned from the window and squealed at seeing Joe back to his old self. She darted to his side and pointedly ignored the sour look on Neeps face. Joe was looking from one to the other, his Adam's apple bobbing alarmingly again. Ned decided to leave him to it.

'What about Sparks?' He tugged Jenni's coat arm. 'Any sign?'

Jenni looked at the still empty shelf. She had no idea where the little bug might be. They ran on light and happiness, so if all the happiness had been sucked away perhaps, they had to wait for it to return to normal before the light bugs came back. 'We should get out there, Boss, 'elp the others.'

Ned hauled Joe up from the floor, bringing Willow with him. 'Right you two, er three.' Neeps had bounced up to stand unbelievably close to Joe. 'We need to get out into the city and spread the love. Sounds hokey, I know, but in order for the Great Sadness to clear we've got to help everyone find their love.' They all stared at him. 'Look, I don't know how it works, it just does alright, so get out there and get it done.'

Chapter 22

Ned put Joe and Neeps on her street, the one that included *The Daily Blag* and any people working at the paper or rather anyone who had sunk into sadness whilst at work. Once done there, they were to start on the next street and keep going door to door making sure everyone they sorted out began doing the same. That way it would not take long to sort the city out. Ned and Jenni went back to the Druid Grove, he felt he owed that nun for doing what she could at such a difficult time. Besides he didn't particularly like any of his neighbours – they could wait for the general happiness sweep. Willow had rushed off to her orchard and thinking about how vibrant and ripe she was right now; Ned was fairly certain that anyone who looked at her would be cured. She positively radiated... well, something that most young men and women took as love. He stomped along, thinking back to what had happened with the Upper Circle or the Emperor or whoever the hell she was. They hadn't spoken at all; he had hugged her. Someone must have already helped her to find her love and she had taken a long time to recover. Yes, that was it. She was delicate or something.

They arrived at the Druid Grove and it was still dark

and quiet. They tried to find their way back to the room where they had seen all the sad cases but became a little muddled and ended up in the kitchens. There were some freshly baked honey cakes and cheese twists on the table. Ned's tummy rumbled loudly - he felt like he hadn't eaten in forever. There was a pitcher of milk as well. He gave in and sat down pouring himself a tumbler and stuffing several honey cakes in his mouth.

'What?' he muttered at a glare from Jenni, spraying crumbs everywhere. 'I'm starving.' He downed the milk and grabbed another handful of honey cakes to eat on the way, putting a handful of cheese twists in his pockets. Who knew how long it would be before he would get another meal? They wandered around a little more and then saw some flickering candlelight ahead. Pushing the doors open they found the druids and the nun. She was slumped in a corner, chin on hand, staring off into space. It looked like the sadness had finally claimed her. Jenni gestured for Ned to start helping people and he glared back, he still didn't understand exactly what it was he was supposed to do. He accidentally touched the foot of one of the young women laying nearby, she stirred and stretched becoming animated again. Blinking, she looked around in concern, 'What's happened?'

'It's a Great Sadness, 'e saved ya,' replied Jenni.

'But I didn't do anything,' muttered Ned to Jenni under his breath.

'Just lay 'ands, Boss.'

'Lay hands?'

'Yeah – touch 'em. Like you just did.'

'Okay Jenni, I'll touch them.' Ned shook his head and walked down one side of the room, hand out to the side, sweeping across the various bare feet that were poking out. As he walked by, each foot stirred, its owner waking up and realising they still had love in their hearts. Ned stepped back and stared in disbelief. How could his touch be having such a big effect? Jenni dragged him over to the other side, making him touch Sister Eustacia's hand as he passed. She came to with a beaming smile and a bustle and instantly began mothering the young druids who were waking up confused, hungry and in some cases naked. It's a druid thing.

Ned marched down the other side of the room, hand out, touching feet as he went. Thank goodness druids didn't wear shoes indoors otherwise it might have been a little awkward trying to find bare skin. The druids all stirred and came to.

'How is this possible Jenni? Are the others doing it like this?' asked Ned, a tinge of doubt in his voice.

'Naw, just you, Boss.' Jenni was grinning from ear to ear. 'You're in luv.'

'Love,' Ned spluttered. 'Love?' He began laughing a touch hysterically. 'You're way off there Jenni. Love – ha!' But when she had told him what she thought, the first thing that popped into his head was the Upper Circle in his arms and the unexpected tender feelings that had awakened within him.

They left Sister Eustacia in charge, she could sort out the doctrine issues later. To be honest, druidry was not massively popular and now that their High Priestess had been brutally murdered, it could be time to try out a new religion for a change. They could still dance naked in the moonlight, nothing but your own shame stops you from doing that.

As they walked, Ned felt peculiar emotions surging within him. He hadn't felt like this for... he hadn't felt this way since... he hadn't – he didn't bloody know how he felt except for confused as heck. All he knew was that whatever was happening to him seemed to be getting stronger and stronger. As he walked along, people recovered. The Great Sadness seemed to be literally melting away.

'Is this all me?'

'Some, Boss,' replied Jenni. 'Collective power is at work n'all. The more luv there is right, the more it grows. S'powerful really.'

'Right, let's head back to HQ. I need a drink.'

The Noose was rocking. Literally. There were so many people inside getting roaring drunk, singing and carousing that they were moving the wonky floorboards. Even Reg had a smile on his face and whilst he wasn't exactly singing, he was certainly humming enthusiastically along. A pity he was about five songs behind everyone else, but no one seemed to have noticed. Ned and Jenni pushed and shoved and squeezed their way to the stairwell, which was full of lazy revellers. You get them in every pub. They want to go out with their mates for a drink but all they really want to do is sit down somewhere that isn't home, with a beverage that isn't tea, and company that isn't their wife. You could do a roaring trade if you opened up front rooms for hire.

Ned couldn't be bothered with niceties anymore. He walked up the stairs, ignoring the various body parts he stepped on. Nothing popped or snapped so he figured he hadn't done any lasting damage and by the time he had made it to the top of the stairs, the lazy loungers at the bottom had forgotten they had been walked all over. Story of their life.

The office was quiet except for a well-known hum. It was Sparks – he was back, brighter and zippier than ever.

'Where you been, Sparks?' asked Ned, then he shook his head. 'Never mind, I can't be bothered to gear up. Go tell Jenni.'

There was a brief pause as Sparks flew dizzying loops around Jenni's head, creating a halo-like effect.

'E says 'e was 'ere the whole time but we couldn't see 'im cos 'e lost 'is light,' she reported.

'Fair enough.' Ned plopped down into the nearest chair and closed his eyes. It felt like a hundred years since he had last had a decent nights' sleep. Idly he began to wonder what the beds felt like in the Palace and whether they did have hot falling rain as well as baths big enough to swim in. He was beginning to enjoy his daydream when Jenni coughed. He sat up abruptly, colouring vividly and was about to shout about something or other when the rest of the catchers returned.

'I think everything's back to normal, Boss.' Willow was glowing radioactively, clearly, she was extremely pleased with herself. 'I helped at least seventeen fruit trees pollinate and there will be several brand-new blooming flower beds throughout the city in the morning. It's like spring has gone into overdrive. It feels so, so, alive!'

Joe and Neeps were nodding in tandem. She was holding his hand tightly, her eyes shining in happiness. Joe looked a little pale.

'Right you lot – shift's over. Go home. Take the rest of the day off. Let's recover from all this and then it'll be back to normal tomorrow.' Ned tried to settle back into his chair for some more daydreaming but everyone stayed where they were. He looked up at them annoyed. 'Didn't you hear me?'

161

'Erm, what about the usurper, Boss?' asked Jenni.

'Yeah – we need to do something about my sister.' Joe tried to look brave. 'Where is Brogan anyway?'

Before Ned could summon the energy to reply, there was a polite knock at the door and Fred, the Palace Guard, poked his head around the door.

'Oh good – you're here. I have a proclamation. And it's from the real one as well.' He came the rest of the way into the room, his plume tickling the ceiling. 'Uh-um. The honourable and rightful Emperor of Roshaven, *may he live for ever and ever*, has decreed that the Chief Thief-Catcher Ned Spinks may keep his neck from the noose for a period of twenty-four hours for successfully breaking the Great Sadness. However, the Rose-Thief has yet to be brought to justice and thrown down in chains.'

'She won't agree to that,' murmured Joe.

'Ahem,' Fred scowled at the interruption. 'The Emperor, *may he live for ever and ever*, requests the Chief Thief-Catcher's presence this evening to discuss how justice shall prevail.'

Jenni gave Ned several nudges and winks.

'Ah, that's the end of the message, but I'm to remind you that dinner is served at six and that you don't want to be late unless you mind making Ma Bowl cross and between you and me...'

'Yes, thank you, Fred,' replied Ned. 'Please tell the Emperor that I will be seeing her, er, him at dinner.'

Fred was looking at Ned with a pleading look on his face.

'Oh, may he live for ever and ever.'

'Great, thank you, Sir. See you later, Sir. Brilliant. Okay.' Fred trailed off as he and his plume made it out of the room and began to re-navigate the stairwell.

'Why do you keep calling the Emperor, *may he live for ever and ever*, her?' Willow twirled a strand of green hair around her finger, looking up at him through thick lashes, her deep, deep green eyes luring him in. Thank the gods for that hair charm.

'None of your beeswax,' retorted Ned. 'How long have I got?'

'Couple of hours, Boss,' replied Jenni.

'Right, I'm going home for a kip. You lot piss off. Back here tomorrow, first light.' He left them to sort themselves out - if they decided to spend the night in the office, that was their problem. He walked without seeing, feet taking him home on autopilot, thinking about what was going to happen later. Dinner with the Emperor. Would that mean full state function? Would the Highs be there? Could the Emperor appear at the same time as the Upper Circle? Surely a state dinner would mean all dignitaries so not only Lower Circle and Stalls but all the Guild Heads as well. Would he have to wear his posh uniform? He didn't think anyone actually knew what thief-catcher posh uniform looked like. To be fair no one probably knew what the everyday thief-catcher uniform looked like either - it was a relaxed dress code, giving them the ability to blend in. As much as a nymph, sprite, and firefly can blend. Realising he had made it home, Ned searched for something to drink, there was some ground something or other left over from Momma K's gift basket. He sniffed it warily and grinned. It was coffee. There was a good chance it had some ground beetle in there as well, but Ned wasn't going to dwell on that.

He got water on the boil then went to find his dress uniform. The boots were so stiff they creaked like mad when he tried to put them on. It was no good, they didn't fit. Too small and he didn't have time to try and widen the fit. His old faithfuls would have to do, a bit of spit and polish would do them the world of good. Pity he didn't have any polish. Ah well, spit clean it was then. He would wait until he had had his coffee. The trousers looked alright, if you could call them trousers. They looked more like skin-tight leggings and was that... yes, it was. A codpiece. Well, that wasn't happening. Special dinner or no special dinner. Ned looked down at the trousers he was wearing, they were, at best, filthy. He rummaged in his trunk; he was sure he had a fresh pair somewhere. Finding them eventually he pulled them out and remembered the roof chase they had done two months ago and that death-defying knee skid. Shame about the missing knees. Feeling thoroughly dispirited he decided against looking at the dress shirt and jacket. Thank the Gods he didn't have to worry about a stupid hat with plumes. No thief-catcher would ever be seen dead in plumes.

Going back to the kitchen, Ned was mulling over whether it was worth washing behind his ears or not when something caught his eye. There was a man hanging from the doorway. He started then realised it wasn't a man, it was a suit of clothes. Dark blue trousers, a crisp white shirt and dark blue waistcoat. It didn't look like thief-catcher clothes. He was going to be Ned. 'Thanks, Jenni,' he whispered. Right, where was that tin bath?

Chapter 23

Butterflies flooded Ned's stomach as he walked up to the Palace. He hadn't felt this nervous since... since... since ever. His hands had been shaking so much when he tried to shave, he had left it. The last thing he needed was a million little cuts all over his face or even worse those little pieces of tissue that you stuck on them to stop the bleeding then forget to take off. He had washed his hair, after all, it was a special occasion and he had been rather grimy. If he was completely honest with himself there had been a funky smell about it. He felt good, he hoped it wasn't going to be a state function, but if it was, he would eat and run. No harm, no foul.

Fred was posted at the entrance. He greeted Ned with a smart salute, nearly knocking himself out and grinning hugely as he accompanied Ned to the fourth floor. Ned frowned; he had forgotten about the usurper. Everything fell out of his head when he walked through the double doors. All the wives, children, and maids of various stature lined the walkway from the door to the side room he had seen the Emperor in earlier. No one said a word but there was a lot of smiling, winking and a few catcalls. Someone pinched his bottom. Ned focused on putting one foot in front of the other. He felt like a prize bull on show.

As he entered the side room, he was surprised by the transformation. Gone were all signs of the drunkenness, the Great Sadness, the bathtub, and the Highs. Instead, candles flickered all over the room creating warm and cosy lighting. Ned could smell the Emperor's spicy, warm perfume with those delicious hints of caramel. He breathed in deeply. She was standing by the fireside, her dark hair hanging down, wearing a simple blue silk dress that perfectly complemented his own attire. She smiled nervously and took half a step towards him. At that moment a servant swept in with glasses of champagne for them both. Ned took them and walked over to the fireplace.

'You look beautiful,' he said, handing her a glass.

'Thank you. So do you. I mean, handsome.'

Ned smiled and drank some bubbles. 'How do you feel?'

'I'm fine now. Thank you for everything you did.'

'It was nothing.'

They lapsed into an awkward silence, both racking their brains for something to say. The silence stretched on and on - Ned was beginning to think this whole thing was a bad idea when servants swept in again. This time with their first course. They sat wordlessly down at a small table. He looked at the perfect face in-front of him. Her face was heart shaped with beautiful big brown eyes and a faint sprinkling of freckles over her nose. Her mouth was a delicate pink, lips not too large or too small, laughter lines crinkling as she smiled to herself watching him, watching her. He flushed and knocked the salt cellar over.

'Sorry,' he muttered.

'It's alright. This is a bit awkward, isn't it?'

Ned nodded. He inspected the plate in front of him. Ma Bowl had outdone herself. Potato skins loaded with bacon and cheese, artfully arranged on the plate with a splodge of BBQ sauce for dipping. His favourite. Tucking in with gusto he decided to tackle the elephant in the room.

'Why the subterfuge?' he asked thickly, forgetting his manners in hunger.

'Which one?' The Emperor was eating delicately - clearly, she'd never tackled potato skins before.

'Okay, why are you pretending to be the Emperor?'

'I am the Emperor.'

'So why be the Upper Circle?'

She sighed. 'It's restricting to be Emperor all the time. As Upper Circle at least I can force policy through the bureaucratic chain. As Emperor all I ever get are nods and smiles before everyone goes and does the same as they always have.'

'Why pretend to be a man? Why not just be the Empress and force change?'

The Emperor arched a brow at him. 'It's not as straightforward as it might seem. For instance, would you bow down to a woman?'

'Well, I, er, don't have a preference, to be honest.' Ned's ears began to turn pink. 'I don't have much to do with people in high places.'

'I can see.' Ned's plate was empty, BBQ sauce smeared over it and he was licking his fingers in enjoyment. The cutlery lay to the side of his plate untouched. The Emperor smiled and touched her napkin to her lips. Reacting to this signal the servants reappeared and swept the finished plates away from them.

'Not a fan?' Ned was worried, did she not eat?

167

'I asked Ma Bowl to prepare a meal you would enjoy. After all, I invited you.'

Ned was beginning to feel like he was under a microscope, being scrutinised, weighed and evaluated. He didn't think he was going to measure up. He decided to change the subject.

'What happened to the er, previous Emperor?' He was about to say real but caught the flash of temper in his dinner partners' eyes and swiftly changed his mind.

'My father? He passed away peacefully. He had been ill for a long time. I had been covering for him, so it was natural that I continued.'

'Are there no other heirs?'

'He had all his sons killed at birth.'

'How very... imperial of him.' Ned didn't know what to say, he had heard the rumours of course but to have it confirmed, and so calmly, by a survivor was surprising.

'All Roshaven's Emperors choose one heir to succeed them. Any others are deemed superfluous. Luckily, I was chosen.'

'So who are all the other children I saw running around?' Ned was curious.

'My father tired of his wives quickly. They were free to dally and procreate once he'd moved on. He was a kind man.'

Ned snorted. 'Apart from the filicide.'

'Yes, well. We all have difficult roles to play.' The Emperor replied crisply.

Another uncomfortable silence fell as the servants bought the next course. Pie and mash with thick gravy. Ned felt like he had died and gone to heaven. The Emperor looked at the carb stack in front of her and swallowed. 'Where are the vegetables?'

'Depends on the pie. Let's have a look.' Ned cut into

the golden pastry, releasing a plume of steam and the delicious aroma of steak and kidney. 'Sorry your 'Ness. Meat pie, no veggies.' He was grinning, somehow, he had started to enjoy himself. He piled his fork high and began eating. The Emperor watched him, amusement dancing in her eyes before she too tucked in. This was different from her usual fare and she liked it.

'So, what's your name?' Ned asked.

'I'm sorry?'

'You know mine. I can't call you Empress all the time. Can I?'

She smiled. 'I think it's my turn for questions. Why thief-catching?'

Ned shrugged. 'I've got a nose for trouble. Not causing it, finding it. I tried lots of other things but kept finding the dishonest apprentice or discovering defective goods sold at a premium. It was fate. I worked the night shift for a long time before my predecessor met with his end.'

'That wasn't my fault.'

'I never said it was.' Ned waited for an explanation.

'He was rude to the Highs. They executed him before I could step in.'

'He was a knob,' Ned shrugged. 'No love lost.'

The Emperor put her knife and fork down but motioned for Ned to continue. She twirled her wine glass around in her hands, the candlelight catching at the crystal making rainbows dance.

'Ever been married?' she asked idly.

'Yes.'

'And?'

'I don't want to talk about it. You?'

She laughed; it was like beautiful music piercing his soul. 'My father tried to find me a suitor before he fell ill, but thankfully he didn't get far. There aren't many suitable candidates for an Emperor.'

'Will you reveal yourself?' asked Ned.

'I don't know. I need to get rid of the imposter first before the rest of the city finds out.'

'Which is what I'm here for.'

'Partly. Let's have dessert first.' She inclined her head a particular way and the servants came rushing back in to clear the plates.

'How do they see that? Is it magic?'

'Imperial secrets.' She was laughing at him now, eyes dancing, cheeks flushed, lips parted. Ned felt a sudden desire to lean over and kiss her. Dessert stopped him. Ma Bowl had won his stomach forever. Before him, in a delicate chocolate bowl was a slice of her famous tiramisu. It was so delicious she only made it once a year. There had been fights over this legendary dessert and now she had made it for her Emperor. To have with him.

'Oh, my favourite.' The Emperor was delighted.

'Mine too.' They locked eyes and smiled, sharing a moment and for the first time that evening the chasm between them didn't seem so wide. They did not speak as they ate the delicious dessert. After all, when you have finally made it through the boring courses to the finale, the thing you only came out to eat in the first place, who wants to talk through it? Dessert should be savoured and enjoyed to its fullest because that second slice is never as good as the first. Ever.

It didn't take long for it to be over. They both found every single scrap of dessert within their bowls, then Ned threw caution to the wind and lifted the bowl with his hands before taking a large bite. The Emperor giggled, then did the same. The bowls melted quickly, and they ended up with chocolatey fingers and mouths.

'If the Highs could see me now.' The Emperor inclined her head again and servants bought warm water and towels for them both.

'Do they know you're you?'

'Yes, but they don't know who the Upper Circle is. I have a double who can act for me at state events. She is well protected and compensated.' The Emperor rose and moved over to where two chairs sat closer to the fire, she sat gracefully waiting for Ned to follow.

'I need this imposter gone, Ned.'

'I know.'

'Do you have a plan?'

Ned thought for a moment. 'Brogan.'

'What is a Brogan?'

'He's her love,' Ned explained. 'She sent him to the middle of nowhere with the rose so that love would die. That's what caused the Great Sadness. Jenni took us there so I could get him and bring him back. I lost track of him when we came back here. He was helping others find their love but I'm not sure where he went.'

'You mean the barbarian?'

'Yes, have you've seen him?' asked Ned.

'He's in the dungeon.'

Ned stared at her in disbelief. 'Why?'

'There was a hulking barbarian in my chambers. I wasn't sure why he was here – I'd found out I lov... I mean, I'd been, you'd...'

Ned grinned. 'I'd hugged you.'

'Yes. That's it.' The Emperor's cheeks were rosy. 'Anyway, you ran out of here before I could talk to you about anything and he was mingling with my wives, so I panicked. He's been well treated.'

'I bloody hope so, otherwise, he might be disinclined

to help us.'

'He can be persuaded.'

'You can't persuade love, Empress. It just is.'

They gazed at each other, the flickering flames of the fire dancing in their eyes. He was the first to look away. She turned as if hearing a commotion and Brogan came rumbling into the room.

'Ned!' he boomed. 'Tell her I'm on your side. I want to share the love.'

'It's okay Brogan, you're free to go.' Ned reassured him. 'Well, you're not actually free to go, I need you to help me sort out Mia but other than that you are a free man.'

'I love her, you know?'

'I know you do, pal, I know you do.'

'What exactly is your plan, Thief-Catcher?' The Emperor was gone, the Upper Circle sat next to Ned. He had been so distracted with Brogan's entrance that he hadn't noticed her put her enormous headdress on. To be honest, he hadn't even noticed it was anywhere in the room. Had she used magic? He knew the Upper Circle had some power; she was a truth-catcher after all. But as the Emperor she couldn't use it in public. Emperors were not allowed to be magical. He decided not to dwell on it right now, he had had enough things he couldn't explain happen today. A headache loomed behind his eyes.

'Brogan, if I provide magical cover, do you think you could convince Mia to stand down?' Ned asked.

'I love her.'

'I know you do. The question is does she love you back?'

'She sent me away, but I know she didn't mean it. If I could just talk to her,' pleaded Brogan. 'I love her so much.'

It was like trying to talk to a broken record and not a good one at that.

'Let's hope he manages to wear her down with his undying love and not whip her into a greater fury.' The Upper Circle looked at Ned with eyes full to the brim with unspoken emotion. 'Is there anything more I can do?'

He wanted to say yes. He wanted to ask her to throw down these disguises and run away with him to some secluded bedroom where they could properly get to know each other. He fought down the urge to kiss her passionately. What had been in that dessert? Mentally shaking himself, he spoke rather hoarsely. 'Is she still in the throne room?'

The Upper Circle let out a small sigh of disappointment before nodding. Ned half bowed to her and pulled Brogan along with him, out of the room.

'Pull yourself together man,' Ned snapped. 'She wants a hero, not a snivelling wreck.'

Brogan blew his nose loudly on some unidentifiable piece of fabric which vanished back into his breastplates. He buffed his armour as well as he could striding along and used wet fingers to muss his hair the way she liked it. 'Be honest, Ned, do I smell?' he asked.

'Singularly. But we don't have time to deal with that. Hopefully, she likes overripe barbarian.'

Leaving the fourth floor felt like ripping a plaster off his most tender parts. All Ned wanted to do was run back to his Emperor and declare his passionate love. As they pushed the doors open, an unidentifiable maid grabbed Ned's arm and slipped a piece of paper into his hand. He looked down in surprise. The paper smelled of her perfume and in beautiful script were the following words – *My name is Fourteen*. Ned's heart ached, that wasn't a name. It was a number, her heir number. Which meant thirteen brothers and sisters were murdered before her and countless others removed after her. He tried to push his compassion aside and focus on the task ahead, he needed a clear head. He was there to provide magical protection for Brogan against a warlock whom, so far had been unstoppable. He felt his power wells, they weren't bad, but he didn't have any extra juice. Then he spotted a familiar face lurking between two statues.

'Jenni.' Ned was relieved.

'Boss. Fawt you could do wiv a power surge.'

'Excellent timing, as always.'

The sprite beamed and joined the unlikely heroes as they walked to the main throne room. It was rather dark and decidedly empty within, but Jenni pointed to the throne which, although shrouded in shadow, seemed to have a bundle of something upon it. The bundle stirred and came undone.

'I said I didn't want to be disturbed.'

'Mia?' Brogan's voice broke.

'Brogan? Is it really you? How?'

'I came back for you. I love you, I...' He couldn't finish as she flew down the steps and launched herself at him sobbing incoherently and clutching at his large body. The smell didn't seem to bother her in the slightest.

Ned felt slightly put out, after all, it had been a joint effort coming back from the middle of nowhere and if he and Jenni hadn't gone there in the first place, Brogan would still be there. Jenni was lighting the candles in the room, so Ned focused his ire on the fireplace and lit it with a giant whoomp. The flames burnt bright green for the first few seconds before returning to their normal hue. It caught the attention of the reunited lovers and

174

Ned flexed his magical fingers, ready to do battle if need be.

The door burst open and in ran Joe.

'Joe? What are you doing here?' Ned asked.

'Don't hurt my sister! We can work something out – she didn't mean it.'

'She killed the High Priestess and Two-Face Bob, Joe. She's facing murder charges even if we let everything else go.'

'And she doesn't appreciate being spoken to like the cat's mother,' Mia interrupted icily. 'Joseph, pull yourself together. Now that you're here, I'm more than a match for this catcher and his imp.' Mia scowled at them all.

'Sprite,' Ned said.

'Sorry?'

'She's a sprite, she doesn't like it when people get it wrong.' Ned explained.

'Whatever. Now that my brother is here, my magic is amplified, and I doubt the two of you would be able to overpower me.'

'Mia – don't.' Brogan pleaded with big barbarian eyes, one hand on her arm, the other on his heart. Ned seriously thought he might start batting his eyelashes soon.

'Brogan, you don't understand. It's out of my hands. I have no choice.'

'Who do you work for?' Ned was beginning to see a way out of this mess.

'How did you know?' Mia was startled, she half looked behind her as if expecting her mysterious boss to be standing there.

'Just tell me.'

Mia licked her lips and shot a look at her brother who was frowning at her. 'My father. I'm working for

175

my father.'

'But he died... he's dead. Mother told us...'

'Mother fed us a pack of lies to keep us away from him. He's not dead, he left her. He left us.' Mia's voice wobbled but she took strength from Brogan's hand which had now encircled her own. 'I never believed her, so I went looking for him. I found him experimenting in the Purple Mountain. But he was trapped there. I wanted to make him proud, so I agreed to be his apprentice and help him escape.' She gave a half laugh. 'He made me the warlock I am today.'

'So you admit you are responsible for the murder of Two-Face Bob and the High Priestess?' Ned asked.

'No.' Mia shook her head. 'That wasn't me. Believe me or not but I swear I didn't kill them. My father released the wraith that killed Two-Face and used me to steal power from the druid vigil. I'm his conduit.'

'I'm not sure that absolves you of all wrongdoing,' Ned said.

'I know,' Mia replied quietly.

Joe was frowning. 'But, but, I followed you. You pulled me along. This whole time you never said anything about it to me.'

'I couldn't. I took an oath of secrecy, but it looks like the Great Sadness broke its hold.' She flexed her fingers and looked around in startled wonder. 'I can't feel him. I'm free of his chains.' The wonderment quickly fled her face. 'We need to leave now. He wanted an update; he'll be here soon. I was meant to hand this empire over to him. If we go, this very second, we might be lucky.'

'Lucky enough for what?' A tall, thin man had walked unnoticed into the throne room. His aura radiated so much power that even those who could not read such things were intensely aware of his deadliness. Black eyes bore out from under thick black eyebrows as the man evaluated everyone in the room. He dismissed Ned immediately. Free from his attention, Ned motioned for Jenni, who was half-hidden behind him and had not yet been noticed, to make a sharp exit so she discreetly popped. The man's head whipped back at the use of fae magic and frowned at Ned suspiciously.

'Is this how show your respect?'

Mia fell to her knees and prostrated herself on the floor. Thinking that it might be a good idea to emulate the second most powerful person in the room, Brogan and Ned followed suit. Joe looked as if he had seen a ghost.

'Who are these unworthy souls, my child?'

'No one Father. Just vassals coming to the end of their usefulness. I was about to discharge their services.'

'Allow me.' The sorcerer raised one hand, a spark of power glinting from the tip of his finger.

'NO!' Mia exclaimed then tried to smooth over her reaction. 'They have given faithful service. I wish to retain them for any future works.'

'Are you sure? I feel certain more worthy worms could be found if you spread your net a little further.'

'Yes, Father. I am sure.'

'Very well – dismissed.'

And before Ned knew what was happening, an unseen force had pushed him, Brogan, and Joe out of the throne room and dumped them unceremoniously in the corridor outside. Brogan had a broken puppy dog look on his face. Ned grabbed his arm before he could try and do anything more stupid than fall in love with a psychotic sorcerer's daughter and dragged both him and a catatonic Joe away.

'Let's get out of here. We need a better plan.'

Chapter 24

Joe finally came to in Ned's kitchen. If he was surprised to find himself there again, he gave no sign. He stared down at the peanut butter and banana sandwich in front of him. Ma Bowl had dropped off a little something for Ned to keep his strength up. There was rather a lot of little somethings, most of them fattening, some of them aphrodisiacs.

'That was my dad.' Joe sounded stunned.

'Yeah, we met him. Seemed like a lovely chap.' Ned was eyeing up the corner of an apple turnover that peeked out from the hamper on the table, hoping no one else had noticed it was there.

'No. You don't understand,' Joe said. 'He died fifteen years ago. In a fire. He was trying to rescue his grimoire. It was horrible.'

'Looks like he made a full recovery. You two not hungry?' Ned looked hopefully from Brogan to Joe, they both shook their heads. Each one preoccupied with his own heartache. 'Excellent.' Ned rubbed his hands together in glee. If you have never been fortunate enough to have one of Ma Bowl's legendary apple turnovers then it would take about four chapters to explain to you how mouth-wateringly delicious they are and how very, very rarely she bakes them. Ned began to have paroxysms of ecstasy, lost in a heaven of pastry, cream and apple. Secret spice? Ginger. Who knew?

Ned's moans finally brought the others out of their respective funks. Mostly because it sounded like he was having a one-man orgy and neither Brogan nor Joe felt like being present at such an event.

'If that was my father, then Mia must be working for him under duress,' Joe said.

'And nothing she did was her fault,' Brogan grinned. 'We can rescue her, pardon her and love her forever.'

'I wonder what he has over her, to make her do what he wants. She never does what anyone else wants – ever.'

'And she still loves me. Can you believe how lucky I am?'

'I can't believe she never told me about him. I've been following her all over the place and for what? She didn't even tell him about me!'

'I need to make a good impression. I need to ask him for her hand in marriage, it's the right thing to do.'

'I need to speak to him,' they chorused.

Ned sat back in his chair, amusement flitting around all over his face. He looked like the cat that got the cream and judging by the crumbs on the table before him, he certainly had. All of it.

'Boys, we do nothing tonight,' Ned said. 'Let's sleep on what we know and regroup tomorrow. If this guy is more powerful than Mia, we need to make sure we're fully loaded.'

'But he's my father, I have the right to speak to him.' Joe objected.

'He may have sired you, kid, but he's not your father and from the looks of things he wants nothing to do with you.' Ned glanced at Brogan. 'And as for you, Cupid, cool your heels a little. She loves you; you love her. What could possibly go wrong?'

They both looked glumly at Ned, but he didn't care, he was riding the sugar high of his life. Who cared about the withdrawal headache of tomorrow? This was better than beer, better than smokes, better than – well probably not better than that, but he was so out of practice, for now, it was the best thing that had happened to him in a good long while. He showed the others the spare room. It had two pallets available, so they didn't have to top and tail. Ned sat on the edge of his own bed and kicked his boots off with abandonment, not caring where they fell or what they broke. He flopped backwards into his bed and was asleep within seconds. Dreaming of Fourteen and how pretty she looked in candlelight.

Mia trembled in the throne room. She hadn't thought her father would ever be able to physically follow her here. Yet here he seemed to be. Had he finally managed to escape his prison? Did that mean he didn't need the red rose anymore? Which would be great, seeing as she had lost it.

Get the rose of love. It had seemed like such a straightforward errand. But on the way here Brogan had been a stupid oaf and allowed himself to be sweet-talked by that floozy of a doxie. Well, she wouldn't be sweet talking anyone anymore. Mia had pulled her tongue out of her mouth. With a pair of pliers. She didn't know whether the woman would live, and she didn't care. She had been so angry that when she arrived in Roshaven, she had decided to have some fun first. If only she had stolen the red rose her father had asked for in the first place. Now she had to try and explain that she had lost it.

It must have cost her father magically to be here, he had never left his prison before. She peered at him sideways, trying to gauge his wells but as always, he was impervious to her senses. Something to do with the family bloodline.

'How long are you planning to stay?' She asked nervously.

Her father was pacing around the throne room. 'I like what you've done here. Finally consolidated a position of power. It was forward thinking, a little out of your league but you show promise. However misguided your initial thought process was, the fruits of your labour will bear greatness. Have you destroyed the Emperor?'

'No, the refuge is still warded. I've been dealing with... something else.'

'You have failed to kill the person you are pretending to be. Did you learn nothing in Canva?'

Mia flushed. That had not been her fault. It had been her first kill and the girl had been so gentle and naïve, she hadn't been able to go through with it. She had spent several weeks in the box for refusing to carry out that order and she had no idea whether the fragile girl still lived. Probably not.

'The Emperor is powerfully warded. I was building up a counterspell when things got sidetracked.'

'You refer of course to sending the hulking barbarian, who is hopelessly in love with you, to the middle of nowhere.'

'Yes, Father.' *Dammit* she thought. She had hoped he wouldn't have noticed.

'I felt the Great Sadness across the miles. It was a good try but lacked the proper power base. Do you know why you failed?'

Mia shook her head. It looked like her father was on

a lecturing ramble rather than a punishment jaunt so she tried to look as interested as possible while thinking furiously about what she could do to rectify the situation.

'True love has blossomed here. A powerful magic that cannot be swayed by anything we might try. A pity you didn't lay plague to everyone when you arrived. Still, I'm sure you thought your methods adequate. Tell me, do you still have the rose of love?'

'No, Father.'

The sorcerer's eyes narrowed. 'Where is it?'

'I sent it to the middle of nowhere.'

'Then I should send you to go fetch it.' He lifted a hand menacingly.

'It's too late, someone already went.' Mia broke in hurriedly. 'They returned bringing back love and breaking the Great Sadness. I assume the rose was destroyed in the process.'

'You should never assume anything, child.' The sorcerer began pacing. 'Who are these star crossed lovers that broke the Great Sadness? Something like that takes power. Power I can use.'

'The Emperor and the thief-catcher.'

'If you had killed your quarry in the first place instead of wasting your time building a popular rogue in the papers, our mission would have already succeeded. Now we have true love to deal with.'

'Yes, Father.'

'Luckily for you, I did not need this pathetic rose specifically. My goal was to use its power of love. True love, however, that power will sustain me indefinitely and I can finally leave my prison for good.'

Mia watched as her father began to flicker. His spell was weakening. She tried to hide her surprise; she had honestly thought he was here in flesh not projected in spirit. It had been a powerful projection; he had opened the doors. She tried not to show the relief coursing through her veins, she still had time to get out of here. To run as far and as fast as she could and save Roshaven in the process.

'Do not think of running, my child. We are blood. I will find you. You can tell your brother that I look forward to reacquainting myself with his gifts when I see him next. He not only boosts you but his father as well, a useful tool to have in times of need. We must be cautious we don't drain him too early.'

Mia swallowed and bowed her head. There was no getting out of this situation for any of them. All she could do was try to warn those involved and suffer the consequences.

'You will send the Emperor and the thief-catcher to me. I shall not trust their deaths to you.' He waved a hand and the image of her mother suspended in a cage appeared. Mia's heart ached as she looked at how thin and frail her mother had become. The woman in the cage began coughing, a deep wracking sound that seemed to tear her apart. Blood flecked her lips as she fought for breath. The image disappeared. 'If you want to keep your worthless mother alive, I suggest you do what I say. Or would the loss of one of your own limbs be more motivating?'

'Yes Father, I mean, no Father, that's not necessary. I will send the Emperor and the thief-catcher to you. I just need a little time.'

'You have one week. If they are not with me by then, your mother dies and you lose an arm.' He smiled warmly. 'I'll let you decide which one.'

With that he faded from view, his borrowed power source completely drained. Mia tried not to think what that might have been. An unsuspecting fae more than likely. She hoped it had only been one. What adrenalin there had been coursing through her body had run out and she collapsed in a heap, sobbing. There was no way out. She had to do what he said. She had to.

Chapter 25

Joe slept fitfully; he couldn't stop thinking about his sister. He could feel her emotional pain and he wanted to go to her side and make everything better, but he was scared of his father. How was he alive? That fire had been all-consuming, they had lost everything and lived in near poverty since. Their mother had never allowed them to use their magic for personal gain, she had always commented darkly on the corruption of spirit that using magic caused. It was one of the reasons Mia had left home at fifteen and why Joe had reluctantly been dragged along. Where possible, he fixed the things she broke but he could do nothing for the High Priestess she had apparently killed. He was worried his sister's soul was now broken beyond repair. At least she still showed a little love and compassion - she hadn't let their father kill him, Ned or Brogan. Fed up with tossing and turning for what felt like forever, he got up. Brogan's pallet was empty. Joe headed downstairs cautiously, girding himself for an argument.

'Morning sleepy-head.' Ned had absolutely no idea why, but he was feeling cheerful. Seeing as happiness had decided to try and start the day off, he thought he'd go with it and enjoy the experience.

'Morning,' muttered Joe. Brogan was sitting with an enormous stack of pancakes in front of him. Despite everything, his tummy rumbled in anticipation and it was with pathetic gratitude that he slid into an empty chair and accepted a similarly piled plate.

'It's the only thing I can cook,' Ned said as way of explanation. The three men sat in harmonious silence while they methodically polished off their respective stacks. 'So, what's the plan?' Ned asked, scraping his plate clean.

'I need to help my sister.'

'I must save Mia.'

'Thought so. I think we ought to go and speak to her again but with a little firepower in our corner this time,' Ned said.

The men all turned as a huge bang reverberated in the kitchen. Jenni and Momma K appeared. Momma K looked even smaller and more delicate than she did in her own realm.

'Ya owe me big fo' dis, boy,' she said.

'Yes, Momma K.'

'Where me suga'?'

Joe thought Ned was going to kiss the diminutive sprite but instead, he reverently placed a large sugar bowl in front of her. The fae glowed with pleasure and settled herself in front of the sugar cubes. She may or may not have been eating them. It was difficult to tell without staring and Joe felt that staring might not be the best idea. He vaguely remembered his time in Momma K's realm and that she was not a person, individual, fae, to be crossed lightly.

Once everyone had eaten their fill, they filed out of Ned's odd little house. 'Shall we walk or pop?' Ned

186

deferred to Momma K. She appraised them as if weighing up their usefulness then closed her eyes. Great, thought Joe, she's doing a diva. But then he realised, they were in the throne room. Just like that. No pop, no noise, no disorientation. Whoa. His next thought fell out of his head and he ran to the heap on the floor.

'Mia? Are you okay? Talk to me!' Joe grabbed one of her hands.

Brogan was a millisecond behind Joe and had Mia's other hand in his, stroking it gently and whispering messages of love in her general direction. Mia groaned slightly and woke, taking her hands away from both of them and pushed herself up to sitting.

'What are you doing back here?' she asked.

'Making sure you're okay,' began Brogan but Joe cut across him angrily.

'Who was that, Mia? I thought Dad was dead. You said he died. Why didn't you tell me about him? What are you doing with him? What is going on?'

Mia smiled faintly but before she had time to answer, Momma K threw a powerful jolt of magic into her and lifted her upside-down in the air.

'What? What are you doing? Put me down!' Mia yelled.

Joe and Brogan leapt up, shouting recriminations which suddenly disappeared as Momma K silenced their voice boxes.

'Chil', wha' darkness ya playing?' asked Momma K. 'Dere is evil here, spreading, like cancer. It know ya but it's no define ya. It's dark, dark, dark and it took de life of one o' mine.' She paused, sniffing the air. 'Maybe more dan one. Speak.'

'It's my father, not me. He is trapped in a magical prison, but by using the blood of fae he can project for a

187

short while.' Mia looked desperately at Ned. 'But now that true love has blossomed in the kingdom, he says can use that to free himself, forever.'

Momma K turned to look at Ned with sadness in her eyes.

'What? Why are you looking at me?' asked Ned.

'Me poor sweet chil'. We got to stop dis.' She gestured and Mia fell back to the floor, luckily Brogan's instincts were ready, and he caught her. They smiled tentatively at each other.

'We've got to stop him, right? We can stop him, can't we?' Joe looked at the people in the room hopefully. 'She never meant to do all these things - he made her. Didn't he Mia? Tell them.'

'It's complicated.' Mia looked nervous, unsure of her audience.

'I suggest you un-complicate it, fast.' Ned was in no mood for being given the run-around. His feet hurt.

'Right, okay then. Short version,' Mia said. 'I didn't believe Mum when she said he'd died in the fire. I remembered Father saying that any warlock who couldn't survive the gentle tickle of flames didn't deserve to wield magic, so I performed a locator spell. It was a weak signal, but I kept following it as best as I could until I found him.'

'Where?' Joe's voice was small, and he looked lost.

'It's not important. He wasn't pleased to see me, in fact, he sent me away. Said I would interfere with his work. I was devastated. All I ever wanted was to be as powerful a warlock as he was. I just wanted to make him proud. Then something happened. I don't know what, but he disappeared, and the locator stopped working. I bummed around for a bit before I started to get these weird dreams of Father calling out to me. Eventually, I realised he was.'

'Was what?' Ned was watching Mia closely for any signs she was concealing the truth.

'Calling me. He was trapped in his prison. It's in the Purple Mountains, somewhere. I'm not sure where.'

'Ya say dis, chil' but me tink ya lying.' Momma K's eyes were flashing, a bad sign.

'I'm not, I swear it. He has only ever given me instructions to do other things. He wanted me to get him things. Small things at first, then larger and larger items. He's trying to free himself from the prison.'

'Do you know how he got trapped in there?' asked Ned.

'No.'

'But I do,' Joe said. 'It was me, I did it.'

Mia laughed a touch hysterically. 'How could you possibly trap our Father?'

'I read a spell from his grimoire'

Mia scoffed. 'The grimoire burnt in the fire.'

'No, it didn't. I had it. When the fire started.'

'Where is it now?' Mia reached her hands out aggressively as if Joe would be able to produce the book there and then. The whole room fell silent, even Momma K's eyes were weighing up how useful the grimoire might be, in her hands.

'I, I, I, I'm not telling,' Joe stammered. 'It's a bad book for doing bad things and you can't be trusted. Neither of you.'

'Aargh! You stupid idiot!' Mia threw her hands up. 'If we give the grimoire back to him, he won't need me anymore, and I'll be free to get on with my life.' She glared at her brother. 'And get Mum away from him.'

'What do you mean? Get Mum away from him? She's at home, isn't she?'

'No. She's his prisoner. Why do you think I'm doing all this? This isn't the person I want to be you know.' Mia was glaring at her brother who stared back at her disbelieving.

'We have to save her. We have to get her back,' Joe said in a small voice.

'Yes, we do. And get away from all of... this!' Mia gestured around her in disgust at the throne room.

'Sounds like an excellent idea to me.' The Upper Circle had appeared.

How does she do that? wondered Ned and hoped his ears weren't pink. Every muscle in his body wanted to run over to her and fold her into his arms but he restrained himself with a nod in her direction. Between equals. She didn't respond.

'I suggest we give the sorcerer what he wants so I can be rid of you once and for all.' The Upper Circle looked around the room. 'The Emperor, *may he live for ever and ever*, wishes to continue his imperial rule of Roshaven in peace.'

'We all know, you know.' Mia was smiling sweetly.

'Know what?' asked the Upper Circle.

'That you're the Emperor and he's you,' replied Mia.

The Upper Circle stood completely still for several moments before gracefully lifting the enormous headdress off her head. 'Thank goodness for that, it's hard to see in this thing,' she said calmly. 'You killed my subjects and stole my property. Thief-Catcher – arrest her.'

Ned was inwardly cursing. 'Now isn't the best time, Your Grace. We need her to help us stop her father. Then she can pay for her crimes.'

'Crimes I didn't commit!' Mia snapped.

'Me see to it, dat she pay. Believe.' Momma K was

190

appraising the revealed Emperor with frank approval. She was a big fan of strong female leaders. She performed a complex spell and silver spirals shot out of her fingertips and sank into Mia's skin. It burned with a satisfying sizzle. After Mia's screams had finished Momma K explained herself. 'Dis will anchor her to us. She will no get far. Her so-called magic has been bound.'

'So we're doing this? We're going to try and stop a psychotic sorcerer.' Ned glanced around the room.

'It's not like you've got anything else to do next week.' The Emperor, Fourteen, was smiling at Ned.

'Fine, but we need a good plan and I pick the people,' he replied. The room erupted as everyone began arguing who should go and what they should do when they got there.

Momma K solved that problem. She threw a silencio spell at everyone as well as sticky glue which meant everyone was stuck in an odd posture. No one could move anything apart from their eyeballs and every set of those was staring daggers at Momma K.

'Me doh have time for dis – ya gotta move. Big magic man tink he in charge. Well, he no. No one in charge of fae and no one ride de magic for nottin'. Skinny boy,' Momma K pointed at Joe. 'Ya will take dem to de grimoire, no question. Who else? Barbarian can carry.' She hawked and spat loudly as she looked at Mia. 'Chil' of evil. Ya go but bound, no magics fo' ya. Jenni look to ya. Thief-Catcher, ya in love, boy. It's true and strong. He needs it but I woh ask ya to risk it. Boy, it ya choice. It precious and powerful but if ya lose it, it gone for good.' Her gaze and voice softened. 'Me can' no protect you.' She released the spell, there was a whoosh of air from everyone, but no one spoke.

Ned looked at Fourteen. 'What do you want to do?'

he asked her.

'I want my empire back.'

Ned looked back at Momma K. 'We're in.'

Momma K nodded in satisfaction. 'Me give ya what me can, chil', but me no join dis quest. Me realm needs me presence to survive. Jenni will be me link to ya. She speaks for me.'

Jenni swelled with pride under the scrutiny. It wasn't well known that she was one of Momma K's favoured children. It was the reason she was so powerful.

Momma K came and spoke to each person, doling out power where she could. It was a different magic to that Ned was used to, raw and full of a life of its own. It sparked and leapt under his touch, rippling with pleasure at the chance to be used. It was difficult not to be tempted.

When she came to Mia, Momma K scowled at her then her expression softened, and she placed a hand on Mia's head. 'Chil', ya bin used poorly. In dis, he is no father. Me release ya from he chains and bind ya magic, transferring it to Jenni. In time, when ya earned it, yo power will return. But chil', ya have atoning to do.'

Tears streamed down Mia's face, she looked younger and more innocent. Joe and Brogan both rushed to her side and she accepted their hugs gratefully. Jenni flexed her magical muscles and red stars shot out of her fingers; this was a different kind of magic than she was used to. The warlock power fought for a moment with her fae magic, but it was a short battle. Silvery swirls glowed along the length of Jenni's arms and the red stars gradually faded, becoming pale pink sparkles in the silver swirls.

Fourteen and Ned stood close together. His power wells were thrumming, he had never felt so charged.

'What happens now?' she asked.

'We go on this quest and win the day I suppose,' Ned replied. 'Are you allowed time off for this sort of thing?'

Fourteen smiled. 'The Highs will see to it that everything carries on as normal. They're very good at that. I will have to deal with things when I get back, though. I mean, now that everyone knows.'

'Yeah, you'll have to come clean to the rest of the city I suppose,' Ned said.

'Do you think people will judge me harshly?'

'It's quite a big secret.'

'It's not like the Highs don't have secrets of their own,' objected Fourteen.

'Yeah but nothing like this.'

'Don't flatter yourself. Ma Bowl and the High Right have been caught canoodling on three different occasions.'

'What are you talking about?' asked Ned.

'What are *you* talking about?' asked Fourteen.

'You declaring yourself a female Emperor,' he replied.

'Our ... relationship?' she countered.

'Oh,' they both chimed and coloured slightly. 'I'm sure it will be alright.' They continued to speak in unison and then laughed. Both of them felt unstoppable, the way you do when that first flush of love hits you. You can do anything, conquer anyone and are more in love with each other than anyone has ever been before in the history of all time. No one ever had a love like yours. That is until your first argument and then love is rubbish and what kind of idiot ever thought of it in the first place.

Chapter 26

It was never going to work. Even if it was one of those million-to-one plans. There were too many ifs. Too many unknowns. Too many people involved. And Ned had a problem with his socks. Every single pair he owned had holes in them. Every single one. He was about to go on a quest with the women he thought he might - you know - and there was a high chance that he would have to take his boots off. What would she think of a man with holey socks? Would she think it debonair? He hoped so because they were the only clean ones he had, and he didn't have time to get any more. In fact, he should have left five minutes ago. They had decided to meet on the Dead Pier. That's where the first part of the plan - that wasn't going to work - started.

When Ned arrived, he saw the others were even later than him. Good. It was important that he stamped his authority on this quest, even if it was his first official one. He was Chief Thief-Catcher and held the highest rank. Apart from Fourteen. Ah. There could be an issue. He was distracted by the approaching cavalcade.

Mia and Brogan were in front, both of them bristling with knives and axes. Seeing as she was unable to use her magic, Mia had fallen back on her other talent.

Vicious weapons master. She was a pro at most things with a pointy end and a keen shot with an arrow even without enhanced sight from her powers. The only downside was all this artillery was bloody heavy to carry. She had every intention of giving most of it to Brogan, but it was important she made a strong impression on the others at the start. This quest was about her family and as senior warlock, lack of power notwithstanding, she was going to be in charge of these mismatched idiots. Brogan was thinking he could have probably brought a few more weapons.

Following them were Willow, Jenni and Sparks. Sparks was back to full strength and glowing brightly despite it being the middle of the morning. He may or may not have acquired some additional light juice from Momma K. The fireflies and the fairies had a long history - it was best not to ask about it in too much detail – it could be illuminating. Willow was thorny. She knew they were going into a battle of sorts, so she had tapped into every plant-based protection system she could think of. She had new poison sacs growing on the insides of her wrist, perfect for throwing globules of the stuff out at the unsuspecting - not so good for accidentally dripping into your tea. Her skin had grown exceedingly waxy which was making her feel hot, but no one would be able to damage her dermis. She had thorns positioned strategically all over her body, wherever a person might try to get a handhold. It was a singular image. Jenni was Jenni. She shimmered in the building heat of the day but that was to do with her personal odour, no stronger or weaker than usual. Momma K had given her an additional direct tap to her own magics, not that Jenni would need them, she didn't think. Being fae meant you had an unlimited supply as long as you didn't burn out or

195

let some cretin of an evil warlock drain you. The other thief-catchers had no desire to be in charge of this quest, that meant writing the reports and Ned was well and truly welcome to those. They were aiming for looking menacing. It was a hit and miss result.

Bringing up the rear came Fourteen. Not the Emperor or the Upper Circle, just Fourteen. She was without her ridiculous costume and headdress, there was no entourage or fanfare, and she had shed all Emperor-like items. She wore suspiciously well-worn grey trousers, a blue shirt, a dark leather jerkin, and shouldered a travel pack that looked like it knew what it was doing. Clearly, this wasn't her first quest. Ned was impressed. His lady had layers; he couldn't wait to peel them back. Not like that. Focus.

The group arranged themselves in front of Ned. He broke the bad news first.

'Sparks, you've got to stay here. Man the HQ, look after things while we deal with this... er... quest.'

The firefly dimmed and settled on a nearby skull, then he brightened again and zipped to attention. A firefly in charge of the Thief-Catchers, it was a proud moment indeed. He flashed his butt at Ned and flew off, back into the city.

'Right, you all know why we're here. Look after each other and maybe, just maybe, we'll make it through this in one piece. Is everybody ready?' Ned looked at his team.

There were various nods, some filled with excitement, others wondering what the bloody hell they had got themselves into. Ned steadied his nerves and bent down at the side of the pier. He dipped his fingers into the water and swirled them around. He didn't have to wait long.

'Reporting for duty, Sir.' Pearl had changed her scales to match the Emperors' royal colours of purple and gold. It was a stunning display.

'We need safe transport to the Isle of Illusion,' Ned explained.

'We? As in everyone up there?' Pearl eyed the team doubtfully.

'Yes. Problem?' asked Ned.

'Does everyone have to make it there in one piece?'

Ned frowned.

'I'm kidding, Boss,' said Pearl lightly. 'It's no problem but I'll need blood payment for safe passage.'

Ned sighed. 'Even though you work for the catchers, now?'

'It's not my fault.' Pearl's spikes bristled. 'We'll have to go right through a heavily populated area, Mermaid City. Without the appropriate blood, I can't guarantee your safety.'

'How much?' Ned asked.

Pearl appraised the group. 'One vial each should do it,' she said, passing a bag up to Ned. 'Two for the big fella.'

Ned took the bag out of the water and stood to face the others. 'You all heard?' They nodded, faces a lot paler than before. 'Right, form a line and I'll collect. Squeamish first, it's worse waiting, believe me.'

There was a lot of pushing and shoving but eventually, a line was formed. Brogan was first. Just goes to show you never can tell with barbarians. Brogan was actually pale and sweating slightly. Ned hoped that the bloke didn't faint but then if he had a heap of barbarian on the pier at least he would be relatively easy to roll into the water. Ned took a knife from his belt and stabbed the tip of one of Brogan's fingers. He yelped and then glowered at Ned as he began to squeeze the same finger so that droplets of blood fell out into the tiny vial he was holding.

'Is that all?' Brogan was relieved. 'I thought it was a blood sacrifice.'

'You were willing to sacrifice yourself for me?' Mia was dumbfounded. No one had ever done anything as selfless as that for her before, except for her brother, but he was family and it didn't count if it was family.

'Yer. I told you, I love you and I'll do whatever I can to fix things.' Brogan was beaming at Mia. They were having a moment.

It was all getting a bit too hero-esque for Ned. Thank goodness they hadn't decided to meet at sunrise. He jabbed another of Brogan's fingers and got a womanly yelp in response. It made him feel slightly better. Once that finger had dripped its drops, Mia stepped up and defiantly slashed her own palm for Ned to collect her blood.

'That was clever,' remarked Ned.

'What do you mean?' Mia glared at him.

'Because now you have an open wound and you're about to go into carnivorous mermaid territory. Finger pricks give us everything we need.' Ned grinned at her. 'Watch your back.'

Jenni was trying so hard not to laugh that tears were leaking out of her eyes. She waved a hand and the cut was gone but everyone had seen how Mia's bravado act had misfired and she stalked over to the other side of the pier. Her hulking barbarian shadow followed.

Jenni cheerfully had her finger jabbed; the sparkly silvery blood drops dutifully collected. Next up was Willow who gasped at the metal of the knife but gave up her green sap happily. Joe watched with interest and held out his finger bravely but had to shut his eyes the entire time. Once the drops were collected, he sucked his finger hard.

Fourteen stood in front of Ned. 'Shall I do you?' she asked.

'What?' Ned was confused.

'Shall I prick you and you prick me? Together.'

Although he knew what she meant Ned couldn't stop the blush. *Just play it cool, play it cool.* Ned's inner thoughts were getting far too loud, so he coughed and took Fourteen's slender, soft hand in his. He had never felt more rough and awkward in his entire life. She flourished a blade from somewhere and together they pricked fingers. The blood began to drip on the floor until Ned blushed again and fumbled a vial, one for each of them. The others watched in amusement.

Now that all the blood had been collected, Ned put the vials back in the waterproof bag and knelt down to speak to Pearl. 'Is it payment in advance?'

'No, pay at the Way Gate when we get there. Are you ready?'

Ned nodded and asked Willow for some rope - he didn't look to see where she got it from, but it was hemp, good and strong. He looped the rope around the waist of each of them, tying them to each other, himself in the lead, the vials of blood bag dangling from his waist.

Ned gave them final instructions. 'Stay together. Don't touch anything. Don't interact with anyone. Focus on the person in front of you, ignore everything else around you. Jenni?'

The sprite nodded and muttered her spell. Instantly everyone began clawing at their necks as gills formed and the air became unbreathable. There was a mad dash for the water as everyone hurried to get in the ocean and ended up falling in a tangle. Luckily Pearl was on hand to right everyone and help them reorient themselves. She was particularly interested in Willow whose wiles seemed to work just as well underwater as they did above. Joe had trouble keeping his eyes away from the mermaid's shape, so he had resorted to closing them.

'Okay, Pearl. I think we're ready.' Ned said.

The mermaid took Ned's hand. He looked back at Fourteen who was studying them coolly but there was nothing he could do. Without Pearl's touch to lighten them all they would never be able to keep up with her. As it was, it was going to be a long slog through the inky waters to get to the Isle of Illusion but first, they had to make it past the Way Gate and Mermaid City.

They set off. It was quiet and cold. No one felt much like talking. Shoals of fish glinted from time to time as they came to investigate the strange procession. Large shapes loomed in the distance – they could have been boats or whales or well, better not to think of the 'or'. Thankfully, this being mermaid territory meant they didn't have to worry about sharks - mermaids hunted them for sport. All they had to worry about were the bloodthirsty merpeople.

Pearl's hand tightened on Neds. A mermaid was approaching, fast.

'Darla.'

'Pearl.'

They greeted each other warmly.

'What treats do you bring to lunch?' asked Darla.

Pearl chuckled. 'They are not for you, Darla. They seek passage to the Isle of Illusion and have their blood payment for the Way Gate.'

Darla pouted. 'Well, let me know if anyone falls behind. I'll see to them.' She swam to the edge of Ned's vision, but he knew she was keeping pace with them. A ridiculously easy thing for her to do as a single man swimming as fast as possible was no match for a hungry mermaid and a long train of edible delights like this? It was temptation on a seaweed platter.

More mermaids joined Darla's peripheral swim. None came to speak to Pearl, clearly, Darla had told them why they were there, but it was beginning to feel more and more dangerous to Ned to be in the water.

After what seemed like an eternity, but was only about ten minutes, the Way Gate finally appeared. It was a rusty old gate that had somehow found its way to the bottom of the ocean. It marked the beginning of the mermaid settlement and they guarded the gate at all times. Anything that went through the gate had to pay the blood price. They were, after all, asking permission to travel through Mermaid City and most importantly pay for protection from their children. Juvenile mermaids were even more vicious than the adults. They were like piranhas with the faces of angels. Blood payment ensured that the children would be kept inside, but only for a short time. Food that freely walked in couldn't be ignored. Ned hoped for mermaids in a good mood at the gate otherwise they might have to swim for their lives.

'How many?' The first guard asked, his eyes raking over the travellers hungrily. Ned decided his muscles looked much bigger than Brogan's. It was not a comforting thought.

'Seven,' replied Pearl.

'Two for the big guy?' The second guard chimed in. He was smaller but looked speedy to Ned, all streamlined and eel-like.

'Yes.' Pearl smiled widely. There was a short pause.

'Make the payment,' demanded the big guard.

Ned fumbled with cold fingers to undo the bag at his waist. It seemed to take forever but he finally managed to pass the bag over. They rooted through it, hooting with delight at the fae vial and looking intrigued by Willow's contribution. Finally, the larger guard looked at the line of wary travellers.

'You've got ten minutes.' And he moved aside to let them through.

Ned sighed with relief. You could traverse Mermaid City in seven minutes, so ten was pretty reasonable. He tugged on the line to get everyone's attention. 'We've got ten minutes to get through the city. Do not interact with anyone, especially the children. If we swim fast and close together, we'll make it without any problems. Everyone alright with that?'

There were lots of nervous nods. The guards held the gates open and smiled toothily at the food passing through.

'Did you tell them it was ten minutes from the moment they set their toes in the ocean?' asked the speedy one.

'Nah. Spoils the fun.'

The guards watched the slow swimmers.

'How much time do they have left?' Speedy was feeling hungry.

'None. Ready for some lunch?'

The two guards left their post and swam after the meal train.

Jenni was behind Ned and she yanked his rope. 'Boss, summik ain't right. There's a helluva lot of fish faces following us, including those guards.'

'It's probably because they've not seen this many of us in one place before.' Ned tried to sound convincing.

'I ain't 'appy about this, Boss.'

'Aren't we protected magically?' asked Ned.

'Momma K's magic doesn't work down 'ere. You'll have to ask nancy boy.'

Ned sighed and pulled on the rope connecting Jenni to Joe. 'Joe, hey buddy, focus.'

Joe was circling the edge of pure panic, his eyes were wide and pupils hugely dilated, he was panting slightly on the verge of hyperventilating. If indeed it is possible to hyperventilate underwater when you are breathing ocean. He managed to bring his wild, frightened gaze to Ned's face and nodded barely.

'Joe, buddy, I need you with me, okay? Can you extend a protection spell around us?' asked Ned.

Joe looked around fearfully, expecting an attack from every side. He shook his head. 'I can't, I can't do that kind of magic. Just simple stuff. Usually, I either amplify or quash.'

Ned inwardly cursed. 'Which is it with me?'

'I don't know, I've never tried with you.' Joe flinched at a piece of seaweed dancing in the water.

'Let's try now then shall we?' asked Ned. 'Joe? Hey, Joe – buddy – with me.'

Joe nodded and held out his hand. Ned grabbed it and gave it a little squeeze of reassurance, unsure whether that was for his or Joe's benefit. He tried to quieten his mind and think about a protective shield over his friends. When his thoughts drifted towards Fourteen, an enormous surge of power pulsed through his body, making Joe jolt in surprise and a blue ring of protection appear around the group. Impressed, Ned let go of Joe's hands. 'Thanks kid, that was great.'

Joe looked shocked. 'I think that was all you, Boss.'

Ned smiled and nodded to himself. Being in love

wasn't so bad after all.

A juvenile mermaid bounced off the shield. It looked annoyed. As if it was being denied a free lunch. Ned shouted for Pearl's attention. She turned and her eyes widened at what she saw. Ned followed her gaze and saw at least a hundred or so hungry mermaids swimming behind them.

'I thought we had ten minutes?' he asked.

Pearl thought for a moment. 'Um, did you check when that ten minutes started from?' She sounded sheepish.

'No, I did not ask when that ten minutes started from,' snapped Ned. 'Ten minutes is ten minutes. Right? Right?'

Pearl looked even more embarrassed. She shrugged fluidly, making things jiggle, but not quite enough to distract Ned from his impending death.

'Stop that. Get us out of here, Pearl. You still work for me, okay?' Ned was hedging his bets.

Pearl nodded and then peered more closely at the mostly human group in front of her. 'Who is protecting us? Fae magic doesn't work down here.'

'Me,' growled Ned.

A new light of respect grew in Pearl's eyes and she grabbed his hand, tugging him forwards. The others hurried as quickly as their land-loving limbs would let them move through the water. Mia was feeling the drag of the additional knives but there was no way she was going to let any of them go now. They might be protected for the moment, but that magical barrier had no guarantee of lasting forever and she had delved Ned before, he was patchy at best. That is why she'd dismissed him as a credible threat earlier. Now he was the only thing she could count on and she didn't like it.

More mermaids bounced off the shield, but Ned only had eyes for the gates in front of him. Like the entrance gate, these were rusted and clearly from an abandoned wreckage of some kind or other. Somehow or for some unknown reason, they delineated the mermaid territory. If they could get everyone past those gates, they would be safe. Or as safe as prey is in open water. The juveniles would not be allowed to pass through the gates and hopefully, most of the adult mermaids would see it as too much trouble.

Everyone was feeling tense. Time slowed. The shield started to boing as more and more mermaids hurled themselves at it, trying to pop its protection. It held, barely. Ned could feel his grip on the magic begin to dwindle. They had to make it to the gates. He had to keep Fourteen safe. They surged forward, swimming for their lives and passed through the gates. No one followed them. Yet. Pearl turned and made a half bow to them.

'I should stay here. Hopefully, I can encourage my family not to follow you or try to eat you.'

'I hope so.' Ned could almost feel sharp teeth boring into the back of his neck so without looking around or even thanking Pearl for getting them that far, he set off as fast as he could. Without the mermaid's buoyant touch, it was hard going so he ordered everyone to swim to the surface and for Jenni to remove the gills. As they broke the waves, they could see the Isle of Illusion. It wasn't far. Or was that part of the illusion? With true grit and determination, they swam, conscious of the many fins that had begun to flash beneath them. Just a little further. There. Ned felt sand beneath his boots. He stood and tried unsuccessfully to run out of the water. At best he managed a semi-hobble. The others followed as fast as they were able, most falling to a crawl but all of them moving forward. Anything to get away from the mermaids. They had all forgotten they had no idea what waited for them on the island.

Chapter 27

The Isle of Illusion could not be accessed except by travelling through the Mermaid City. Boats that tried to sail across the stretch of water either didn't make it that far or they never came back, so the mermaids' blood price was always paid, one way or another. Fae were unable to pop to the island due to a strong magical force-field repelling them, hence the intrepid group's journey through the ocean. None of them ever wanted to put a single digit in that body of water ever again. They lay gasping and heaving on the beach looking like rather well-armoured seals. Eventually, Ned marshalled his thoughts enough to do a headcount. Everyone was still here. The hot sun that blazed above them seemed to be good for drying them out quickly, if not for anything else. It was time to figure out how to achieve the next stage of their quest.

'Joe, you alive?' asked Ned.

'Yes, Boss.'

'Where on the Isle did this guy say he was going to hide the grimoire?'

'He told me he lived in the fire grove or something.' Joe didn't sound certain.

'Fire grove. Sounds great.'

Ned heaved himself to his feet and did a body check. Then he looked around him and his heart felt like it fell out of his chest as he looked at Fourteen lying motionless on the sand. Then he saw her chest move. She was breathing. He had trouble catching one of his own for a moment and was studiously trying to avoid looking at Jenni, who was grinning at him from ear to ear.

'Okay, troops, up and at 'em,' barked Ned.

There was quite a lot of groaning, the sort you normally come across when everyone knows they should be doing something, but they can't be bothered to actually get down to it.

'Can't we stay on the beach for a while? There's some interesting seaweed here.' Willow pouted. The seaweed in close proximity to her looked glossy and swollen like it was doing its best to impress.

'No,' replied Ned. 'Let's get going. Where are these fire groves, Joe? Any idea?'

Joe scratched his head. 'I think they're in the middle of the island.'

'Great. Let's head for the middle then.'

Ten minutes later and the group came out of the dense forest back to the pristine beach. It looked a lot like the beach they had left. Indeed, Ned was fairly sure that pile of seaweed plumped and ready for Willow's attention was the same piece as earlier. That can't have been right. Surely the island wasn't that small. And anyway, if they were walking away from themselves then they couldn't come out on themselves, could they?

'Wait here,' he ordered and went backwards through the forest. He came out in front of himself and everyone was stood waiting for him. 'Right, there's no middle.'

'What do you mean there's no middle?' Mia scoffed

at him and dragging Brogan, set off into the forest. Moments later she reappeared on the beach coming back the way she had gone but from the other direction. It was disconcerting. No one else believed it until each and every one of them had done the exact same thing. Ned felt that Jenni and Fourteen only did it because everyone else had and they didn't want to miss out on anything, but his pride was certainly a little dented that no one took him at his word.

The light was beginning to fade. It would soon be dark out here in the middle of the ocean, on a tiny island, with no city to light their way.

'We'd best build up a fire and get some sort of shelter set up. We can figure out what to do in the morning.' Ned tried to sound a lot more positive than he felt.

'If we make it 'til morning,' Joe said gloomily, setting off to look for driftwood on the beach.

Within half an hour they had a fire blazing merrily and everyone seemed to be waiting for everyone else to produce some dinner.

'Who had the food pack?' Ned demanded.

No one answered.

'C'mon, someone must have bought the food pack.'

'Er, that was meant to be you, Boss,' Jenni smiled up at Ned with rather too much hope glistening in her eyes.

Dammit, he thought. All that distraction this morning about bloody socks and boots and he had forgotten to pick up the ruddy satchel with all the provisions in it. 'Does anyone have anything at all?'

A quick whip-round produced a couple of sticky toffees and half a hank of dry bread that Brogan said he was saving for something special. No one liked to ask for what exactly.

'Jenni, can you do anything?'

'Not here – the isle protects against magic.'

'Anything from the ocean maybe? Now that we're beyond the mermaid's territory?'

She looked at the glittering water with distrust then held her hand out. There was considerable resistance to her magic. She was going to have to stand in the water. In the end, Ned and Brogan stood either side of Jenni on some handily jutting rocks and dipped her feet ever so slightly into the water, ready to yank her out at the slightest show of mermaid fin. Once her feet were in the water, fish began flying out at regular intervals until at least twenty of varying size and colour lay in a heap by the fireside. Mia and Fourteen proved the depth of their knife skills by gutting and filleting the fish for supper. There was a competitive edge in the air, the sort you get when any two women are doing the same task, at the same time, together. It happens amongst family members, very good friends and even Emperors and their usurpers. In the end, it was an even match, ten fishes filleted on either side but the last few to go under the blade were somewhat sloppily done. No one cared, they were all too hungry.

'Nothing poisonous, was there, Jenni?' Ned asked after half the fish had been consumed. Everyone stopped eating to look at her. She shrugged and carried on munching regardless. The pace of consumption slowed somewhat but, to be honest, the idea of warm, full bellies outweighed the possibility of crippling stomach aches and potential death. Everyone felt they had been through quite enough already that day.

Gradually people stopped eating, stopped talking and started falling asleep. A small part of Ned was telling him to set watches and keep the fire burning through the night. They didn't know what dangers might be lurking on the island. Despite their inability to walk into the interior, it didn't mean that something nasty couldn't walk out. He hushed the voice. Fourteen was leaning on him. It felt safe and warm and she smelled heavenly. He never wanted to move again, ever.

Early that morning, or indeed later that night – hard to tell when you are sleeping on the beach and your fire has gone out – Ned woke up with a crick in his neck and a dead weight lying on his arm. Fourteen was snoring. It was still endearing even if it did sound like a saw cutting through wood. But now he had to pee, it was probably that which had woken him up. He eased himself out from under Fourteen and went to find a suitable rock. When he turned to come back, everyone was gone. He blinked, stared for a while, rubbed his eyes, turned around, and then stared for a bit longer. Yep, no one there except a few discarded fish bones, which may or may not have been theirs to begin with.

Ned eyed a small crab suspiciously.

'Right, I've had enough of this,' he said aloud. 'I demand to see the man who runs this place.' He stalked off into the jungle and returned immediately to his spot on the beach.

'Arrrgggghhhhhhhh.'

The yell relieved his frustration slightly, but it didn't solve the problem that he could not get off this blasted sand and he had lost his fellow questers. He closed his eyes and walked forward once more. He stopped when a tree branch slapped him in the face. It sounded different, it felt denser, warmer and more green. Cautiously he opened his eyes and saw that he was in the forest. At last.

'Forgive my foibles, but it is the Isle of Illusion you know, you have to let go of what you think you can see.'

An old man with a long dirty white beard and scruffy looking brown robes pushed through some foliage on the left and stood smiling at Ned as if he were inordinately proud of himself.

'Where are the rest of my people?' asked Ned.

'Oh, they're still asleep on the beach.'

'Then why couldn't I see them?'

'Because you were ready to see me. That is not something I control but come, be welcome. I have hot broth, which will do you the world of good. You can tell me why you braved the mermaids to come here.' The old man smiled toothily.

'I'm here for the grimoire.' Ned felt he might as well be upfront about it.

'All in good time, Thief-Catcher, all in good time.' The old man turned and went back the way he had come. Ned debated it for a millisecond but decided that he wanted to get off this island and if dealing with a mad old coot was the way to do it then he would drink the broth and talk the talk. As long as he didn't have to cut any toenails. He had a bad experience as a young man visiting a Great-Uncle who had smelt similarly to this old hermit.

They walked without speaking for a few minutes through the jungle until they came to a clearing. A simple wooden hut stood in the middle, the chimney merrily puffing away and all signs of life looking extremely inviting. It was like something out of a fairy-tale, so much so that Ned fingered the knife he kept in his back pocket for emergencies. He didn't want to end up cooking in the oven. And he hadn't seen a single puff of fire grove smoke.

The two men entered the hut and the most mouth-wateringly, delicious aroma hit Ned's nostrils. He inhaled deeply. This might even be worth the toenails, but he still could not shake the feeling that something wasn't quite right.

'What's wrong with him?'

'Dunno.'

Those voices - they sounded far away but Ned knew them, he was sure he did. They sounded like his friends, but they weren't physically there. There was no one here but Ned and the old man. He was sitting at the fireside now with a bowl of soup in his hands offering it up to Ned, smiling benignly.

'I fink you should kiss 'im.'

'Well, if you think it would work.'

'I'd do it, but it might kill 'im not cure.'

Ned shook his head; he knew those voices and he half wanted to laugh at that last comment but he could not for the life of him remember why. The bowl was in his hands now, the spoon halfway to his mouth and then it suddenly got stuck, as if he couldn't move it any closer to him. There was softness and warmth and that familiar, delicate perfume that made his heart beat faster. She was kissing him.

Bloody hell, the Emperor was kissing him! Ned's eyes flew open and he was back on the beach, lips locked with Fourteen and the rest of the group standing around staring. He broke contact and began coughing and apologising and wishing he had found a way to clean his teeth or shave or something when he suddenly remembered the old man. He looked around wildly then rounded on Joe.

'Kid, who exactly did you give the grimoire to?'

Chapter 28

'I don't know his name. It was this old guy I met on my travels.' Joe frowned. 'Come to think of it, it was a bit weird. You see, he already knew about the grimoire. I remember thinking I must have told him about it at some pub one evening but do you know what, I don't think I did. I can't remember how we met at all.' He scratched his head. 'What I do remember is that he knew of somewhere to keep the grimoire safe and offered to do it for nothing. I thought it sounded like a good idea at the time.'

'You are incredibly idiotic at times.' Mia scowled at her brother. 'I would never let the grimoire out of my sight, and you gave it to some daft old man, on a whim.'

'Hey, that's not fair. I found it. You didn't.' Joe scowled at his sister. 'And anyway, you started to do all kinds of odd things that I had to try and cover up for you. So what if I gave a stupid old book away. It didn't work anyway.'

'How would you know? You can't even do basic magic.'

'I tried some of the spells,' Joe retorted. 'Duds – every one.'

Mia shouted louder. 'You fool – you don't read spells

out of the grimoire like some daft adventure novel. You have to prepare a safe space. Anything could crawl through from the other side.' She shook her head. 'You could have killed thousands and thousands of people.'

'Ha! Nothing happened. Well, apart from trapping dad in the mountain, that could've been me. But otherwise - not a single, bloody thing. So stop acting like you're so much better than me. Without my twin tie, you'd be nothing.'

'Fine – let's get rid of it then.' Mia glared at him.

'Fine.' Joe glared right back.

The twins stood nose to nose, left hands outstretched with identical tiny red sparks shooting out of their fingertips aimed at each other's hearts.

No one else in the group moved. The sparks kept flying at each other and cancelling themselves out when they touched. Little soft poofs of smoke kept appearing. It was never going to work because Joe was too weak, and Mia's power was blocked. Finally, Ned pulled the two of them apart and stood gingerly between them.

'I think we have enough danger to contend with without having to worry about wiping each other out. Okay?' He glanced at each of them.

Both twins glared at him and he could feel the heat of their anger. They slowly lowered their hands and extinguished the spells. Ned let out a breath he didn't know he had been holding.

'This old guy – scruffy looking with a dirty white beard? Master of illusion that sort of thing?' Ned asked Joe.

'I don't know about the illusion bit, but yeah he was old and had a beard.' Joe flexed his fingers. 'He said he couldn't do magic to me. Said I had a powerful gift.'

'Right, he's a real charmer.' Ned thought for a

moment. 'How did you know he would be here?'

'He told me that if I ever needed him, I could find him here, on the Isle of Illusion. That's it. That's all I know.' Joe retreated to the other side of the dying fire. Willow went with him, to make sure he was alright. Her tendrils stroked his head gently.

Mia stalked off to where Brogan was sitting and huffed at him. He hadn't even stepped in to protect her honour, not that she needed protecting. Brogan smiled to himself and continued to sharpen his blades. He might not be the smartest barbarian in the box, but he knew better than to get involved in brother and sister quarrels.

Ned sat down next to Fourteen and cleared his throat. 'Thank you for the er, for the kiss. It was… nice.' The tips of his ears were getting rather pink.

'You're welcome. I was trying to wake you up before you came to any harm.'

'Yes, yes of course.' He tried to keep his voice light and carefree, but he was a little disappointed.

Fourteen leaned over and kissed him softly on the cheek. 'That one was just for you.' She got up to go and see Joe and Willow, her scent wafting seductively behind her. Ned watched her with an ache in his heart. Realising Mia and Brogan were watching him, he reddened, coughed and called for everyone's attention again.

'I suppose this old guy trapped me in some kind of illusion. He wanted me to eat soup.' Ned looked at Jenni. 'I'm guessing that would have been bad?'

Jenni piped up. 'If you eat something in an illusion, nine times out of ten you're trapped there until the illusionist either dies or lets you go. It's an effective way of catching your enemy. Who doesn't love to eat or drink, right?' She didn't sound her usual grammatically

216

incorrect self, some of her sparkiness had disappeared.

'What's up Jenni?'

'Nuffink, Boss.'

Ned wasn't convinced, but if she didn't want to talk about then he wasn't about to waste time trying to make her. He spoke to the team.

'I think we need to see if we can find this old man together, as a group. With everyone keeping an eye on each other we should be alright. No one drink anything, no one eat anything and whatever you do, don't break anything. Who knows what he'd do if we broke something.'

'How do we find him?' Jenni asked.

Ned frowned at Jenni. She hadn't dropped any h's. 'We'll walk backwards and find our way into the forest.'

'Walk backwards into the sea? What a stupid idea – who put you in charge anyway?' Mia was sneering down at Ned, spoiling for a fight.

'You don't get a say,' Ned retorted. 'You're lucky you're not in irons.'

She shut up but didn't stop scowling at his back. Ned waited while the others gathered their things and then walked backwards away from them. Any minute now he thought. He stopped when the sea reached his knees. Clearly, this was not going to work.

'Alright then, let's try forwards again.' He sloshed out of the ocean and onto the beach trying to ignore the squelching. He reached the foliage line and held his breath as he stepped forwards. He vanished into greenery. The others followed quickly, reluctant to lose sight of him.

The forest loomed at them from all sides. Everything looked a bit too green and a bit too lush. Ned knew it must all be an illusion because Willow was walking stiffly trying to avoid touching a single leaf or twig with any part of her body. She had gathered all her tendril-like hair into her arms and was hugging it to herself. The path stretched on and on and on.

'Didn't you say there was a hut or something?' Joe was poking through foliage willy nilly, seemingly oblivious to the green menace that grew around them. He stripped some leaves from an overhanging branch, and everyone held their breath to see what would happen. The leaves in Joe's hands melted whilst new ones grew instantly. Joe yelped and wiped his hands vigorously on his trousers leaving bright green stains behind. The marks fizzled slightly and smoked alarmingly, but nothing else happened.

'Remember that conversation we had, like two minutes ago, about not touching anything?' Ned shook his head. 'Jenni, will his trousers be alright?'

Jenni stared blankly at Ned, then slowly turned around and disappeared into the brush.

'What was that?' Fourteen took half a step after her.

'Not Jenni.' Ned frowned. 'We'd better go after her, it. Maybe it will lead us to where we need to be.'

The group drew closer together as they carried on through the foliage. There is something incredibly comforting about snuggling up to someone you barely know when danger threatens. It's like you are saying to the world, here, eat this one, not me. It's about giving the enemy choice, getting your odds down. Smart group behaviour. Ned found himself walking next to Fourteen. She slipped a cool hand into his and he felt a bit better, but he was worried about Jenni. She wasn't just his deputy and she was much more than his magic supply on tap. She had saved his life on countless occasions, he owed her everything. She was his partner; he couldn't let anything bad happen to her.

It was fairly obvious which direction Jenni was headed. Every step she had taken had resulted in the plants nearby withering and dying. Not that any of it felt the slightest bit natural in the first place. They walked cautiously onwards. Willow was crying softly, wilting against Joe's shoulder. Mia and Brogan brought up the rear. She was looking daggers at Ned whilst Brogan was merely enjoying being alive.

A clearing opened up in front of them.

'That's the hut. His hut, I mean.' Ned looked about for Jenni but there was no sign. The hut looked as welcoming and inviting as it did before. 'C'mon.'

The front door swung open as they reached it, a delicious aroma wafted out to meet them. Cinnamon twists, just like Aggie's Bakery back home. Ned could actually feel his knees going weak.

'Here have some of this.' Willow shoved some sap up his nose. Ned coughed and blinked. The sap was strong and the breaded goods smell had gone. He decided not to ask where the sap had come from but muttered his thanks as she did the same for the rest of the group. They now all looked like they had a really, really, bad cold.

The old man was sitting by the fire. Jenni was burning in it. Ned shot forwards without thinking and rebounded hard as he hit a magical shield.

'Release her - now!' Ned was furious he had allowed Jenni to be burnt alive.

'Don't worry. She's fine, they can't burn, you know.' The old man smiled fondly at his hearth. 'It puts fae in a sort of stasis. I thought we'd be able to have a better chat if I outgunned you. Firepower to firepower, so to speak.'

'I thought fae magic didn't work on this blasted

island.' Ned growled and drew as much power from his wells into himself, with no clear idea of what he was going to do but with Joe and Fourteen standing at his back, one of them was going to be able to amplify his rage. He waited for the old man's next move. Despite the rage coursing through him, he didn't want to hurt Jenni further.

'On the island, no. But my home, well let's call it a nexus point. A point of great strength and of course great weakness.' The old man's gaze passed over the group. 'Welcome, welcome one and all. Ah, young master Joseph – how good to see you again. You are keeping well I trust?'

Joe nodded and reddened. 'Erm, look we've come about that book I gave you. I need it back.'

'That's impossible I'm afraid. I cannot allow the grimoire to go back out into the world. Your father stole it from me and now it has been returned.'

'Look I didn't know he stole it, but we need it to stop him,' said Joe. 'He's going to get free and we can't let him.'

'Not my problem,' replied the old man cheerfully. 'He can't come here, I am protected. What care do I have for the rest of the world? I was here before and I will be here afterwards. It is but a blink of an eye to me.'

Ned was only half listening to Joe stammer and the old man pontificate. He was watching Jenni. Her eyes were rolling in her head like they were moving through treacle. He looked up and saw some rafters. Nothing special, you would expect rafters in a wooden hut like this. Then something caught his eye. A corner of a well-worn book peeking at him. His attention was diverted by a bellow of rage from Brogan who leapt at the old man with his broadsword drawn. He passed through the

220

magical shield and loped the old man's head off. Everyone watched as the head fell to the floor and slowly rolled away. The old man's body slumped in the chair. There was a stunned silence.

'He was irritating me.' Brogan smiled broadly at the others.

'Well done thickhead, did you think to ask him where the book was before you killed him? Or how we get out of his illusion?' Mia glared at him.

'Er.' Brogan shuffled his feet then perked up again and put his hand in the fire, fishing Jenni out and placing her gently on the floor.

'How did you do that?' Fourteen was amazed and slightly suspicious.

'Six times out of ten.' Brogan held out one of his amulets.

Ned reached up to the rafters and plucked the book down. He shoved it into Joe's arms then knelt down by Jenni's prone form. He stroked her hair. 'You can't leave me now Jen, I need you. Who else will see me through this alive?' he whispered.

'I ain't going nowhere, Boss. Momma K'd kill me.' Jenni grinned without opening her eyes. She still felt somewhat discombobulated.

'Well, that's alright then.' Ned fought the urge to kiss the sprite on the forehead. He felt she might not appreciate it and there was a good chance of catching something.

Everyone was milling. That thing that happens when no one is sure what to say or what to do. The hut seemed small, dark and claustrophobic with everyone inside. Ned went through the door to the outside and inhaled the fresh air deeply. The forest was gone, the hut was on a sandy beach. The beach was a small strip on a rocky

221

base. In fact, the whole island looked smaller and less green.

'Illusions broke then,' remarked Jenni, opening her eyes.

'What now?' Joe was fingering the grimoire uneasily.

'Now we pop out of here – right? I mean the illusionist is gone, isn't he? So we can get off this rock?' Mia was sounding slightly hysterical. Ned eyed her suspiciously.

Jenni popped out and then came back grinning. 'Yep, we can move, but I can't take us far. Too many. I can manage the nearest mainland.' She swivelled and fixed Mia with an evil grin. 'And you need lockin' up again.' There was a blast of power that knocked Mia to her rump. She scowled at the sprite and muttered a string of curses under her breath.

Ned felt a mixture of alarm and relief. The last thing he needed was an unstable warlock armed with her powers, plotting behind his back. It was bad enough he had an unstable warlock. He was not entirely sure which side she was on. Her father had coerced her into doing some terrible things, but most people had a moral line they wouldn't cross. Torture, murder and total destruction of villages would be way past it for most people. Trouble was, Mia wasn't most people.

'Everyone hold hands, let's do this!' Jenni was smiling hugely. The group formed into a loose circle easily enough, but the hand holding was a little awkward. Ned jumped when Fourteen slipped her hand into his and groaned inwardly as Willow took the other side - he could feel attraction for her grow unasked for, thanks to physical touch. He tried to look nonchalant. Joe zipped in and took Willow's other hand, making himself blush and stuck his hand out for Mia but Jenni took it and attached herself to Mia instead. Mia looked a little green around the edges but clung on to Brogan's paw with a certain death grip which put Brogan standing next to Fourteen. He looked a little unsure. She was, after all, royalty. Barbarians and royalty do not, as a rule, get on too well. But Fourteen smiled sweetly up at him and placed her hand within his. Brogan grinned and Ned felt a flare of jealousy whip through him. He tried to ignore it, mentally calling himself a fool but couldn't help glaring at the hulking brute.

Jenni closed her eyes and focused on bringing everyone with her, there was a loud sucking noise as the party lifted off the rock and then squelched out of view. It's difficult to pop when carrying a large mass. They reappeared on a dusty road in the middle of nowhere. Not *that* middle of nowhere, but another one. A road that led in the direction of a mountain pass where the evil sorcerer was trapped. For now.

Chapter 29

Landing back onto solid ground, the group quickly let go of each other, hands dropping like hot coals and most people falling down to the ground. There was retching from those unused to popping. Even Ned felt a little queasy, but at least he had been able to keep his feet. Fourteen was clinging on grimly to his hand, reluctant to let go. *Fine with me* thought Ned and he gave hers a little squeeze.

'Joe, how do we stop him, then?' asked Ned. 'We got you the book. We got you onto the mountain trail. More or less. What's next?' Ned was concerned. They had never moved past this part of the plan in the discussion before, it had always been glossed over, somewhat.

'Well,' Joe sounded nervous. Everyone was looking at him. 'We got a ways to walk to get to the Purple Mountains, we need to go through Fidelia but at least we can resupply there. And then...' He fumbled with the book trying to open it and turn the pages one-handed. In the end, he had to sit down and place the tome on his knees. 'Ah, here it is. This is the spell which will strip him of his powers. Hmm, we need to get some unusual ingredients, but we should find them in Fidelia.' He looked up with a smile. 'And if not, Jenni can pop to wherever we need, right?' Jenni looked at him, raising an eyebrow. Joe faltered, 'I mean if we ask nicely of course and um...'

'Yes Joe, she'll help us get what we need.' Ned frowned at the sprite who shrugged and went back to picking her fingers.

'Anyone know which direction to Fidelia?' Ned looked around at the blank faces. He thought he knew but was hoping someone else might have an idea as well, Ned didn't feel like explaining how he knew where Fidelia was. Brogan was the only one who seemed to be paying attention, for once. He turned slowly, frowning and then pointed.

'That way.'

'Are you sure?' Ned was relieved, that was the direction he thought Fidelia was as well.

'Yep.'

'Okay, let's move out. The sooner we get to Fidelia the better.' This trip had already turned out to be more than he had bargained for. Still, at least he could spend more quality time with Fourteen. She wasn't holding his hand anymore. She had moved physically away as if she was trying to build a bit of distance between them. Like she had remembered who she was. Ned felt a little hurt but passed it off as a woman, imperial, Upper Circle thing.

The group fell into a natural order. Brogan and Mia marched off in front with Joe and Willow traipsing behind. Jenni was zigzagging here and there as if she were incredibly bored with walking in a straight line. Fourteen and Ned brought up the rear. Hopefully, there wouldn't be any bandits. Or snakes. Or rain.

They walked along the track for what felt like hours. No one was talking. Ned kept an eye on the building clouds behind them. So far, they were not getting any closer, but they were definitely getting blacker. He called Brogan over.

'How far do you think we have to go? Looks like we might need to find some shelter.' He pointed to the cloud.

'We're about halfway I reckon. We won't get there by nightfall.' Brogan didn't sound remotely bothered by this fact.

'Are you sure you can't pop us, Jenni?' asked Ned.

'Nope. Not all of you. I'm starving. You got anyfink?' She looked hopeful.

Ned shook his head. What they needed was a miracle. As if by magic when they rounded the next corner, they saw a small farmstead which looked abandoned. The farmer's house was nothing but ruins, however, the roof of the barn next to it seemed to be intact and as large fat raindrops began to pelt them, there was little consideration as to what to do next. A night in an abandoned barn was better than walking through the night in the pouring rain.

The barn door squealed as Brogan pushed it open. It was dark and smelled mildewy inside. There was no sign of life except for the desperate scrambling of rats trying to find their hidey holes. Ned felt he could manage the magic required for some light and delved deep into his wells, flinging soft glowing balls up into the rafters. There was a screechy flurry from the bats in the eaves and when the lights stayed where they were, the bats flew out in a huff, leaving guano in their wake. There was no hay in the barn, so the visitors would have to make do with their own coats as bedding in order to get a decent night's sleep. The only equipment inside was a wicked looking scythe, which despite the abandoned air of the rest of the place, looked like it was well oiled and cared for, a beloved tool used regularly. It was rather menacing.

Everyone set up on the opposite side of the barn to the scythe, trying to ignore the implement of death. It took a while for them to settle down. It was too quiet, too dark, too close, and at times, too loud with strange noises that couldn't be explained. Eventually though everyone fell asleep. Everyone except for Ned. His eyes roved the barn, catching at every shadow, every wisp of movement although there seemed to be nothing there at all when he focused his gaze. Fourteen was leaning on him, her warmth felt delightful. He snaked his arm around her. He might as well hold her close, while no one was judging them. His hand touched something sticky. Ned frowned, whatever could that be? He bought his hand back to his face and sniffed, it smelt metallic and looked dark and thick. Fumbling for a fire-starter, Ned lit the candle stub that lay nearby and frowned at the stuff on his fingers. It looked like blood. He shifted to get a better look at Fourteen. Her head lolled to the side at an unnatural angle. Her throat had been slashed. It was her blood that lay thick on his fingers.

He looked up in horror, hoping someone else was awake. Someone had seen the light or heard something. Brogan and Mia were leaning against each other. Twin slashes across their necks. Matching sheets of congealing blood lay upon their breasts. Ned's gaze moved on in sick slow motion. Jenni's body lay like a broken rag doll. She had been literally bent in half. Her skin was grey, her limbs sticking out at unnatural angles. Willow had been cleaved in two from neck to navel, like a tree struck by lightning. There was no blood just green sap oozing from the cut edges. Her features were wooden, lifeless. Joe had been pinned to the wall by a pitchfork. His young face was frozen in fear. Ned could not comprehend the horror that lay around him. He let out a low keening moan, full of pain and loss and hurt.

'Ned? Ned! Whatever is the matter?' Fourteen was shaking Ned's arm as he tossed and turned, caught in the horrific nightmare.

He woke gasping, eyes darting around the barn as the others roused. They were all alive. He scrambled to his feet. 'We have to leave – all of us. Right now. It's not safe here.' He pulled Fourteen to her feet. Everyone was looking at him oddly. He knew he was still in the cold grip of fear, his skin felt clammy and he was sweating. He didn't care whether he looked like a crazy man, he was desperate to get them out of that barn.

'Huh.' Joe sounded surprised.

'What? What?' Ned looked around wildly.

'The scythe's moved.' He pointed to the other side of the barn where the scythe stood inverted this time, its blade still glinting wickedly. 'And we have one of these now.' Joe hefted the large pitchfork in his hands.

'Put that down!' yelled Ned. 'Up, up, all of you. Move. NOW!' His voice carried desperation and a lifetime of shouting for survival in the Black Narrows. Undertones of menace delicately entwined with forceful authority.

Unbidden, feet began to shuffle out of the barn. Soon everyone had left it behind. Ned herded the group down the lane away from the building of his nightmare. A sudden whoosh made them stop and turn back to look. The entire structure was engulfed in flame, thick smoke billowing into the sky. As one the group turned to look at Ned in disbelief. Then they all smartly marched away, their feet eating up the road towards Fidelia. The further they went from the barn, the brighter the moon seemed, and friendly stars began to appear in the night sky, lighting the way. Ned breathed easier.

'Are you alright?' Fourteen's brow was wrinkled in concern, she touched Ned's arm gently and he flinched.

'Yes, I think so. The further we get away from that place, the better.'

'What happened?'

'I don't know. You were all asleep and it was so quiet and then I looked and... and... you were all...' He gulped. 'You were all dead. You three had your throats slashed.' He looked at Fourteen then nodded towards Brogan and Mia. Pointing at the others he went on. 'She was split in half, he was pitchforked to the barn door and Jenni, Jenni was... she was...' His voice broke and he had to take a moment to collect himself.

Fourteen didn't know what to say. It wasn't that she didn't believe Ned, but it all sounded so far-fetched. Obviously, he had had some kind of nightmare, probably fuelled by lack of sleep and only one half decent meal recently. But she considered the facts, the scythe had moved and the pitchfork had appeared, then the barn had ignited itself. A leftover threat from the old man on the island perhaps? There was no denying the whole thing had an intense air of evil malice. Instead of trying to find the right words, she held his hand, trying to reassure him by just being physically there.

Chapter 30

The road was empty and the journey uneventful as they drew closer to Fidelia. The only thing that changed was Ned's mood - he grew grimmer at each footfall.

'Why do you dislike Fidelia so much?' Fourteen asked casually. Everyone throughout the day had approached her, separately, begging her to find out the reason for Ned's mood. She wasn't sure how much good she could do. She knew next to nothing about the man. She only loved him, that was all.

Ned was watching the flight of a lone crow as it flapped lazily in the sky. He squinted against the brightness of the sun before dropping his gaze. 'My brother is there.'

'And you don't get on.'

'Not especially.'

The silence dragged. It likes to drag. It takes extreme pleasure in digging its heels and seeing how far it can push the absence of sound. Most people can't take it. Those who can are rewarded and become a member of the Silent Order who live in The Mountains of Absentia. It is not a pleasant place.

'You want to talk about it?' Fourteen asked. Fortunately, she couldn't stand dragged out silences. She would not have to give up all noise and wear wisps of air anytime soon.

Ned went to kick a pebble viciously. He missed and stubbed his toe on the hard-packed mud instead, making his eyes water and forcing him to swallow several excellent swearwords. He began to limp slightly.

'My brother is Chief of T.A.R.T.S,' he finally replied.

'Oh.'

'Wossat?' Jenni gave up trying to pretend she wasn't earwigging. In fact, the whole group were clustered within easy earshot of Ned, trying hard to look nonchalant. Most of them were doing a bad job.

'He is in charge of Thieves, Arsonists, Raconteurs, Tarts and Solicitors.'

'But you're...' Willow had bloomed in surprise.

'Yep.'

'Wow, what do your parents think about it?' Joe was walking backwards at this point; he didn't want to miss anything that deflected his own current family nightmare.

'They are extremely proud.'

'Well, that's good then.'

'Of my brother. They disowned me.'

'Ah.' Joe wheeled back round to hide the grin from his face. He failed miserably.

Ned could feel the tips of his ears getting hotter and hotter. Jenni earned herself several free rounds at the next inn from the others as she blithely continued.

'Wot do they do then?' she asked.

Ned frowned down at her. 'Father is a retired T.A.R.T.S handler and Mother, well, she was a member of the T guild.'

'Thieves?' Jenni asked innocently.

'No.' The ice in Ned's voice cut off any further discussion and he stomped off in front of them all. The others couldn't help grinning at each other at this juicy information but wisely stopped themselves from discussing it there and then. It would certainly give them something to talk about for the next few hours of travel before they got to Fidelia. The journey had now taken on a festive air. Ned attempted to ignore the lot of them, but it was too difficult when they kept whispering and nudging each other. Finally, after he had threatened to knock Joe out with an awesome right hook for making a rather lewd joke at his expense, the rest of them dropped the topic. Rather reluctantly, true, but no one wanted a black eye.

Late that afternoon, the city of Fidelia appeared in the distance like a dirty mark on the horizon. Its chimneys of industry happily polluted the sky above and rained soot down on its unfortunate inhabitants.

'Don't drink the water,' Ned said. 'It'll more than likely kill you. I'd tell you not to eat the food, but hopefully, you've got a little sense about you. If it's still moving, don't eat it.'

The others were nodding. Ned had been giving short speeches for the last hour or so as they drew closer and closer to the city. They were getting more and more excited to see the sights, whereas Ned was feeling more and more tense. He hoped they would be able to get in, get the ingredients they needed and get out again. As they neared the outer city gates, he stopped walking and spoke to them all, one last time.

'Everyone got their shopping list?'

Nods.

'And you're not to buy anything else, that includes any plants that need saving, Willow. You hear?'

More reluctant nodding.

'Stay in your pairs, know where your buddy is at all times and make the rendezvous spot at what time?

'Six chimes,' they chorused.

'And where is the rendezvous?' Ned asked.

'The far east gate, passed the statue of the naked elephant,' said everyone except for Jenni.

'Er Boss, 'ow zactly is a n'elephant nekkid?' she asked.

'You wait and see, Jenni, just wait and see.' Ned rubbed his hand through his hair. This still felt like such a bad idea. 'Just be careful, alright? It's not like Roshaven. This place has no morals whatsoever.'

'It'll be alright.' Fourteen patted his arm. She was rather looking forward to seeing a city other than her own.

They walked the rest of the way to the gate in silence and were met by a couple of shifty looking geezers wearing the acronym T.A.R.T.S embroidered wonkily upon the breast of their jerkins.

'You him?' The greasiest of the lot addressed Ned.

'Who's asking?'

'You're him. Come with us. You lot, stay 'ere.'

Ned looked back at the group. Everyone looked worried except for Brogan who possibly didn't even know what day of the week it was. Ned tried to smile confidently. 'Stay together. Just say no to everything and you'll be alright.' He squared his shoulders and gestured for the grease ball to lead the way. He didn't look back, so didn't see more ruffians spill out of a nearby building and throw hessian sacks over his friends. It all happened so quickly that any shouts were instantly muffled and Ned's grease ball walked faster than expected. Ned was struggling to get his bearings. It had been a long time

233

since he had last been in Fidelia. The streets were known to move.

After about the seventh turning, Ned gave up and tried to go with the flow. He reasoned that if his brother wanted to kill him, he would have done it already. All this was pure posturing, all for show, trying to make out that he was the big cheese. Finally, they arrived at a plain looking building on a nondescript street. The only thing that set it apart from the rest of the city was that there were no other citizens in sight; no beggars, no urchins, no hawkers. This was headquarters. Ned went in.

On a raised dais towards the back of the room sprawled his brother in a ridiculous looking throne-like chair that towered above him, making him look even more weaselly than he actually was.

'Ted.'

'Edmund! Darling! It's Theo now. Fancy you coming to my lickle city. How ever did you dare?' He smiled but it didn't touch his eyes which bored into Ned as if trying to decide whether he was worth doing anything about or not.

'I'm only passing through, brother. I need to resupply and then I'll be on my way.'

'Here in Fidelia we thrive on need, it's what we do best. I'm sure we can come to some sort of arrangement.' Theo slunk off the throne and began to pace the dais. 'The question is, do you have anything I need?'

'What do you want?' Ned asked bluntly.

'Eddie, darling, don't rush me! Let's have dinner tonight. Mother and Father will be dying to see you. It's been an age. You can bring your little friends once I've finished with them.'

'What do you mean, finished with them?' Ned had

hoped not to draw attention to the rest of his travelling companions.

'Just a light interrogation, nothing to worry about.'

Before Ned had chance to react, the building's doors blew open, shards of wood scattering across the floor and a very, very angry looking sprite stalked in with the rest of Ned's troupe behind her.

'Boss! You good?'

'Yes, thanks, Jenni.' Ned pointed to the dais. 'Everyone, this is my brother, Ted.'

'Theo, please, charmed I'm sure.' Theo extended a limp wrist in their general direction. Jenni sniffed then hawked over her shoulder. 'What a delightful little fae,' said Theo. 'I simply have to get one.'

Ned groaned inwardly. The last thing he wanted was his brother to take any interest in why he was here. He had always taken a perverse delight in taking Ned's things.

'Theo, we don't want to take up any more of your time than we already have,' Ned said. 'I'll pay for the doors, we'll resupply and be on our way, okay?'

'Brother, dearest. You must stay here, freshen up. Then you can all join me for dinner, and we will discuss your needs.' Theo's eyes glinted. His gaze roved over the party. He instantly dismissed Joe as a wet lettuce and Brogan as another barbarian. Mia's good looks earned her a second, appraising look whilst Willow's charms seemed to have no effect on him, whatsoever. He didn't do plants. Fourteen had her hood up and was trying to blend into the back of the group but all that managed to do was pique his interest. Theo motioned and the others moved sideways without even realising, their bodies reacting on instinct to the most powerful thing in the room and the intense desire for self-preservation.

Fourteen shrank in on herself, but it was too late. Theo had already reached her and tipped back the hood. He smiled the fat cat cream smile of having just found the price for his brother's need.

'I'll take her. Thank you, brother. You always have such exquisite taste.'

'She is not for you.' Ned shook his head ever so slightly at Fourteen, begging her mentally to be quiet.

'But Eddie – I want her!' Theo pouted.

Things were starting to deteriorate. Ned knew what his brother's mood swings were like. He tried to rally. 'Let us freshen up for dinner and then we can discuss everything, as a family.'

Theo watched his brother for a few moments before clapping his hands. 'Yes, yes. A family meal, that's what we need. Go, go, go. Rooms have been made available. Bathe, freshen, choose something new to wear, it's all available for my beloved brother and his friends. I will see you for dinner. Don't be late!' And he clapped his hands in dismissal. Thugs appeared at the doorway but were unsure what to do as the doors no longer existed. Should they sweep the fragments open?

Jenni smirked at their indecision and as everyone walked through the doorway she clicked her fingers and the doors reassembled themselves, looking better than ever. It was possibly not the wisest thing she could have done. Theo watched greedily, mentally rubbing his hands in glee and already putting together a list of things the sprite could do for him. All he had to do was buy his brother off. Shouldn't be difficult. He would threaten to kill everyone. Ned always did have a bleeding heart. So it should be a decent bargaining chip. Theo yelled for his underlings and began telling them his evening plans. Tonight was going to be fun.

Chapter 31

The group gathered in Ned's room. They were all nervous.

'What should we do?'

'Are we safe here?'

'Is he going to help us?'

Ned held up his hands to stop the questions becoming a hysterical flood. 'My brother is... a handful. He always has been, but he can be reasoned with. Sometimes. The main thing is not to get him too interested in us. So far we haven't done that well.' He frowned at Jenni who at least had the decency to look slightly sheepish. Which was tricky as she didn't have the wool for it. Fourteen was doing a better job.

'I am sorry, Ned, I was trying to stay out of sight. I was worried he might recognise me.'

Ned took half a step towards her, trying to think of something to say. They looked at each in silence which got awkward, fast. Neither one was entirely sure how exactly to express themselves. Mia coughed loudly.

'Look, sorry to interrupt *the moment* but can we trust Theo?' she asked.

'No, but he will expect us to bathe and change. He's a stickler for good manners and we need to start off on the right foot when we go down to dinner. So, here's what we'll do...' The others leant in as Ned outlined his plan for survival. They had to get through one meal. And then find the supplies they needed. And then get out of Fidelia alive. No problem.

Ned waited in the corridor for the others. He had taken one look at the outfit his dear brother had laid out for him and decided that his torn and dirty thief-catcher uniform was a darn sight more decent than the scraps of lace and silk Ted - sorry Theo - had ordered for him to wear. Parts of it were transparent! He had questioned the maid as to whether she had bought the right garments, the poor thing was shaking like a leaf towards the end of his interrogation. Either scared or she was trying her damnedest not to laugh out loud. I mean – silk and lace! For a grown man! He had managed to get the worst of the road out of his leathers, they wiped down well, besides he thought a bit of wear and tear added to his general *don't mess with me* air and he certainly felt like he needed bags of that around him tonight. He hadn't seen his parents in a decade. They didn't approve of his career choice. He was fairly sure they would, however, approve of his love interest. Anything to help them get their hands on more gold and more power. He would have to try and speak to Fourteen before they went down to dinner, see if they couldn't concoct some kind of cover story.

Fourteen's door opened and out swept Willow and Jenni. Willow had also declined Theo's clothing suggestions - far too restrictive. Instead, she had opted for well-placed bloomage. *It certainly made the blood rush along*, thought Ned as he did his best to avert his eyes. Jenni was Jenni. She had decided to wear her filthy red coat with pride. The fact that she didn't own anything else was neither here nor there. She was fae. She could get anything she wanted in a blink of an eye. And Ned certainly had to blink, several times, furiously as Fourteen came through the doorway. She was resplendent. She wore her official Emperor robes, but they had been altered to take into account the fact that she was a woman, so they curved in here and sculpted there. Making sinuous shapes that suggested so much. Ned was adamant they had not been like that before. He was also adamant that they had not bought such robes with them. And as for her imperial crown, they definitely had not brought that.

'Did my brother give you that to wear?' Ned asked.

'No. Jenni popped for me. I wanted to make a good impression.' She looked him up and down disdainfully. 'Unlike some people.'

Ned flushed and stammered. 'You look, of course, you do, I mean, that is, I meant to say.' He took the defeat and turned away, mentally kicking himself for being such an idiot but he hadn't been able to help himself. When he had seen her standing there looking so beautiful, jealously had coursed through his veins at the thought, the idea, of his brother having anything to do with Fourteen at all. Ned's hands were clenched to stop them from shaking as he tried to overcome his sudden anger. Brogan, Mia and Joe came out of the other door in the corridor, all of them opting for their own clothes, which made Fourteen stand out even more. She stretched her neck elegantly and proceeded to lead them all towards the dining room.

Some of Theo's street thugs were stood outside. They leered at Fourteen as she glided towards them and stood imperiously, waiting for them to open the doors. They grinned at the rest of them as they allowed the group entrance into the hall. It was lined with more toughs, all of them heavily armed.

So much for getting through dinner in one-piece thought Ned gloomily. He could see his parents and brother down at the far end of the room, where a lavishly laid table waited for them.

'Brother – dearest! Let's sit down and eat, shall we? Here, sit here, brother. Right here.' Theo manoeuvred everyone to his satisfaction. Father sat at the head of the table with Mother on his right hand followed by Ned, Joe and Willow down one side. Fourteen sat at his left hand with Theo, Jenni, Brogan and Mia.

Conversation flitted across the table lightly. Theo doing his best to involve everyone or at least make everyone feel uncomfortable. Ned watched his father speaking to Fourteen from the corner of his eye. He hoped he wasn't being too inappropriate. A shrill voice interrupted him.

'So, come crawling back to your brother, have you?'

It was Ned's mother. She had decided she would speak to the black sheep of the family.

'Just passing through, Mother. Dinner was Ted's idea.'

'It's Theo now.'

'Right.'

'You would do well to follow his example, he's taken T.A.R.T.S to a whole new level of success. Surpassed your Father's efforts.' She turned a critical eye on Ned. 'And you, well, what do you have to show for yourself?'

'I've actually been promoted, Mother.'

'Yes, I heard about that. Letting the family down by becoming a thief-catcher is one thing Edmund but to voluntarily rise through the ranks is shocking. You should be ashamed of yourself. You've tarnished the good family name.'

Ned gritted his teeth and made non-committal noises. For once his mother had kept her voice down and everyone else seemed fully occupied with the delicate canapés and amuse-bouches. Mouthfuls of yumminess designed to fire up everyone's appetite for the main course but also useful for filling your face and preventing any further conversation. Ned watched the main course arrive – a huge roasted pig with all the usual accompaniments.

'Recognise him?' Theo teased his brother, but Ned looked down at his plate, willing the whole night to be over already.

Fourteen was using every ounce of her Emperor skills to both listen to Ned's father and watch the conversation around the table. The meal and the men droned on; the room got stuffy as bellies were filled. Boredom set in and bottoms shifted on hard chairs. Finally, Theo clapped his hands and the table was cleared.

'It has been such fun to catch up and to meet Eddies' friends. So quaint. But I insist you stay the night. We shall discuss your needs in the morning. Come, come, allow me to escort you to your room, my dear.' And he linked his arm to Fourteen who had no option but to be led away from the table. The others scrambled to follow.

Chapter 32

They met in Fourteen's room - it was the biggest and didn't smell of three-day-old socks. Fourteen stood behind a screen making rustling noises and wafting her perfume right across Ned's face. He had his back to the screen and was scowling fiercely at Brogan and Joe, daring them to risk a look. That perfume! Fourteen glided out from behind the screen, looking demure and more Fourteeney than before. Her Emperor get-up didn't suit her natural grace.

'What do we do now?' she asked the group but meaning Ned. She felt afraid of the power-crazed man related to Ned and unnerved by the leering looks she had endured from the many, many roughnecks who had lined the hallway, not to mention the crude suggestions whispered to her by Ned's father, of all people. What she wanted to do was scrub this place right out of her hair and body, but she reflected sourly, there were probably a dozen peepholes in the bathrooms. Involuntarily she shuddered and realised everyone was looking at her. 'Sorry, what did I miss?' she asked.

'I was just talking about Ted.' Ned reached for a nearby blanket to drape around Fourteen's shoulders. 'We shouldn't underestimate my brother. If we stay here too long, he will have found ways to keep us here. I think we should leave tonight.'

'Tonight? But aren't his men watching us?' asked Fourteen.

'Yes, but Jenni – you could pop us out of here couldn't you?'

Jenni flexed her arms and stretched her magical muscles. 'To be 'onest, I fink I can only do one atta time but lemme use 'im to boost me and see if I can get a bit o' distance.' She jerked her thumb at Joe who started nervously and began nodding.

'Why can't you do us all at once, like before?' demanded Mia. She was feeling very left out. Theo had paid her no attention whatsoever and she'd had to sit through a boring dinner.

'Cos there's an old magical shield in place innit.' She eyed Joe. 'You 'elping?'

'Yes, yes I can help.' Joe was still nodding. 'Whatever you need.'

'Fine, let's pop to the central fountain in Fidelia,' said Ned. 'There will still be people around at this time, they haven't started inn kick outs yet. If we time it right, the drunken mob will cover our tracks for us. I know a merchant who should be able to help us with our resupply.'

'Won't he be asleep?' Fourteen was sceptical.

'He works, er, unusual hours.'

'You mean he's a smuggler.'

'Look, Griff is about the only person in this town who has the nerve to help us out, so I say we forget what he does for a living and be grateful we've got an out.' Ned's nerves were beginning to fray. They had all been in here far too long. Spy holes were going to be reporting back empty rooms. 'Does everyone have their gear with them?'

There were nods and Brogan looked confused until Mia dangled a backpack in front of his face. Honestly, how barbarians make it through life Ned had no idea. People must decide they are too dumb to kill.

'Jenni – let's get going.' Ned ordered.

Joe stood awkwardly at her side, not sure what he was supposed to do. Jenni spat on her hand and grabbed his, making a water seal, of sorts. It helped to have a little bit of elemental support in these things, made the power transfer smooth. She took a moment and focused on Willow. Then the nymph was gone, leaving a few leaves falling through the air in her place. Brogan barely had time to open his mouth in surprise before he too had gone. Next up, Mia. But there was a problem. She wavered. Not really here – not really there.

'It's the binding. She's sticky. Can't shift 'er. Boss?'

Ned came over and endured a spit handclasp, gasping at the sheer breadth of power that coursed through him. Ned looked at Fourteen and there was an extra power surge, surprising even Jenni. Mia vanished and Jenni let go of them both, gasping for breath.

'Bloody 'ell, Boss.' She peered into his face. 'You unblocked?'

Ned shifted uncomfortably. 'Let's get on with it, eh, Jenni?' He wanted Fourteen out of here.

She grinned, tightened her grip on Joe and turned her gaze to Fourteen. But before she could focus their energies there was a wet pop and then Ned felt his belly button swirl.

'Gods!' The world spun around him and suddenly he was deposited in the fountain. Water gushed into his boots and the others looked at him in surprise, including Fourteen, who staggered at the edge of the fountain.

Jenni and Joe appeared. Jenni was excited. 'Boss! 'ow'd you do it? I never showed you that one afore, you never 'ad the juice. And then you just – whoosh!' She gestured excitedly at the others. 'Did you see? 'e went for it. And then 'e'd gone! Took 'er as well.' Turning back to Ned she beamed proudly. 'That were right good, Boss, real fae work. Proud of ya.'

Ned didn't have a clue what she was talking about, but they were all here and it was going to be inn kick-out time soon, so he tried to get his bearings. If memory served then Griff was west of here, near the port. They probably didn't have long; their rooms would have been watched. He herded everyone together and led them towards the port, certain his memory would kick in and they would find Griff before his brother found them.

It took a few wrong turns and one tense moment in an alley, watching some of Theo's toughs stagger back from a late one before they found the nondescript building that housed the most successful smuggler of all time. The paint was peeling and two of the windows were cracked, although they were so dirty you couldn't see in anyway. When Ned tried to open the door it got stuck, warped with damp and old age. It took him, Brogan and Joe several attempts before admitting defeat and standing aside for Willow to rekindle what spark was left in the wood, coaxing it back to life and giving it some strength to open. She caressed the beaten down planks sensuously and left a tiny sapling growing from an old knot as a farewell.

'What?' she blushed green as she became aware of the others staring at her. 'He's lonely. Bit of company never hurt anyone.'

They made their way into the gloom of an abandoned shop. Cobwebs hung everywhere and dust lay thickly over everything except for a brass bell that shone with a dim glow on an empty bench. Ned twonged it decisively. It reverberated throughout the shop and as the dong echoed into nothingness, an old man – woman – hard to tell, an old person shuffled through a half-hidden doorway out the back.

'Eh? Eh? What you for?'

'I'm here to see Griff. Tell him it's Edmund de Silverthorpe.' Ned's ears went red as he heard the hushed whispers behind him at hearing his full name.

'What? What? Speak up you sonofabitch? Eh?'

'Yeah, alright. Good one Griff, come on, let us in.'

The old thing paused in its general shuffling and let out a loud shout of laughter before unfolding to reveal a rather wide, rather dashing pirate. It was the gold hoop earrings and the skull & crossbones pattern on his shirt that gave it away. Pirates can't resist skull and crossbones. The glamour of the old person and the ramshackle shop fell away although the knackered old door remained, treasuring its sapling.

'Edmundo! Good to see you, good to see you. You better not have pissed off your brother and be running to me with your balls in your hand!' Loud guffaws accompanied every statement.

Fourteen was delighted and a little shocked at such a vibrant and loud man. This was going to be interesting.

'Look, Griff, we need some help. Theo's being Theo and trying to keep us here. We're just passing through, heading for the Purple Mountain. I need some supplies and then I'll be on my way.'

'So soon – so soon? Eddie my boy, surely time for a drink and a smoke eh? Come, come away in, my girls will see to your lists. Sit, sit, have a small one eh? Leads to good times eh, Eddie Boy?'

Griff led them through to a richly furnished sitting room and rang a bell. Serving girls instantly filled the room, taking bags, jackets, boots, and piling them unobtrusively in the corner, pushing everyone into soft pillows and plying drinks, sugared dates and saltines upon them. Someone began striking a dulcimer softly and incense wafted across the room.

'We can't stay long, Griff. Theo will be looking to make someone suffer,' Ned said.

'Let me worry about that jumped up piece of shit. He may own the roughs and think he owns Fidelia's ladies of the night, but it's me they come to for their needs and it's me they whisper their little secrets too. I own the ladies and you can't get anything done in Fidelia without the ladies eh? Boobs make the world go around eh? Eh?' Griff dug his elbow into Ned's ribs and guffawed loudly.

Fourteen was being practical. She had already taken a list of supplies from Joe and was handing it to one of Griff's young things. The girl was pursing her lips as she read the list then she nodded and disappeared. There was nothing to do now but wait.

And so they slept. It wasn't their fault - Griff had spiked their refreshments. He was worried. He might be Fidelia's best smuggler and he might own the ladies of this town, but lately, Theo had been getting vicious in the extreme when he was ignored. The boy had far too much power for such a dangerous mind. Griff wanted everyone moved, no questions asked so he could lie convincingly when Theo's roughs came knocking. And they would come knocking. Theo had not yet managed to extend his maniacal rule over the ocean water in the port of Fidelia. It belonged to the Sea-Witch and she loved Griff as fiercely as a mercurial beast can. He fed her regularly and left many, many gifts. Sometimes on purpose. But he had no plans in feeding Ned and his party to the Sea-Witch. He liked Ned, always had. Such a shame the sensible one had decided on an honest life. Such a waste.

Griff had his people cram the visitors into empty barrels with hidden fillers, so even if the lids were opened, they would look like barrels of salted fish and not barrels of wanted people. Time had run out. Theo had noticed his guests were gone and an underground missive had been sent out with a hefty reward for scalped heads and even more for entire skins. Griff had received several versions from his network of spies. Theo didn't seem too bothered about whether the group returned inside their skins or not. Clearly, he felt that murdering the Emperor of Roshaven wasn't a big deal. Griff smiled to himself as he remembered the quickly masked surprise on Fourteen's face as she registered who he was. He had travelled far and wide, even spending a little time in Roshaven's Imperial Court. He knew the Emperor's secret and held it along with many of his own and he was doubly pleased that Ned had hitched his wagon there. About time that lad had some happiness 'twixt the sheets. Ah, young love! He pondered on the wonderfulness of it as an arrow slammed into his chest with a wet thunk. 'Huh.' Griff toppled to the floor, mouth open in surprise. That wasn't supposed to happen.

Ned woke up feeling like he had been stuffed into a barrel. Then he realised he was actually stuffed in a barrel. It appeared to be bobbing and that smell! Salted fish. His stomach was churning, and panic was setting in as he realised he couldn't move his arms, or his legs, or his head. And now all the air was disappearing. It wasn't, but panic said it was. He tried to flex his muscles, such as they were to see if the barrel would magically

248

collapse around him. All that happened was a slight cramp developed in his left foot. So now he was trapped, about to suffocate, and in pain - great. His thoughts jumped to Fourteen and his panic level tripled. What if she were trapped in a barrel too? What if her air was running out? What if – a sob caught in his throat – she was dead?

Something coursed through his veins and the poor innocent barrel that encased him was blown to smithereens and a trembling Ned stretched to standing on a decrepit looking skiff. There were five other barrels, one of which was spinning wildly before it too exploded. Ned ducked, covering his face to avoid splinter missiles and peeked out to see an angry looking sprite. Jenni clicked her fingers and the rest of the barrels disappeared. Everyone else was still comatose. Ned dragged his gaze away from Fourteen, not knowing whether he should try and wake her or not.

'Wot 'appened, Boss? Where are we?' asked Jenni.

Jenni and Ned looked around. They were bobbing on the ocean. Fidelia Quay was still visible in the distance, but the skiff had been cut loose. There were several oiled brown paper parcels piled in the centre of the skiff, one or two had arrows in them and one had a note with a jewelled dagger holding it in place. Ned reached out with an unsteady hand and plucked the note loose. It was badly smeared with what looked like blood.

Theo too far. Betrayed. Done for. Right this. G

Ned blinked several times, damn grit in his eye. His brother had murdered Griff for helping them. It had been a mistake to come here, supplies or no supplies. The others were beginning to stir. Stiff limbs stretched out and consciousness came back. Everyone was surprised and confused, Ned gave them a run down.

'We're in Fidelia's port. Theo tried to kill us. Griff saved us.' He paused for that damn dust in his eye. 'Joe, check through the supplies, make sure we've got everything we need. Jenni, can we get this skiff moving? We need to get closer to the mountain. Finish this bloody quest.'

Jenni peered over the edge of the skiff and sniffed. 'Dunno Boss. This is Sea-Witch territory. She don't get on wiv Momma K but she might talk wiv me. I'll see.' She licked her finger, leant over the skiff and stuck her finger in the water. Nothing happened.

Joe called softly for Ned's attention. 'We've got everything, Boss, it's all here. I don't know how they found it so quickly, but we've got everything we need.' He rubbed his nose anxiously. 'It will work, won't it?'

Ned didn't reply. He bloody hoped so. How had it come to this anyway? He was tasked with chasing a bloody rose thief – who he had found, thank you very much. Now he was helping the thief defeat her sorcerer father. A sorcerer! He didn't even know they still existed. I mean magic was magic, but sorcery was old school tomfoolery. And then what happened when the evil sorcerer was defeated? Could Fourteen love him publicly? Would he have to become a concubine – concubus – concubina? Whatever. His head hurt. 'Any food?' he asked.

Joe passed him a pasty. It was still warm. Guilt sloshed over him as he thought of his mate Griff and that belly laugh that was not going to shake again anytime soon.

Chapter 33

The skiff wallowed somewhat in the ocean, neither drifting forwards or backwards, the wind half-heartedly ruffling Willow's leaves and keeping the passengers cool, but not helping them move in any particular direction. This was beginning to cause a problem as Theo's men had now noticed the skiff, eyeglasses had confirmed the inhabitants and heavily armed rowboats were being assembled.

'Jenni, anything?' asked Ned.

The sprite was now elbow deep in ocean and concentrating. 'She wants payment upfront, Boss.'

Right. *Payment for the Sea Witch, what would that be?* Ned cast his eyes over the skiff looking at the different bags and boxes piled in the centre. The pitiful wind had perked up and was making some paper dance in the breeze. *Hang on, paper?* Ned eased the note out from under two boxes and his heart banged harder as he recognised the scrawl.

You'll have to pay the witch. Look in the red bag, it's no one you know eh!

Griff. Bloody Griff saving their lives, again. The red bag was sitting soggily off to one side. It was with some trepidation Ned peered inside. The head and entrails of

251

grease ball looked up at him. Squashing the squeamishness out of his stomach Ned picked the bag up and hurled the contents out into the water. Instantly Jenni yanked her hand out and the sea began to boil. Eddies began to appear and then white topped waves caressing the skiff were the only sign they were moving and moving fast. That and the sudden lurch away from Fidelia. And the splash as Joe fell in.

Before anyone had time to react, a huge hand of water hoicked Joe out and threw him back to the skiff with surprising accuracy. He landed wetly and gasped, much like a fish out of water. Ned decided not to dwell too much on the size of the helping hand and instead looked out across the bay. They didn't want to go too far out into the real ocean where monsters roamed eating ships for fun. Just that headland, in the distance, you know - the one that looked like a load of knobbly old rocks. The one that was coming into focus more and more quickly. How fast were they travelling? Ned risked a look backwards and could no longer make out the rowboats as anything other than faint dots on the horizon. Didn't mean Theo would not come. Just meant they had a slight advantage.

Fourteen's gasp turned his attention back to the headland which was now in your face-land as the skiff careered out of the water and broke across a particularly jagged rock. There was a lot of groaning. Amazingly the piece of skiff with all the supplies on was still in one piece. It was the periphery and the people who had been banged out of shape. Ned lay still for a moment. He knew he had to get up and do a headcount, get people moving to a safe place to camp and lick their wounds, but right now he lacked the energy to even lift his head. Griff was dead. And it was his fault.

'Come on, up you get. You alright, Willow? See to Joe will you, love. Mia, all good? Yes, I can see. Here, Jenni, use mine.' It was Fourteen. She was marshalling everyone, checking, reassuring, being a leader. Exactly what he should be doing. Damn that dust in his eye.

The group left Ned alone for about three and a half minutes.

'Boss, we're good to go,' Jenni said.

He sat up and saw that all the supplies had been stowed and were now being carried, mostly by Brogan but then, you have got to make use of a hulking barbarian where you can. The group looked resolute, a little dented but determined to make it through.

'Right.' Ned's voice sounded thick in his own ears as he stood. 'Let's try and find some shelter.' He led them off the jagged shoreline, not believing he should be in front but feeling better with each step he took. It was like his old boss, Norm, always used to say – fake it till you make it, then run off with the gold. There might not be any gold here, but Ned could fake it with the best of them.

They trudged wearily off the sands and into the desolate countryside. They were nearing mountain territory and that meant trolls, ogres, giants, anything of large mass that hadn't managed to make it down into civilisation yet. It was hard trying to teach a rock with a pea brain that it couldn't do what it liked and yes it owed taxes and no, I'm not going to collect them, thank you very much for the offer of what to do with your club but if it's all the same, I'm going to run away screaming. Well, that is not entirely fair. The trolls, ogres, giants and other creatures of large size and indeterminate nature understood the last part well. They called it dinner and a show.

253

At last they found a cave. It looked to be abandoned but you never can tell this close to the mountains, so Jenni let a spell loose inside. A few bats, snakes, spiders, lizards, rats, and other creepy crawlies made a fast exit, but other than that it was free and clear of things trying to kill you in your sleep. Except for any nocturnal visitors. And a cave-in. Ned wished his brain would shut up. He had always disliked the mountains. Give him the crowded, smelly streets of Roshaven any day. Fourteen matched his dislike of *outdoors*. At least in the city, you knew who was trying to kill you, out here you had to be on guard for everything. That plant over there? Probably toxic. Those innocuous looking ants? Probably eat the flesh right off your face. That boulder? That will crush you in the night. Nature had the last laugh out here, back in Roshaven no one even knew what nature was.

They huddled near the entrance, all of them reluctant to venture any further into the cave which was probably for the best. Jenni started a magical fire, iridescent flames flickered warmly reflecting unusual colours on the pale faces that surrounded it.

Joe began rummaging through the various bags and boxes piled on the floor beside him, muttering to himself and making several excited exclamations. He finally flourished a bag of marshmallows. 'C'mon guys, let's forget everything for a little while.' He passed out the bag, which had helpful toasting sticks included and they all became busy burning sugar. It actually made the group feel better. The marshmallows were sticky, ooey and gooey and while you were trying to get the perfect blend between charring and burning you couldn't think of anything else. Peace descended, if only for a short while.

Once the marshmallows were gone Ned turned to

Joe. 'You sure you've got everything for this spell?'

'I think so.'

'Are you going to tell us about it now?' Ned asked.

Joe flushed. Up until now, he had managed to avoid talking about it. To be honest, he wasn't even entirely sure he could perform the spell but had sort of been hoping that something else would happen and he wouldn't have to. Sons performing magic against their fathers never ended well in the legends. Not that Joe thought he was legend material, but you can have hope that your quest will at least be successful. He realised he had been inner monologuing a touch too long and now everyone was watching him with exasperated expectation.

'Right, yes, well. It's relatively simple.' He drew the grimoire out of his satchel and flipped to the correct page. 'Um, you've got to make a magical broth and then dip the weapon of choice into it, imbue it with a couple more spells and incantations and then er, hope for the best I guess.'

'Hope for the best?' Mia asked flatly. 'You're putting all our lives on the line with hope for the best? Do you have any idea the kind of person you're dealing with Joe? He's not going to stand around waiting for you to stutter and stammer your way through the spells. You've got to be on it. You've got to be in control, looking like you know what you're doing.'

'I do know what I'm doing!' Joe retorted.

'What's the first part of the spell?' Mia asked.

'Er, um, just a minute, let me see.' Joe began flipping pages frantically.

'See, you don't even know. You're a joke, Joe. Can't someone else do this spell?' She looked meaningfully at Jenni.

'Nope. I ain't got the right kind of whoosh. S'gotta be 'uman, see.'

Willow was whispering to Joe, trying to boost his confidence and stroking his hair with various tendrils. She turned to stare at Mia, thorns in her eyes.

'Well, maybe you could give me my magic back?' There was a hint of desperation in Mia's voice.

'You have to answer for the murders you were involved with. No magic for you.' Ned was emphatic. 'Hey Joe, maybe I can be your understudy. Spells seem to be working for me at the moment, wouldn't hurt for two of us to know what we're doing.'

Joe seemed to melt with gratitude, and he looked like he might cry. Clearly, the boy was not cut out for this sort of thing. He scooted around the fire so he could sit closer to Ned and began to show him the various spell pages. It was long and complicated, and Ned could feel his head hurting already. Then Fourteen put her hand in his and everything felt like it was going to be okay.

Several hours and a banging headache later Ned made himself recite back the elements he had mastered so far, to Joe and Jenni. Everyone else was out looking for food.

'So, we have to boil the magical berries, I forget what they're called but we've only got one sort so we can't muck that up. Yes, so boil berries in the enchanted water from the spring of eternal happiness.' He clattered through the various bottles and vials lined up in front of him, finally choosing a bright pink one with a sunshine yellow stopper. 'This. And then, and then mash 'em all up with a pinch of, a pinch of...' He trailed off as he searched through the various packets on the ground. 'This! A pinch of this. Sand from somewhere or other. That's right, isn't it?'

Joe was fascinated at how nonchalantly Ned dealt with the incredibly rare magical ingredients that littered the ground in front of him. Some of them could kill them all instantly if not handled properly. No wonder Ned's magic was blocked - he had no respect for it.

'Yes, Boss,' said Joe. 'That will create the paste to cover the weapon. Have we decided what to go with, yet?'

Ned shook his head. They had few options. Within the party, they owned one rather rusty sword, which was more for show than anything else. Griff had provided a snazzy looking mini crossbow, but no one knew how to work the mechanisms - it looked extremely new-fangled. Most of them had throwing knives of one sort or another but the problem with knives was you either had to be up close and personal to jab 'em in good or have superb aim that wouldn't be put off by any magical force-fields that may or may not be in place. The most sensible idea would be to give everyone a knife dipped in the magical paste and orchestrate a complex attack so the evil sorcerer wouldn't know which direction his death was coming from. Only they didn't have enough knives. The only other weapon Griff had supplied was a bow and arrow. Ned had instantly dismissed that. Bows and arrows were gentry weapons of choice - no use here at all.

'Let's make as much as we can and then put it on everything. Fights rarely go to plan in my experience.'

Joe nodded miserably. He thought his father would easily deflect any such attack, but he didn't want to tell Ned that.

'What do we do with him once we've managed to stab him? I mean this paste should rob him of his power and hopefully hit a vital organ but what then?' asked

Ned.

Joe stared blankly at Ned. 'I hadn't thought about that.'

'Maybe we could tie him up somewhere?' called Willow as she investigated the nearby vegetation.

'Maybe,' agreed Ned but privately he thought tying up would only lead to an escape. They needed a more permanent solution.

'Wot about sending 'im to the middle of nowhere, Boss? 'E ain't gonna get out of there.' Jenni nudged Joe and winked at him.

'That is not a bad idea, Jenni. Not a bad idea at all.' Ned started putting the ingredients together into the sturdy pestle Griff had supplied. How had that guy anticipated exactly what they needed? 'You alright to have that spell ready?' He asked as he steadily ground each new ingredient to a fine powder and finally mixed them all together. Jenni nodded confidently and looked over his shoulder in approval. It looked like glittery black sand. By the time he was ready to pour in the liquid part of the mixture, the others had returned from the hunt. Willow had gathered every conceivable edible plant you might think to find betwixt mountain and sea whilst Brogan proudly lay a fat fish on a nearby rock. His smile faltered somewhat as Fourteen put down a brace of conies.

'Snares,' she explained shyly.

Mia looked over everything and then nodded towards her brother. 'We gathered; you cook.'

'I can't right now Mia, we're making the paste.'

'Well I'm not doing it,' Mia retorted.

'But you didn't even catch anything by the look of things,' Joe argued.

'Brogan's counts as mine.' And Mia stalked off to go

258

sit as far away from the cooking pot as possible but close enough to be able to see when it was ready.

'It's alright, I don't mind doing it.' Fourteen began to gut the fish with her belt knife. 'I don't get to cook often.'

Ned watched her skill with surprised appreciation. 'How do you even know how to do this stuff? Surely that's not standard emperor training?'

'You'd be surprised.' Fourteen smiled fondly in memory of her training. Some of the happiest days of her childhood had been spent with the various imperial groundsmen her father had employed. She had been liberal in using the phrase, *But I am the Emperor's daughter!* Besides, folk didn't mind when it was clear she was actually interested in their trade and more to the point showed deft aptitude to everything she turned her hand at.

Joe continued to work the ingredients into a paste. There was some muttering, a few surprising colour changes and once a huge smoke ball that smelt strongly of rotten eggs which wafted across the campsite, lingering a lot longer than anyone cared for.

'It's ready.' Joe and Fourteen spoke at once. He had made the deadly paste. She had concocted a rabbit stew that smelt rich and inviting and had somehow fried fish strips in butter – in butter! Goodness only knows where she found that.

Ned gathered the various knives and began dipping them into the paste, rubbing it in with a piece of dragonhide they had found in one of the supply bags whilst the rest of them helped themselves to food and in Brogan's case to seconds. Ned had nearly finished when Fourteen apologetically placed four more knives on the floor.

'Let me do these. You get some food before it's all

gone.'

Ned smiled gratefully, what a woman the Emperor was turning out to be. He, indeed no one, noticed Fourteen surreptitiously dip the discarded arrowheads into the mixture and then rolling up the arrows and bow into her saddlebag. Such things could come in handy. Waste not, want not as Ma Bowl always used to say.

The campfire was full of the happy silence of well-fed people. Even Mia had to begrudgingly agree – to herself, not verbally – that it was a fine feast for people effectively on the run and halfway up a mountain.

Chapter 34

They slept well. They did not notice the nocturnal visitors who were swiftly deterred by Jenni's *you don't want nuffink to do wiv this place* ward. It was probably for the best. Five humans, a nymph and a sprite do not turn up in the mountains every day. It looked like fast food had finally slowed down and decided to deliver itself, so the variety of bloodthirsty predators were wide-ranging. A couple of them considered camping outside to wait for whatever was inside to emerge, but the dawning of a bright ball of sunshine made them think it was probably best to go home and sleep.

Ned looked at the ground in front of the cave curiously. Had every single creature in the mountains come to look at the outside of the cave? How strange. He was the first awake and waited impatiently for everyone else to rouse. Eventually, some slightly squashed breakfast rolls were handed out and somehow Fourteen put the coffee on to boil. This camping out lark was easy peasy when you had Griff to supply you. The group finally got on their way and began the climb up the side of the Purple Mountain.

No one spoke much. The air was a little thinner and the ground a little looser. You had to watch every step so

261

that you didn't turn an ankle. Then there were the midges. Attracted by an abundance of warm bodies, they were having the time of their life. So much blood to choose from. Mother midges were bringing their whole families out and soon a hazy swarm surrounded the group.

'Jenni! Can't you do something about this?' yelled Ned, spitting out a few midges that decided to dive-bomb his mouth.

'Nope.'

'Why not?'

'S'nature ain't it, gotta let it be. First law an' all.'

Ned glared at the sprite, but she wasn't bothered by him or the midges, her unique smell kept most of them at arms' length and tough sprite skin meant that even those who made it through her singular odour were unable to bite. Willow was also midge free and doing her best to swish the air around Fourteen and Joe with various tendrils. Brogan still didn't even know which day of the week it was, let alone what mountain he was climbing or what bug was biting him. Bug biting was a common ailment for barbarians. Came with the line of work. Mia looked as miserable as Ned felt.

They continued trudging on and eventually, the midges left them alone. In fact, every bush, plant, bug, lizard, spider, snake and probably a multitude of other nature, disappeared. The power of the sorcerer was beginning to show. It got quiet, even the sky began to forebode. Everything about the place was screaming at them to leave now and never come back. Except for Jenni, she was capering in delight. To her, it was like some kind of natural Eden. Magic called to her and she felt intoxicated.

'Ned, have you seen Jenni?' Fourteen asked in

concern.

'She looks happy. Glad someone is.'

'Yes, but didn't Mia say her father was preying on fae? What if there's an enchantment at work that we can't see but she can.'

Ned watched as Jenni skipped delightedly. She never skipped. 'You might be right. Hey Jenni, come here a minute, would you?'

She danced over to him and he ran a quick decontamination sweep over her. Standard thief-catcher issue - you never knew what you'd come up against in Roshaven.

'Boss? Wassup?' Jenni shook her head, trying to clear the fuzziness.

'Just checking up on you. We want to keep you safe, Jenni. We need you at full strength.'

She nodded rather dreamily, still basking in the magical glow that only she could see. Ned frowned. Jenni would never normally allow herself to be swept like this, she claimed the decontamination removed vital layers of her personal aroma. He hoped she would snap out of whatever this was before they reached the sorcerer. She was their main firepower. She was their only firepower. No one else had anything close.

They trudged and trudged, the top of the mountain creeping closer and closer. No one felt inclined to stop nor did they particularly want to hurry. They ate in silence whilst on the move. There was much dagger flourishing by everyone, bar Jenni and Willow, as the group checked they could reach their blades easily and quickly. Surely the sorcerer would not be able to stop all of them at once? Besides, all they needed was for one blade to nick him. The paste was potent.

The dark clouds gathered above them, menacing and

grumbling to themselves. Thunder rolled and lightning began to crack the sky.

'Ah, the theatrics have begun,' Mia said sourly, trying to feel like she was doing the right thing but all she could think about was that her father had told her to bring Ned and Fourteen to him. She had now done that; however, she was also involved in the plan to confront and stop him. It didn't seem like such a good idea now they were so close. Perhaps she could offer the others up as extra payment. Father could always make use of parts. And if she gave him a nymph and a sprite there was a miniscule chance he would let Brogan be. After all, he couldn't possibly have any use for her stupid barbarian.

As they rounded a corner everyone suddenly stopped. It was involuntary. No one had decided to stop; they just couldn't move anymore. Except breathe. They could still breathe. And they could still roll their eyes theatrically at each other as they tried to figure out exactly what had happened. Mia's nose itched. Without thinking she scratched her nose and instantly seven sets of accusing eyeballs were riveted on her.

'Okay, fine, I can move but look, it isn't my fault.'

Before she could say any more there was a crack of violent lightning and the sorcerer who had been so threatening in the Emperor's throne room stood before them. Not stood. More like loomed. He crackled with raw energy and glowed darkly, somehow. As if touching him would rot you from the outside in.

'Child. I see you finally kept your promise. But why do I have all this extra baggage?' He gauged Joe's magical ability and frowned. 'He is of no use to me. He cannot even amplify his own father. What a waste.' He crooked a finger and Joe crumpled to the ground.

Ned felt like he had been kicked in the stomach by

ten horses. Just like that Joe was finished. This was a suicide mission - they didn't stand a chance. He caught Fourteen's eye and tried in vain to tell her he loved her with all the force he could muster into an eyeball.

Mia had gone white, her voice trembled as she spoke. 'Am I free to go, Father?'

'Yes, yes. I have no further use for you or your Mother. I will allow you to fetch her.' He looked her up and down. 'Before you go, I see you managed to get your magic blocked. As you are no longer using it, I will.' He made a grabbing gesture at his daughter. Her whole body arched backwards, head flung back, fingers curled in pain. She screamed as he ripped her power from her body. When he had finished, he turned disdainfully, and Mia fell to the floor in a silent heap. She was still alive, Ned could see her breathing, but it was erratic, and he had never heard of anyone surviving a power rob like that before. Especially not one as brutal or as complete as that one. Usually, power thieves left a little behind. It could be replenished over time eventually, so it made sense to let it grow back. That way there would always be someone to rob. But occasionally they took too much and the human shell left behind never lasted for long. Ned risked an eyeball at Brogan. His face was stony, muscles clenched as he strained with every fibre of his being to move. A single tear rolled down his cheek.

The sorcerer continued appraising the rest of the party. 'You and you can be drained.' He pointed at Jenni and Willow who were released from the freezing spell only to be magically bound together and gagged. But he had underestimated Willow's power - many do. She was psychically calling all the limited vegetation in the area to her. All she needed was something thorny to help rub these ropes free and the extra plant life would help boost

265

Jenni's power although to Ned's fourth eye she was already glowing incandescently. Surely the sorcerer could see that?

'You, you may leave. I have no need for muscle.' Brogan turned woodenly and began to walk away, completely under the thrall of the sorcerers' suggestion. He didn't turn back to look at Mia once although Ned thought he could see various shoulder muscles rippling as if they were fighting each other.

'You two. Now you are what I really want. I will drain the power of true love from you and release my chains. Lawman, you can then die. You, however, young Empress, you are an interesting figurehead. I can make a pretty little puppet out of you.' The sorcerer was looking at Fourteen with a peculiar light in his eyes. Ned felt hot molten anger pour into his bones and suddenly, he could move. He tried to breathe normally and not give anything away. He risked a glance at Willow and Jenni who nodded slightly at him, they were free. It was now or never. Ned eased the dagger from his belt and threw it with lightning accuracy at the sorcerer. It bounced off his personal shield as he turned with a laugh.

'Did you really think a little blade could defeat me?'

'Worth a shot.'

The sorcerer's eyes narrowed. 'How are you moving? Nothing should be able to penetrate my spell.'

'That's wot you fink.' Jenni threw a fireball at him which glanced away from the sorcerer harmlessly, but it did take his attention away from Ned. Willow was encouraging lichen and moss, fungi and weeds to grow around the sorcerers' feet, to find the smallest crack in the shield and wedge themselves in. Many tendrils were being fried but still more were being thrust forward and purchase was happening. A tiny pore became a chink and microscopic fungal spores flooded through the hole attaching themselves to the sorcerer, encouraged by Willow's loving magic.

The sorcerer wasn't paying the slightest bit of attention to the small amounts of plant life attaching to him. Instead, he was cackling maniacally as he exchanged power balls with Jenni. Different colours, different sizes, being thrown all at once. Fast and slow, high and low, in dizzying patterns bouncing harmlessly off each other but leaving magical residue all over the place. Now that he could move Ned opened his power wells to the utmost of his ability and willed the magic to come to him. Nothing happened for the longest moment, but then a slow trickle began. It was powerful stuff.

The sorcerer began to notice things were happening around him. He looked down and saw that his feet were completely encased in various mountain vegetation. He tried to move but he couldn't, so he aimed releasing spells at his feet. A few shoots withered and died, but otherwise, the vegetation tightened its grip. It was fuelled by Willow's grief and was one hundred times stronger than it should have been. Jenni continued to fire her balls and now that the sorcerer was distracted, his shield began to weaken until a blue ball of electrical fire hit him right in the goolies. He groaned and bent over, blindly sending out a scatter spell of fireballs. They all missed.

In all the distraction Fourteen, now also able to move, unwrapped her bow and arrow. She nocked one of the arrows tipped with the killer paste, lifted the bow and took her shot. The sorcerer jolted as the arrow impacted his chest and went through his heart. Smoke began to rise. He looked down in confusion then rage filled him, and he wrenched his feet from the vegetation instantly killing everything plant-based within a twenty-mile radius. Willow crumpled to the ground.

The sorcerer threw a powerful incantation to his left and knocked Jenni over. She fell and cracked her head on the ground. She didn't move. With his other hand, the sorcerer pulled out the arrow and threw it to the floor. 'How dare you!' he snarled. He advanced on Fourteen who stood her ground, never looking more beautiful. Before the sorcerer could bring about his wrath Ned released a spell. It flew at the sorcerer like black putty, hitting him on the back and began to spread all over his body so fast, Ned's eyes couldn't keep up with it. As the blackness engulfed him, the sorcerer howled in rage before disappearing with a wet plop.

Fourteen ran to Ned, shaking slightly as she clung to him and they hugged each other in relief for a long time.

'Where did you send him?' she asked.

'To the middle of nowhere.' Ned grinned at her.

'Won't he escape?'

'I don't think so. He needs to find love.' Ned tenderly stroked Fourteen's face. 'Not much chance of that, huh?' And he kissed her. It would have been the perfect moment except for Jenni's string of loud abuse as she came to.

Fourteen broke off the kiss and with a quick smile at Ned she rushed to help the sprite. Ned looked over at the direction Brogan had gone and saw that he was hurtling back to Mia. She was groaning, so at least she was still alive. With Brogan's help, she might pull through such a vicious power theft. Or perhaps Momma K could do something for her. Ned knelt down and gathered Willow into his arms. She had lost all colour, all her leaves, all her femininity. She was gnarled bark with arms, legs and a face locked in pain. He stroked her bark gently, whispering nonsense words of comfort. He hadn't realised that she had been *that* sweet on Joe. Poor lad. Look at him, lying there on the floor. Someone must have rolled him over. But, wasn't that his chest rising up and down?

'Willow? Sweetheart. He's alive.' Ned stroked her face.

Willow's dark brown eyes, filled with pain, unfroze and she looked at Ned in confusion then she turned her head and saw Joe dazedly getting up from the ground. Instantly she nymphed. Her lush, thick, green hair sprang out of her head and all her wiles whooshed back with such force that Ned had to take several moments to gather himself against the immense gush of nympheremones. It helped that he could look at Fourteen who was checking Jenni's scalp for any breaks. He looked at their little team and shook his head in wonder. They had made it. Somehow, they had all bloody made it.

Epilogue

Of course, the group then had to release the various trapped fae from the sorcerer's cave as well as rescue Mia & Joe's mum. It was a slow procession back down the mountain and a lengthy return to Roshaven. They avoided Fidelia and went the long way around, no one was keen to swim with the mermaids again. Plus, Ned wanted to pay his respects to Griff's widows.

Mia and Joe's father remains in the middle of nowhere. Or somewhere to the left of it now I believe.

Joe stayed with the Thief-Catchers. Willow is flourishing. I hear on the grapevine there is talk of buds.

Sparks continues to shine light into the depths of Roshaven's criminal underworld and Pearl remains a useful aquatic team player.

Mia eventually worked off her debt and Momma K's binding wore off. The magic came back slowly. Her and Brogan now take on impossible quests. They succeed five times out of seven.

Jenni remains Jenni.

Ned and Fourteen... well now, that is another story!

The End

Huge Thanks

I would like to say thank you, as always, to my beloved husband Kevin for putting up with me as I wrote and edited The Rose Thief. I could not succeed without his love and support.

Thank you to my wonderful team of beta readers - Donna Tyrrell, Claire Evans, Michael Rice, Hannah Bligh, Taron Wade & Kate Bentley. Your fantastic attention to detail and willingness to discuss character intricacies with me at random moments was invaluable.

Huge thanks to Ian Bristow, who saved the day with his wonderful artwork and created the beautiful cover for The Rose Thief. He captured the characters perfectly. You can find out more about his artwork at www.iancbristow.com

About the Author

Sign up to Claire's newsletter for exclusive content and all the latest writing news: http://eepurl.com/csWd0f

Follow Claire on Twitter: @grasshopper2407
Like Claire on Facebook: facebook.com/busswriter
Visit her website: www.cbvisions.weebly.com

Claire Buss is a multi-genre author and poet based in the UK. She wanted to be Lois Lane when she grew up but work experience at her local paper was eye-opening. Instead, Claire went on to work in a variety of admin roles for over a decade but never felt quite at home. An avid reader, baker and Pinterest addict Claire won second place in the Barking and Dagenham Pen to Print writing competition in 2015 with her debut novel, The Gaia Effect, setting her writing career in motion. She continues to write passionately and is hopelessly addicted to cake.

The Interspecies Poker Tournament
Case 27 of The Roshaven Files

Ned Spinks, Chief Thief-Catcher, has a new case. A murderous moustache-wearing cult is killing off members of Roshaven's fae community. At least that's what he's been led to believe by his not-so-trusty sidekick, Jenni the sprite. She has information she's not sharing but plans to get her boss into the Interspecies Poker Tournament so he can catch the bad guy and save the day. If only Ned knew how to play!

The Interspecies Poker Tournament, Case 27 of The Roshaven Files, is a humorous fantasy novella following the adventures of Ned Spinks and Jenni, a prequel to The Rose Thief. If you loved Terry Pratchett's Discworld, you'll love Roshaven.

Printed in Great Britain
by Amazon